THE RELICS OF ERRUS
VOLUME 1

GORDON
GREENHILL

ST. ASINUS
PUBLISHING

Flight of the SkyCricket
Copyright © 2019 by Gordon Greenhill
Published by St. Asinus Publishing
Rockford, MI
gordongreenhill.com

ISBN 978-0-9996795-1-7 (softcover)
ISBN 978-0-9996795-2-4 (ebook)

Editor: David Lambert
Cover design: Jeanette Gillespie
Interior design: Beth Shagene
Cover and interior illustrations: Elisabeth De Cocker/www.liefsbeth.com

Printed in the United States of America

First printing in 2019

For
Kyria, Kristine, and Kassandra
My own three little adventurers

᷾

Contents

THE MERRISIAN SYSTEM

MERRIS

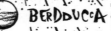
BERDDUCCA

THERRA

AVONIA

ERRUS

LEMERRUS

VERCANDRUS

Quarreling Prefaces

The epic poets, like my histrionic brother, often forget that real historians are interested in beauty as well as truth. The prophecies preserved in stone in the Holy City were both. They were true because they came true. They were beautiful because all true things are beautiful. So without doubt, they are the place we must begin. They predate all other facts. They are the one uncontestable proof that before recorded history "something" happened—something terrible and wonderful, which we have forgotten, but which did in fact happen. In these volumes I will propose what I think that "something" was.

> DR. SONJI RAZHAMANÌAH, *An Attempted History of the Halighyllian Prophecies and Their Fulfillment,* Vol. 1: *Legends of the Arrival of Men and of the First Theso-Hamayunean War,* 6r.

Surely no world has experienced anything like the events that fulfilled the prophecies carved into the walls of the old temple in Halighyll. Yet fulfilled they were, and in ways that are hard to believe. But this is the purpose of epic poetry—of my poetry: to help us believe in the past, to help us be present in events we would otherwise find incredible. Surely we cannot believe what we cannot even imagine. Thus, the poet must first capture the imagination. If all is done well, the mind will follow later and willingly.

When historians, like my famously pedantic sister, speak of "history," they can only speak of facts on a timeline that fade into "myth" at the far end. For them, "myth" is a term of defeat, the ending of the road. But for the poet, who embraces myth, it is the front door. I am quite certain that what is history in one world can be mythology in another and vice versa. I have learned from this to always take several deep breaths before using words like "impossible."

The historians themselves know that before history, buried in that "myth," a war was fought between the greatest powers in our world, and that humans were first brought to Errus to end it. But because it is only myth to them, they struggle to see the connections between that ancient war and the ones that have so recently come to our world.

I have not wasted my career merely cataloging historical facts (as my own sister has done in her interminable volumes of "attempted history"—what a barbarism!). I am a poet. I have sought to awaken the imagination to how unexpectedly, how scandalously, how impossibly those prophecies came to pass before the very eyes of our grandcestors. The historian inevitably begins with the prophecies themselves—that is her mistake. The poet knows better. He always begins with three little lost girls . . .

FRANKO RAZHAMANÌAH, *When Speaking of History: Essays on the Superior Qualities of Epic Poetry*, 45.

BOOK 1

Keddy Manor

Children know it, men forget it.
Poets learn it, sages scorn it.
Which is history? Which is myth?
How can anyone ignore it?

Look again, it is not hard,
Take a risk, and trust the Bard.
For myth and history intermingle
When our bias we discard.

> FRANKO RAZHAMANÌAH,
> from "World to World" in
> *The Ballads of the Ever-War.*

Chapter 1

The front door swung open on creaking hinges. Late summer sunlight poured through the opening, pooling in a rectangle of light on the ancient hardwood of the old manor house. The light painted three long shadows onto the floor.

"Can you believe it?" said one.

"It's kinda spooky," said another.

"Quiet." Anna silenced her sisters and leaned further into the doorway. "Hear that?"

A creak, creak, creak of feet descending old stair treads echoed out of the darkness. It stopped. A moment later, a woman emerged like a ghost from the gloom and stood in the patch of sunlight. Eli and Rose gave a collective start and retreated backward a step. Anna held her ground a moment longer. Then, realizing she was now alone in the doorway, she also withdrew slowly, trying not to show fear.

Her sisters fidgeted nervously on the porch, but Anna stared stubbornly at the tall woman, who seemed to have stepped off the pages of a fairytale—the evil housekeeper.

"How touching." The woman's hands were clasped primly at her waist. Her pursed lips and tight bun of graying hair made her pointed chin even more severe. She carried herself with the seasoned authority of one used to making slackers stand up straight.

"Um . . . Miss Heavernaggie?" Eli held out her hand politely. "I'm *El*-ee Hoover. I know it's spelled E-L-I, but that's how Mom always wanted it. This is Anna and Rose."

Anna, her junior by a year and a half, rolled her eyes at her sister's prattle. *Typical*, she thought. Eli was such a pet.

Miss Heavernaggie looked at the outstretched hand with disdain. "Young persons ought not extend the hand to their elders. You ought better to have curtsied. But residents of this continent have always shunned proper manners, preferring every variety of impertinent cheek." Her British accent and floor-length dress fit perfectly the colossal Victorian mansion, the girls' new home. She and the house, however, were both absurdly out of place in twenty-first-century Dare County, North Carolina.

Rose, a sturdy age eight, looked up at Anna with open mouth, and Anna knew she was about to ask what an "impertinent cheek" was. She squeezed Rose's hand to stop her, but the housekeeper spoke first.

"You need not stand there gawking like birds. Come into the foyer. And where is Master Hoover?"

"You mean Dad?" Rose's face was frozen in a bewildered grimace.

"I mean your father, yes," snapped the housekeeper. "I am quite certain he did not just dump you on the porch like a steamer trunk."

"Steamer trunk?" mumbled Rose.

"He's checking on his books." Anna tramped past her into the house. The housekeeper looked puzzled, but Anna was in no mood to offer explanations.

"The truck with his books hopped the curb coming up the drive," offered Eli, still laboring to sound polite. "He's afraid they were damaged. He told us to come up and . . . um . . . go in." She smiled weakly and pushed a still-fuddled Rose through the door after Anna.

The housekeeper scrutinized first Eli, then Rose. Anna knew what was coming; it was always the same. Eli had her father's dark brunette hair, neatly combed in straight ordered lines, and everyone spoke to her as if she were an adult, although she wasn't even fourteen. Rose, a sweetheart in lovely auburn tresses, had her grandmother's almond-shaped blue eyes, and though most of the time she was as clueless as a guppy, people still cooed, "What a darling!" to every idiotic thing she did.

When Miss Heavernaggie's penetrating gaze fell on Anna, the eyes narrowed slightly. Anna could guess what the housekeeper was thinking, and she wanted to look straight into those eyes and shout, "So I cut my own hair! Big deal! You wanna take a picture?" But she held her tongue, knowing it would just make things harder for Dad. She stuffed a truant strand of ragged blond hair back under her baseball cap and gnawed her tongue. *I just wish I still had the red highlights*, she thought.

But whatever Miss Heavernaggie thought of Anna's most recent act of self-expression, she said only "Come," and walked into the hall. "I'll show you to your rooms. You may freshen up, and I shall have tea served as soon as Master Hoover arrives."

"Why do you keep calling him 'Master'?" asked Rose.

But before Miss Heavernaggie could answer, Anna said, "Wait—did you say 'rooms'? You mean there's more than one?" They had all shared a bedroom in the old house.

The housekeeper didn't even break stride. "I do not know what sort of hovel you are used to calling home, but a young lady ought to have her privacy. So yes, you are each to be assigned your own room."

"Thank the gods!" said Anna, rolling her eyes toward heaven in fake pagan piety.

"Now, there will be none of that!" The housekeeper stopped and waggled a boney finger in her face. "I've been with the house over forty years, and in all that time we have never tolerated flippant speech. And you might as well understand from the start that just because you are Mistress Keddy's last heirs, you do not have the right to do as you please. This is an old house with many oddities that will not abide being disturbed! So from this point on you will be polite, well mannered, and . . . and better groomed than you are at present." And with a final grimace at Anna's cropped locks, she continued her floating ascent.

Anna trailed a few steps behind, contemplating this exotic new form of life. Miss Heavernaggie, however, was just warming up. "And since your father has decided you are to live here, you will be given all the benefits of your new situation. As soon as you are settled, your father will want to arrange for your remedial studies. I have references for an excellent Latin instructor, and another for manners and courtesy, and I think—"

"We do go to school, you know." Anna assumed her "duh" face.

"Not during the summer, and so—"

"Of course not during the summer, but the rest of the—" Anna stopped short. "You don't mean summer too?"

"That is another thing. Do not interrupt. It is rude."

"Have you even met Dad?" Anna did not even try to hide the panic in her voice.

"Certainly not! Nor is there any reason I should have. The trustees have always handled the affairs of the estate. I was only recently informed that he would be relocating you from . . . wherever it is you are coming from."

"Chicago." Eli's feigned cheerfulness was only marginally successful.

"Do not answer questions that have not been asked. It is rude."

"But—" Rose was still working at reconciling the antonyms *school* and *summer*—"if you've never met Dad, how do you know he wants us to do all that?"

Miss Heavernaggie paused. The implacable face quivered as though struck with a tiny hammer. Clearly it seemed an impossibility to her that Master Hoover would *not* want such things. "We shall see." Putting her hand on a doorknob, she added, "Miss Anastasia, this is your room. Miss Eleanor, yours is—"

"Just Anna," said Anna flatly. "And she's Eli, not Eleanor."

The housekeeper turned to Eli, horrified.

"Yes, ma'am," confirmed Eli. "Just Eli. Dad says Mom always hated long names."

"Said they're pretentious," added Rose helpfully. Eli had in fact been named after her mother Elizabeth but had been given the shortened form her mother always wanted herself. Anna had actually gotten an extra letter out of the deal. For Elizabeth Ann Hoover had preferred the longer form of her middle name.

"I should have expected as much," huffed Miss Heavernaggie and shoved the door open, revealing a tomb-like darkness. Despite Anna's excitement about having her own room, now that it came to it, she was not quite ready to leave her sisters for this forbidding hole. Like an angry dog who could sense Anna's fear, the housekeeper harrumphed loudly and strode into the room. A moment later thick draperies had been sundered, and afternoon sunlight was streaming into the large and beautifully appointed bedroom. The wooden writing desk, wardrobe, and four-poster with a thick, white comforter instantly conquered Anna's hesitation. She walked in slowly, eyes wide with wonder.

"There are dolls and other toys in the armoire. You may freshen up in the washroom down the hall, but you are to be downstairs in a half hour for tea. Come along, you two. Your rooms are just further on."

Incredulous, Anna approached the wardrobe. Five minutes later, she was storming down the hallway to Eli's room. She threw the door open to find Eli sitting on the bed. Rose was already there, fiddling with the hair of a doll from her own room. Eli was in the final pages of a thick volume of Charles Dickens.

"Now this is ridiculous! Dolls! What does she think, we're five?" said Anna.

"I like dolls," said Rose.

"And tea! What is this, jolly old England? The old bat's crazy."

"And mean too," added Rose, wide-eyed. "Like Cinderella's stepmother."

"Well, think about it from her side," said Eli in a maddeningly adult way. "Dad said there's never been kids in this house. We wouldn't be here at all if—" She broke off and started over. "Mom never lived here, and neither did Gram and Gramps. I don't even know who we were related to. We're just some kids off the street to her, and Dad's not related to anyone."

"Dad said something about an old aunt," said Rose, "and there were lots of 'greats' in front of her name, like three or four."

"I wonder if she's lonely," said Eli.

Anna threw herself onto the bed. "Any way you slice it, she's gonna be a royal pain in the—"

"Yeah, but the house is like . . . wow!" said Rose.

Even Anna had to concede that the house was a big step up from the dilapidated split-level in Chicago. This was a monstrous thing, as big as a city block, with passages and staircases and spires jutting out in every direction—more like a castle than a house. It was the kind of place where they hung carpets on the walls and posted suits of armor at the tops of staircases—just the sort of thing you'd see on top of a hill in Europe, off in the misty green distance, where some old family with a coat of arms lived. In England or Germany it would have been amazing. But this was the North Carolina coast, and here it just seemed stupid, like some-body trying really hard to pretend he was a rich European. Or just medieval.

Rose hopped off the bed and looked out the window into the woods that surrounded the house. She stood for a moment and then said, "Hope Dad doesn't marry her."

"Who?" said Eli and Anna together.

"Miss Heavernaggie."

"Did you whack your head or something? She's too old for Dad," said Anna.

"Not by much."

"By twenty years, at least! She's got to be sixty! Besides, Dad'll never get married again! I mean, when Mom . . ." Anna pulled up sharp as her throat closed up on her. She'd gotten too close to the line. They didn't talk about Mom very often, but Anna knew that each of them had different memories. When Eli talked about Mom it was always in distinct places—at the store, reading on the couch, climbing into the bathtub with her. Anna had only one memory —a kind face hovering in her mind without anything around it. Rose claimed no memories at all. She could only talk about warm cozy feelings surrounding the word *mom*. Anna knew little about the accident that had taken Mom so suddenly out of her life, but the mere fact was more important to her than the details.

She was painfully aware, however, of the effect of Mom's death on Dad. He had put away all the pictures and boxed up all the memories. He refused to speak of her, and the girls had learned not to ask. He now lived a life somewhere between denial and mourning in alternating breaths.

Anna's mind batted cat-like at the memories that had made up the last year or so of her life. She didn't know exactly what her father did at the Chicago-land university, but it had something do to with long-dead places and people. ("Doctor of all things ancient," a colleague had once said within earshot.) Based on the number of books in his office that bore his name, she knew he possessed a shabby sort of fame—the kind that hung like cobwebs to a professor but is totally not impressive to your friends. Since Mom's death, he'd thrown himself into his work, and it seemed as if the articles and books had issued from his laptop with the ease of Kleenex from a box.

Next to his own books on the shelves were thousands of old volumes in cracked leather covers—in Latin, Greek, and stranger-looking languages she didn't recognize. He even had a large humidor where he stored atrociously ancient folios with shattered bindings and yellowed pages, and dozens of scrolls. Anna called it "the freezer," and the girls were never permitted near it. She'd long made peace with the fact that if the house ever caught fire, she would have to fend for herself, for Dad would burst himself carrying the freezer out before he remembered that he had bio-kids as well.

Recently the university had given him some kind of promotion, so now he was free to live anywhere he wanted so long as the university's name showed up on his books. This promotion had allowed them to make the southern move.

Anna knew only bits of the story—how a year or two before her death, her mom had found herself the beneficiary of an old estate near Roanoke Island on the North Carolina coast. Mother hadn't known the house existed, nor had she known the relative who had left it. Through some long-forgotten event—a poker game, a repossession, or some crazier story— the great house had come into the Keddy family and now came to her (Keddy was her maiden name). But since Dad's work kept them in Chicago and the estate was managed by a trust as a sort of museum and couldn't be sold, they had never thought about it—until, with Elizabeth's death, the estate had passed to her girls.

Dad said the move south was to give the girls a fresh start. Anna thought this a rotten reason.

Eli had quickly figured out that the estate was near the site of the early British colony that had famously disappeared almost without a trace, and Anna had quipped that this was fitting since the same seemed to be happening to them—minus the fame.

"Well," said Eli after a few minutes, "we should go downstairs. We don't want to get on her bad side if we can help it."

Trudging out into the hall and down the stairs, Anna decided that she really wouldn't mind very much at all getting on Miss Heavernaggie's bad side.

"Any idea where to go?" asked Anna.

"The kitchen, maybe?" offered Eli. But none of them had a clue where that was. When they reached the bottom of the stairs, however, they heard voices. They wandered through the library, a room with a piano, and one with a chandelier before coming to a door that was slightly ajar. Light spilled through the crack.

The voices in the next room were agitated. It was their father and the housekeeper, and they seemed to be having a disagreement. The girls looked at each other and hunkered down at the crack to listen.

"But Master Hoover—"

"I'm going to insist you not call me that."

"But . . . but sir, I have standing orders to preserve—"

"Yes, I know all about that. Your position is endowed with the house along with the cook, the gardener, and the maid, and I want all of you to go ahead and run that proper historic English household that you've been instructed to maintain. Give your tours and show off the house as you always have, but please understand, I'm not English, and neither are the girls. We won't fit into all that. So you'll just have to run the house . . . well . . . around us. We only came here because . . . because the girls needed a new start away from the memories of their mother. You understand."

"You mean, *he* needed a new start," hissed Anna.

"I liked the old house," whispered Rose.

"Shut up!" said Eli.

"I've got a conference in a couple of weeks, and the move has put me way behind. So I'll be working long hours in the study and the library. Call me only for meals or if the girls need me. But they're pretty good at looking after themselves. So please continue what you've been doing and . . . well, just pretend we're not here."

"Pretend you're not . . . but sir—"

"Teddy, please."

"Teddy." Anna could almost see the look of disgust on the housekeeper's face at the familiarity.

"Yes. Short for Theodore. Everyone calls me Teddy, or Doc Teddy, if you're feeling funny."

"I cannot say I am in any way pleased with this development . . . er, Doctor Hoover. But as you are the girls' father, you have the final say on their welfare. Now then, where shall I serve the tea?"

"What? Tea? No, see, that's just what I'm talking about. Don't put yourself out for us. Just do what you'd do if we weren't here."

There was a moment of profound silence. Then, "Doctor Hoover, I have served tea at four o'clock every day for forty years, regardless of the circumstances within the house."

Anna was impressed that the housekeeper could sound so in control while being so infuriated.

"Even with no one here?"

"Without exception."

"Oh." The flatness of the reply showed that Dad was only just beginning to realize what he was up against. "Well, then . . . uh, go right ahead. Bring it in here. Where are the girls?"

"I have shown them to their rooms with instructions to come down for tea. They ought to arrive at any moment. If you will excuse me." And a door closed—a little more firmly than was probably good manners. Anna heard her father sigh.

"Well," whispered Anna, "looks like we're having tea. Cheerio, gov'nah." She pushed the door open and walked in.

Chapter 2

Their first week at the old manor was like living in a foreign country. Meals were the hardest. The cook had never learned to cook for children or even apparently for Americans. Oh, the crown roast of lamb with Yorkshire puddings was warmly embraced, and Teddy remarked afterward that he had never eaten so well in his life. But when the following day featured creamed sweetbreads, everyone stared sullenly at their plates. Teddy rose to the challenge and shoveled a big forkful of the calf pancreas into his mouth, loudly complimenting the cook through a repressed gag. Eli also ate a bite to be polite, and Anna too when her dad dared her. But Rose, whose hopes had risen highest at the thought of sweetbread for dinner, just cried, insisting that food shouldn't be called what it isn't.

Then there were the daily confrontations between Dad and the waspish housekeeper (whom the girls had taken to calling Naggie or, predictably, "the Nag" behind her back). Sometimes Teddy got the upper hand, as when the girls were permitted to continue wearing their regular clothes instead of becoming Downton Abbey reenactors for the historical tour groups. And the snooty manners instructor was sent packing. After great consideration, however, the Latin instructor was retained. *"Amo, Amas, Amuck!* Serves us right for having a professor for a father,"* Anna whined. And Naggie was implacable on tea, which continued to be rigidly observed at 4:00 each day.

Before the first week was out, however, and though she would rather die than admit it, Anna began to look forward to the afternoon ritual. It forced Teddy out of his study. This short but predictably regular time with her dad was something new to her, and to have it, she was even willing to put up with the housekeeper's fussing over their "appalling lack of etiquette and troglodyte manners."

Then came a day when Teddy opened tea time by asking Eli what she was currently reading. The question wasn't new, but Eli's red face and hesitations were.

"Oh . . . uh . . ." She glanced sidelong at the housekeeper, who lowered her cup with interest. Eli's goal of reading through all of Dickens's major novels was one of the few things of which she approved. "I finished Dickens the other day."

"Wonderful," said Teddy. "So who's next?"

"Oh, just . . . more like . . . uh, informational reading." Again her eyes bobbed toward the housekeeper, then back to her lap.

"Oh? Like what?" he asked. Anna was confused. This was the one time Eli could be guaranteed Dad's attention, and she had always milked it for all it was worth. Why the meandering?

"Um . . . just some guy named Evelyn Waugh."

"Really," said Teddy, eyebrows raised. "That's a bit more . . . uh, mature than your usual vein. What attracted you to him?"

Eli sat there looking embarrassed, miserable, and silent.

So Rose decided to help. "She told me it's about rich, snotty English people."

The moment of silence that followed was broken by the sound of Eli's saucer shattering on the floor and Anna spewing Earl Grey into her lap. Teddy broke into loud guffaws. Miss Heavernaggie's response was disappointing but admirable. Gathering her dignity up like a shawl, she simply rose and left to fetch a broom.

After the laughter subsided—even Eli snickered a little after the housekeeper had left the room—Teddy said, "Oh my, that felt good." He wiped a tear from his eye, and Anna thought he looked very worn.

"Well, old man," he said to himself, "back to work."

"Daddy, why do call yourself an old man?" asked Rose.

"You mean other than because I am one?" He laughed and cast a sidelong glance at Eli. "There's a story about an old fisherman who went too far out to sea but caught himself the biggest fish he'd ever seen and fought for two days to bring it in."

"*Moby Dick*?" said Anna quickly.

"Sorry, close but no Cuban cigar." He glanced at Eli again.

"*The Old Man and the Sea*—Hemingway," she said neatly. He raised his cup to her. Anna wanted to vomit every time this happened. It was the only game he played with them, and Eli was the only one who was any good at it.

"So whenever I'm feeling overwhelmed by . . . anything—" he paused, as if snagged by a stray thought—"I just think of that old man coaxing in that big fish inch by inch. I realize that whatever I'm doing is a lot easier than that, and I keep going."

"Except didn't the sharks end up eating most of the fish before he could get it back to shore?" said Eli, a little too primly for Anna's stomach. She faked a gag at Rose, who giggled.

"Oh, sometimes that happens too, but that's not the point. See, the old man believed he was put on the good earth to fish, and so he followed his call no matter how hard it was."

"How did he know why he was on earth for?" asked Rose.

Teddy patted her head—she was just young enough for this not to bother her. "You'll understand someday, hon." He got up and walked to the door. "You are trying to get along with Miss Heavernaggie, aren't you?"

"Of course we are," said Eli.

"Trying," added Rose.

"More or less," muttered Anna.

"Good, because she's in a very difficult spot. Her job requires her to keep up the pretense of an Edwardian English house. It's like a museum now, and she's used to doing things in a particular way. Now here we come disrupting everything and trying to actually live here. It's as hard on her as it is on you. See, for all the show-n-tell, this really isn't a museum. It's a home. She is taking care of all this—" he gestured in a way that took in the house, the grounds, and the whole of Keddy Manor—"because she knows it all technically belongs to you—or will someday. It's not easy to watch over something you know you have to give away. So be kind to her, and try not to get in her way when you're exploring." The door closed behind him, leaving the girls feeling chastened and a little ashamed.

A moment later Anna's brain lit up. "Did you hear what he said?"

"Yes." Eli scowled. "But I've really tried to be nice to her."

"No, not that, doofus. The other part. Everything here 'belongs to us,' and we ought to stay out of her way 'while we're exploring.' He just gave us permission to do anything we want, so long as we don't get in Naggie's way."

Rose clapped her hands together. "Oh, hurray! Let's go."

"I don't think he meant—" Eli began.

"Oh, don't throw water on it. Look, we've been moping around in our rooms for a week trying to avoid catching manners from the Nag. Why? There's the woods and the beach and . . . well . . . everything. If we can't find something to do here, we're totally hopeless."

"I suppose," conceded Eli.

"Oh, hurray! Let's go!" cried Rose again.

So the second week in the old house was very different from the first. The girls were up and out of the house right after breakfast. They explored the garden and met the congenial old gardener and caretaker, Mr. Putterly, whom they liked immediately. They roamed the many acres of pine that immediately surrounded the mansion and shielded it from the constant stream of vacationers who drove relentlessly around the back roads, looking for Kodak moments. They found that the trees gave way suddenly to tall grasslands rustling with salty Atlantic breezes. They found the powdery white beach that looked out upon a great inlet of the sea, with its mysterious shadow coast just visible on the other side and the silver thread of a distant causeway lying over the water that connected them to it. By the end of that week, they had completely forgotten any complaint they had about leaving Chicago.

Miss Heavernaggie, however, made up for it with her complaints. She was pleased, of course, to see them out of their rooms—"A budding girl needs her exercise." But she carped bitterly at every meal about the muddy tracks that kept appearing in the front hall, and the mountain of soiled jeans and T-shirts that piled up. And she instituted nightly baths to deal with filthy knees and grimy hair. And even Teddy betrayed them by suggesting that they help with the laundry. Miss Heavernaggie was torn over this suggestion, believing it to be inappropriate for the owners of the estate to wash their own dungarees. But apparently she made peace with it, because the girls spent a large part of the third week spot-treating stains and folding clothes. So they decided to trade their outdoor activities for indoor exploring that produced less time in the laundry room. But Miss Heavernaggie, unhappy if she had nothing to fret over, now complained about having them underfoot, while still wanting them within close enough reach to impose the greater benefits of Western civilization on them.

The house, as it turned out, contained equal opportunities for exploring as the grounds. They found the conservatory, the solarium, and even an observatory in an obscure room on the top floor. They also found countless empty rooms that may have been bedrooms or studies in wealthier days. They even found a wine cellar and, upon reporting the discovery to Teddy and Naggie over tea, received a lecture from the latter on both its unacceptable filthiness and the folly of its existence. It seems that coastal houses never had basements because of the high water table, but apparently the whole mansion had been jacked several feet off the ground just to make room for the several cellars. They were thus more like daylight basements, except without any daylight.

So the cellars were off limits due to dirt. "But especially," they were admonished, "you are to stay out of the south cellar. It was closed up long ago because it is unsafe." This, of course, made it Anna's prime destination, but when they finally found the south cellar door off a mothballed scullery, it was padlocked. "Crud-muffins," she said, and they trooped off.

The best discovery, after the letdown of the forbidden cellar, was the gallery—a long dead-end room with display cases against each wall, like a galley. The walls were covered with oil paintings of men on horses and bishops in red satin, and the displays were filled with old sextants, stone arrowheads, and black-and-white photographs of men in pith helmets. Eli loved it because she had encountered everything here in one book or another. Anna loved it because the whole thing reeked of adventure and mystery. And Rose loved it because she was fond of gadgets and trinkets and things you could fiddle with. So she was also the most frustrated.

"Why do they gotta put everything behind glass so you can't touch it?" she moaned.

"So you don't shoot yourself, stupid," said Anna, pointing at an old derringer pistol.

"Wow, this is curious," said Eli from the far end of the room.

"This is *curious*?" said Anna. "You're channeling the Nag."

"No, seriously, come look at this."

She was examining a free-standing pillar, which was about four feet high with a square glass case on top. It stood near the back wall under a painting of a little boy and girl in old-fashioned clothing.

Anna and Rose joined Eli as she stared into the case. A little glass sphere a smidgen larger than a golf ball rested on a velvet cushion. It was encircled by two bands—a dark brown one, like bronze, running top to bottom, and a bright polished steel one around the middle. There were tiny markings on the bands, but they were hard to see because the room was so dark. Inside the sphere, two needles or arrows were somehow suspended—one pointed somewhat downward, the other pointed straight left.

"It's an old compass. Big deal." Anna walked away.

"Yeah, I guess. But I've never seen one with two needles before." Eli hesitated over the display before following.

"So it's a paperweight. Who cares?" called Anna from the hallway.

Rose remained behind a moment longer, staring at the thing from every angle.

"And don't touch it, Rose," Anna yelled. "Remember that alarm you set off at the museum?"

Rose drew back a guilty hand and followed the girls out of the room, casting a longing look over her shoulder.

Anna had had enough exploration and was ready for some action. "Okay, let's play tag. NOT IT!" she yelled. It was a long shot, because Eli was too old for the game, but Anna hoped the gallery had raised her sense of adventure. It had! Unfortunately for Eli, her "Not it!" trailed Rose's by a split second.

They all knew what was coming from long practice. Anna and Rose leapt in opposite directions, Anna down the hall and Rose back into the gallery.

Well, that was stupid, Anna thought, looking back. *There's no way out. She's trapped herself.* Apparently Eli realized this too and hightailed it into the gallery after her. Having no pursuer, Anna crept back toward the gallery door. But before she could peek around the corner, she heard a crash like the smashing of a picture window. She rushed into the room and, to her horror, found Rose and Eli standing in an epicenter of shattered glass at the far end of the room. The pillar was lying on its side.

"It's her fault," squeaked Rose. "She chased me."

"Of course I chased you! It's called 'tag'! But I didn't make you run headfirst into the—"

"Shut up, shut up, shut up!" shouted Anna. She listened for Naggie's footsteps. The house was so big and had so many rooms, it was possible no one had heard. Her mind raced.

"Quick . . ." She rushed forward and grabbed the pillar. Eli

FLIGHT OF THE SKYCRICKET

bent to help her pick it up. "No! Trust me." She dragged the pillar around and laid it down facing away from the wall. Then she reached up and tried to lift the painting of the two children off the wall. It was too heavy. But now Eli was tracking with her, and between the two of them, they hoisted the painting off its hooks and laid it face down across the pillar.

"There," Anna panted. She looked hard at Rose and enunciated each phrase as though trying to modify her memory, "The painting . . . must have fallen . . . off the wall . . . and broke the glass. Right?"

Now Rose got it and giggled. "Right!"

"And we were never in here, right?"

"Right."

"And we don't even know about this room, right?"

"Right."

"Okay. One more thing for when Rose cracks," said Anna.

"I won't crack!"

"You always crack." Rose looked pleadingly at Eli, who shrugged and nodded. "We were in the hall and heard the crash. So we *did* discover it, but we didn't do it, right?"

"Okay," said Eli. "But why didn't we tell someone when we found it?"

"Oh, good point." Anna fished. "Um . . . because . . . we figured it happened a long time ago, and . . ."

"But we heard the crash," said Eli.

"Oh, yeah. Okay, because Dad told us not to bother Naggie, and we didn't want to get blamed."

"It's not great," sighed Eli.

"You got something better, Sherlock?" snapped Anna.

"No, let's go with it." None of the girls except Anna were any good at lying. But she'd learned that if they worked together, their story was nearly always credible, at least until Rose cracked.

"Got it, Rose?"

"I got it! No, really, I do!" Rose looked back and forth between her sisters, jaw clenched, trying to appear uncrackable.

"Well, it's about time for tea, and we can't be late," said Eli. So they trooped out, trying to force their memories into the new story by sheer will.

Rose came last, tapping her temples and muttering, "I was never here . . . I was never here . . ." But before she reached the hall, she stopped.

Anna turned just in time to see Rose pick something up from under the foot rail of a display case.

"Come on!" Anna urged.

Rose glanced down at the thing in her hand. "Dad said it was all ours anyways," she mumbled and shoved it into her pocket.

Chapter 3

Long after bedtime, Anna awoke to nature's urgent call. On her way back from the bathroom, she passed Rose's room. A light peeped from under the door, faded, then returned—like a flashlight beam searching the room.

What's she doing up? In their shared room in the old house, Rose had always been the first one out cold.

She put her ear to the door and listened, but no sound made it through the oak slab. She gently took hold of the handle. The house was so old that everything creaked and groaned when touched, so Anna figured moving the door even an inch would make it squeak. But remarkably, when she turned the handle and pushed, it made no sound. She inched it open and put her eye to the crack.

The blankets on the bed were piled up in a great hill, and something moved under them like a tunneling mole. A light peaked out from under the edges every so often. *Figures,* thought Anna. Rose used to love playing with her dolls under her covers with a flashlight at the old house. More than once Anna had been forced to dig under Rose's blankets for the flashlight to shut it off after Rose had fallen asleep.

Intending to mock her, Anna squeezed into the room. She leaned against the doorpost, watching the dwarfish shape move to and fro under the mountain of bedclothes. Rose emerged, holding a flashlight in one hand and a small something in the other. She looked wide awake and very intent on the object in her hand. She didn't see Anna.

Rose shook the little something, examined it closely with the flashlight, and kept up a regular mumbling conversation with herself. "And the bands are different, one dark, one light. Well, old man, what does this mean? Can't read the writing—too small. And the arrows don't move . . . except when I do this." She rotated it in her hand. "And then they just kind of snap around." She spent a whole minute rotating the item back and forth in her hand, watching it carefully. She set it on her nightstand, shined the flashlight on it, and gave it a spin. The small globe-like object spun on the table like a top. Rose, perched on hands and knees on the edge of the bed, watched it like a cat ready to pounce.

Anna shook her head. She recognized the thing now. Rose had snagged the compass-paperweight from the crime scene. She couldn't leave it alone! This was just the sort of thing she always did to blow a good cover story. Anna gave a tiny "*Ahem.*"

Rose's hand shot out for the little globe, but as she was also looking up to see who had caught her, she missed and knocked the thing off the table. It rolled across the floor right to Anna's feet. She picked it up.

"Rose . . ." Anna put as much maternal disappointment into her voice as she could muster.

"I was just . . . I was just . . ." Rose's eyes flew around the room as if some miracle might appear to rescue her. None obliged. She deflated. "Look, I know I shouldn't've taken it. But just look at it. It's so cool! Just look at it. The needles don't move . . . or at least, they only snap around a bit when—"

"Of course they don't move. They're just . . ." Anna paused to yawn and changed her tack when she saw Rose redden. Rose wasn't yet beyond throwing a tantrum when she was tired. Anna let it slide. "Look, just promise you'll put it back in the gallery tomorrow." And she handed it back.

"Okay, okay."

Anna's brain recognized the complete lack of sincerity, but her body just wanted to get back in bed.

Naggie was surly at breakfast, but no worse than usual, so Anna figured she didn't know about the flotsam in the gallery. "The house is so big, she probably hasn't been in that room for years," she told Eli as they were coming in for tea. They had spent the day with Mr. Putterly, so they weren't surprised that the housekeeper gave a little squeal of dismay as they entered the parlor and sent them up to wash.

When they returned, Teddy was at the table, looking over his notes. His bags sat by the door. He would leave in a few minutes for his conference and be gone all weekend. Anna and Eli made several attempts at conversation with him, but his answers were short and distracted.

Rose, unusually silent, munched her sandwich with a determined face that made Anna nervous. *She's gonna crack, I can just tell.*

Miss Heavernaggie had just cleared the dishes when Rose suddenly burst like a water balloon. "Dad, have you ever seen a compass with two needles on it?"

Anna froze. Rose always cracked, but never so voluntarily. It usually took at least the threat of a browbeating.

But Teddy, still perusing his notes, didn't even look up. "Why, honey, so they can *both* point north?"

"No, not like that." Rose ignored Anna's withering glare. "Well, maybe one of them. And the other could sort of point down at . . . something else. Only they don't seem to move that much."

"What's the good of a compass if the needle doesn't move?"

"No, *two* needles, and it's not like they don't move. They just don't move much except if you move it a particular way. Then they sort of snap around, like they're looking for something, or can't quite . . . oh, I don't know how to explain it." Thoroughly flummoxed, she finished by blowing a small raspberry.

Teddy finally looked at her over his glasses with mild interest.

"You mean as though they're pointing at something absolutely fixed and keep on trying to point to it even when they can't because of the way you're holding it?"

"Yes, that's it." Rose looked pleased for a moment. Anna face-palmed.

"Honey, where did you hear of such a compass?"

Rose went pale and wide-eyed. Realizing her peril, she looked around, again seeking a miracle to save her. This time it appeared. "Eli was reading about it and told me."

"Eli?" Now he took off his glasses and stared at his eldest. The instinct for self-preservation was strong in Eli, so she played along and nodded. "But this isn't Evelyn Waugh, is it, hon?"

"Uh, no, Dad, just . . . uh, Isaac Asimov," she said with a gulp.

Anna's palm went back to her face. Eli never read science fiction, and Dad knew it. But to her surprise, he chuckled. "It would have to be. Rose, hon, you mustn't believe in things like that. There's a reason it's called fiction."

"I know, Dad." Rose forced a laugh. "I just wondered if it existed."

"It's weird timing that you should mention it, though." He rummaged through his case and produced a stack of bound papers. "Thought for a minute you'd been going through my stuff again." He leafed through the papers until his finger came to rest on one. "Ah, here it is." He pulled a thick article out of the stack and bent over it. He scanned it with remarkable speed, flipping a page every few seconds. Several times he mumbled "Ah, yes," or "Fascinating." Then he said, without looking up, "I was asked to review this paper from a scholar at Notre Dame on objects similar to the one you describe. She's discovered several references to them. The alchemy lists in Euroclide's *Fragments* mentions the *diplasios Magnates lithos*, the double-lodestone. A sort of double compass that could be fixed permanently to a location. No details here, but by the name I guess it somehow pointed out a fixed latitude and longitude, or something like that. And there's an anonymous Latin reference to *ferra sagittae*, the iron arrows, with a similar effect, and, uh, let's see . . ." He continued reading for a moment and then smiled. "Oh, now this is rich. The most detailed account seems to be a legend of an itinerant Germanic monk in the fifteenth century named Stemmathus, doing mission work in France. He claimed to have come across a two-arrowed compass that pointed perpetually toward the gates of hell. The arrows pointed west. So of course he set out in the exact opposite direction, believing it would lead him to heaven."

"What happened to him?" asked Eli, now interested.

"Well . . . and this is just an old story, hon," he said, perusing the article. "You can't take it seriously."

Rose nodded furiously for him to continue.

"It says he traveled eastward across Europe preaching his gospel and attracting quite a group of pilgrims. But when he and his entourage reached Jerusalem, he had a vision or something which persuaded him that he had misread the device." Teddy grinned.

"Misread it?" Eli was aghast.

"Yes, turns out the arrows were pointing the way to heaven, not hell. So he turned around and marched back west again, this time through Egypt and across North Africa—gaining converts the whole time. But when the lot of them reached the Atlantic, the dumb thing was still pointing west."

"So what did they do?" asked Anna, forgetting to glare at Rose.

"What *could* they do?" Teddy actually laughed. "He had hundreds of converts from Gaul, Italy, Greece, Turkey, Jerusalem, and all across North Africa—Christians, Muslims, men, women. Everyone was convinced the kingdom of heaven was upon them. You know, had reached every nation of the earth and all that. So they all booked passage on several large vessels and sailed west."

"And?"

"And what? What do you expect? They were never heard from again."

"Daddy!" Rose deflated. "You made that up!"

"No, honest to God, it's right here in this paper. I'll even bet I've got a medieval history somewhere in the library with the story in it." When Anna saw him glance at his watch, she knew tea time was over. He was leaving now.

"But then the compass exists?" persisted Rose.

"No, of course not, honey. It's just a legend," he said, rising from his chair, "although . . ." He paused, remembering. "A philosophy colleague of mine back in Chicago, Dr. Greenhill—you remember him; he came to the house a few times—told me there is a theoretical plausibility to such things. Something about quantum physics and whatnot, but I never understood it. That may be where Asimov got the idea."

"Yeah, must be," said Rose weakly.

He picked up his bag. "I'll tell you what. I've never met this scholar, but she'll probably be at the conference. If I get a chance, I'll look her up and ask her a few questions about ol' Stemmathus, okay? Now, I'm leaving for the airport. Be good for Miss Heavernaggie. I've asked her not to impose any new colonialist policies while I'm gone, but don't give her a reason to try." The door swung shut behind him.

Chapter 4

"Have you lost your mind?" said Anna.

"Yeah, that was crazy!" said Eli. But the parlor door had already closed behind Rose, who had darted out of the room as soon as Teddy's footsteps had faded. The two sisters looked at each other for a moment and then dashed after her. They caught up to her on the main stairs.

"Hey, slow down! What's going on in that little red head?" panted Anna. But Rose ignored her. She gained the landing and rushed for her bedroom door.

Anna dashed after her and grabbed her wrist just as it landed on the door handle. "Okay, speedy, what's up?" Rose struggled, but Anna held her firm.

Eli arrived, hands on hips. "You want to share what that little stunt was about? Do you know how close you came to—"

"Would you guys just shut up and come in here?" said Rose with some heat. This was not the Rose-meek-and-mild that Anna knew. She let go of her wrist, and Rose threw open the door and rushed to her nightstand. A second later she was holding out something in her hand for them to see.

"It's the paperweight," said Anna nonplussed. She realized that she had already known that Rose wouldn't put it back voluntarily.

"No," said Rose firmly. "It's the loadstone thingy."

"The what?" Anna was in the habit of not listening too closely to Teddy's lectures.

"Oh, Rose," said Eli in her most maternal voice, "you heard Dad. He said that was just a legend."

"No!" Rose stamped her foot. "It's the thingy!" And she shook it in front of their faces.

"Okay, okay," Eli soothed, grabbing her sister's flailing arm and gently extracting the glass globe from her hand. She stared at it, turned it around in her hand, then shook it herself. "Honey, it's just a paperweight. The arrows don't move because they're encased in glass. It's like that sea urchin under glass at the gift shop that one time that frightened you so bad, remember?"

"Don't talk like a grownup!" She grabbed the globe out of Eli's hand and ran out the room, yelling over her shoulder, "And they do too move! Just not a lot!"

"We can't let Naggie find her like this," sighed Eli. "She'll crack for sure."

Anna followed her into the hall. "I think she's already cracked."

Rose had run back down the stairs. She shouted back, "Now come and see this!"

"Geez!" said Anna. "If we don't shut her up, the Nag will catch her for sure." They ran to join her in the main foyer.

"What do you say now?" Rose thrust the sphere under Eli's nose.

Eli sighed again and took it. She looked at it mildly, turning it slowly in her hand. Then she started.

"What!" said Anna, "What's so—"

"The needles moved," Eli said, staring even harder at the globe.

"You just turned it over, that's all," said Anna.

"No, no, they like snapped to a different spot when I turned it over. I watched it happen." Eli scrutinized it.

"See?" said Rose triumphantly. Eli slowly turned it back.

"See, there they go back again. But wait, upstairs the down arrow was pointed almost straight down." Eli held it up to the sunlight coming through the transom above the front door. "Curious.

Now it's at an acute angle to the other one." She turned to Rose. "How did you get it to do *that*?"

"I came down here," said Rose stubbornly. "I moved, then it moved, that's all. It got cute on its own."

"What about the other arrow?" said Anna.

"It's hard to tell," said Eli. "It's pointing . . ." She turned and walked back into the house, holding the sphere in front of her eyes.

"Hey, that's mine," said Rose.

"Just a minute. I'm thinking." Eli walked back to the stairs, paused, and started to go back up. Halfway up she stopped and looked back at them with wide eyes. "It *is* moving," she whispered.

All three girls huddled round the sphere. The downward-pointing arrow had moved back to a forty-five-degree angle; the other arrow pointed more or less up the stairs. Slowly they began to climb again, all eyes on the device. They reached the landing and started down the hall. As they walked past their bedrooms, the downward arrow continued its slow, even descent toward vertical, but now the other arrow began to move slowly too. More slowly but just as deliberately, it began to ease to the right. The long hall ended in a sort of keeping room with a big fireplace, thick carpet, and passages going to the right and left. By the time they reached it, the horizontal arrow was pointing hard to the right.

"This is creepy," said Anna.

"Yeah," said Eli, "but we have to go right." So they did. Two steps into the passage, however, Eli gave a little cry.

"What is it?" said the other two and huddled round her. The horizontal arrow was swinging lazily around in no particular direction.

"What happened?" asked Rose.

"Don't know," said Eli. "I just took a step, and the arrow seemed to come loose."

"You broke it?" Rose gasped.

"No, I don't think so . . ." She turned slowly around and walked back to the keeping room. The needle snapped back to its original position. She turned and stepped back into the hall, and as before, the needle seemed to come loose. "I don't get it."

"Keep walking. See what happens," said Anna.

So they did. They took another four steps, and once more, Eli gasped. "There it goes again! The arrow's locked back up, but this time it's pointing back toward the fireplace room."

"What's the other arrow doing?"

"Pointing straight down."

A light went on in Anna's mind. "Let me see it."

"Okay, but be careful," said Eli.

"Duh. I'm not going to play catch with it."

"I'm just saying . . ."

But Anna had already run to the far end of the hall, where it turned left. She called back, "The down arrow isn't quite point-ing straight down." Then she ran back past them into the keeping room. "And it isn't here either, but now it's off center in the other direction." And then she ran back to the place where the horizon-tal needle floated freely again. "But here it points exactly straight down, as if it's pointing to . . ."

Eli threw her hands over her mouth and gasped. "To . . ."

"To what? To what?" demanded Rose.

"To hell," squeaked Eli.

Chapter 5

"Don't be so emo," said Anna. "Of course it's not pointing to hell."

"It isn't pointing to heaven," said Rose.

"What? No, geez! What's wrong with you people?" said Anna. "It's not pointing at heaven *or* hell. I don't know *what* it's pointing at, but now we know how it works."

"How do you know it's not pointing to hell?" said Rose.

"Look, moron, would you just listen for a minute?" said Anna, turning the compass slowly before their eyes. "You have to hold it with the silver band flat like this, or else the arrows jump all weird, like they can't quite get to where they're supposed to. But if you do hold it flat, this arrow tells you whether you have to go left or right. The other tells you whether you have to go up or down."

"But up or down to what?" said Eli, still worried.

"That's what we have to find out," said Anna. "The horizontal arrow swings loose right here because we're directly over the . . . uh, *whatever*, right now. So it can't point left or right. See, if I turn it so the bronze band is the horizontal one, it still works, only reversed. The two arrows always get as close as they can based on how you're holding it. I bet if we were down on same level with it, this arrow would be pointing right or left, but the vertical arrow would swing free."

"That makes sense," said Eli hesitantly. "But what are we looking for? Dad just said not to get into any trouble while he's gone. He barely left the house, and we're already—"

"Oh, let's go see, please!" Rose seemed to have gotten over her fear of hell for the moment.

"Okay, then," said Anna. "What's below us?" None of them knew, so in a few minutes they were down on the main level and had followed the compass to the point where the horizontal arrow swung free again. They found themselves standing in a room, empty except for an old armoire. The vertical arrow still pointed straight down, and the horizontal one still swung free at this spot.

"No luck here," said Anna, "We've got to get lower."

"But this is the ground floor," said Eli. "Unless there's a basement under us."

"The cellar?" offered Rose.

"Not the south cellar, I hope," said Eli.

Anna closed her eyes for a minute and turned slowly around. "No, I think it would have to be the wine cellar. We're on the north end of the house." But none of them could remember exactly how to get from where they were to the wine cellar door.

"It was just off that large room with the chandelier," said Eli.

"Yes, in that little pantry, or whatever you call it," said Anna.

Ten minutes later they were standing in the butler's pantry looking down a dark flight of stairs. They knew from their previous venture into the cellar that it would be chilly and dark. "I'll get jackets," said Anna.

"And a flashlight," yelled Eli after her.

Even after they had turned the lights on, it was hard to see. The low-wattage bulbs threw a fragile and jaundiced light that barely reached the walls, and some were burned out altogether. When they reached the bottom of the stairs, they checked the compass with the flashlight. As Anna had predicted, the vertical arrow was orbiting in lazy arcs, but the horizontal one pointed firmly ahead and to the left.

"This is the right level." Eli squinted into the gloom. "Now we just have to follow the one arrow."

The wine cellar was a thousand square feet of musty maze,

with long shelves of dust-covered bottles that ran floor to ceiling, which was itself a very low one. An adult would have to stoop to clear the cross beams, but Eli and Anna had only to incline their heads slightly as they crossed the compacted dirt floor. In a strange way, this was the most familiar part of the whole house. The Chicago house had featured a basement much like this, only smaller—called a Michigan basement—and they had spent many a happy afternoon in their "pirate's cave."

They walked slowly down the main aisle, watching the compass needle gradually move to a harder left position. They made false starts down several of the aisles before deciding that the arrow was really leading them to the next one and then the next.

Finally an old cinderblock wall stood in front of them, and the last aisle shot to their left and right. The arrow pointed determinedly down the left-hand aisle, but that bulb was out, so it looked like a mysterious black tunnel or the mouth of a cave. Rose grabbed Eli's hand, and Anna raised her flashlight and pointed it down the aisle.

She had expected to be surprised or shocked or horrified or—well, anything. But the shaft of light revealed only confusion. Several moments elapsed before her mind could make any sense of what it was seeing. At first she thought it was just a large picture hanging on the wall at the end of the aisle. A painting, maybe, of a green forest in half light. But as she stared at it, she began to realize strange things about it. First, it wasn't hanging on the wall at all. The wall was another five feet behind it. It just hung in midair. Second, it had no frame. It was not a painting enclosed by anything; it simply faded near the edges, becoming more and more transparent until it disappeared near the floor and the ceiling.

Now shock and fear began to take hold. As they stared at it, they all realized at the same moment that the trees in the picture were moving, but most unnaturally. They did not rustle as if in a breeze; rather, they shivered, as in a movie on fast forward. Then came the real surprise. The light changed—not instantly but quickly. The patches of sky seen through the leaves broke out in flaming orange and gold, and light flooded that strange forest. The girls had just witnessed a sunrise—in about five seconds.

When Anna, overcome by the strangeness, lowered the flashlight, the vision vanished.

"Quick!" cried Rose, "Put it back! Put it back!" Anna's hand jerked back, and the image was restored by the beam.

"How is it possible?" said Eli. "It doesn't give off any light of its own, but when you shine the light on it, it shows a sunrise."

"It's like a painting," offered Rose.

"But everything moves," added Anna.

"It's like a window," tried Rose again. Anna and Eli looked at Rose in surprise.

"A window," repeated Anna, "but that would mean—"

"We're looking at something real," said Eli, and added, "Be careful," for Anna had taken a step closer to it.

"I just wonder . . ." said Anna as she reached it. She extended her hand to touch it.

"Oh, be careful," said Eli again.

Anna pulled her hand back and thought hard for a minute.

"Rose, let me see the compass," she said, handing the flashlight to Eli. She held the orb up to the window. The horizontal arrow pointed with persistent doggedness at the center and the vertical still swung nonchalantly. She pushed against the surface of the window with the hand holding the compass, and the surface gave like the surface of a pond. The compass passed through, but as it did, a burst of light came from it. The girls blinked, and when Anna could see again, she saw that both needles were now swinging loose. She wiggled her hand, and the needles flopped about their orbits without any resistance. Her fingers tingled a bit, not painfully but enough to make her draw her hand back. Suddenly Eli gasped and dropped the light. The vision vanished as the flashlight rolled across the ground.

"What? What?" cried Rose.

"I saw . . . I thought I saw . . ." said Eli breathlessly, fumbling for the light. But by the time she got it back into position, she was too wrapped up in the vision to finish.

"What? What?" cried Rose again.

"It was just the flash, I suppose. Or a reflection," and she closed up as she always did when thinking.

"It's like putting your hand into a swimming pool," said Anna. "I think you could go through it." She gave the compass back to Rose and rubbed her hand, which felt a little cold and stiff.

"Oh," Eli exhaled in wonder. "Oh, let's go."

Anna looked at her in disbelief. "You mean, you'd go through into . . . there?" She already knew *she* would risk it in a minute, but Eli usually took a little persuasion.

"Yes, I think I would," Eli said in an enchanted voice. "What an amazing chance. I mean, I've read my whole life about people having adventures, and I always wished . . . I mean, deep down . . . I never thought it could happen, of course, but . . . I mean, what else can we do? Just stare at it? Go back and tell Naggie? How do we know it will still be here? And if this is the door to heaven—"

"Or hell." Anna grinned.

"Oh, don't say that. It's got to be heaven," said Eli, still transfixed.

Rose was the holdout, but Eli's hypnotic words had nearly won her over.

"It looks wonderful," she admitted. "But how do we know—"

"There's only one way to know," interrupted Anna. She held out her hand to Eli, who without taking her eyes off the window reached out and grabbed it. Rose, who was already holding Eli's hand, put up no resistance.

The three stood shoulder to shoulder, hand in hand, on the verge of the window.

"Ready?" said Anna.

"Ready," said Eli.

"Ready," said Rose.

As one, the three girls stepped into the unknown.

BOOK 2

Of the Strange and the Impossible

Halighyll was once a great and prosperous city in which the God Thes was worshipped. But then drought came to that city, and in its wake, great war. The old religion was cast aside for a new one—the veneration of the goddess Merris and her divine children. Yet for all that changed, one thing did not: the city remained parched—and no one noticed that the new gods seemed as impotent as the old.

> DR. SONJI RAZHAMANÌAH, *An Attempted History of the Halighyllian Prophecies and Their Fulfillment*, Vol. 5: *The Rise of the Merrisian Cultus*, 12v.

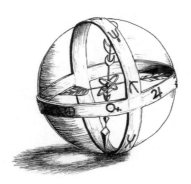

Chapter 6

With a flash of light, the girls found themselves standing in a wooded glade—the very one they had seen through the window, but the light was brighter. It felt like a late morning in spring. Many of the trees were in blossom. The girls shivered a little, for spring in that place was cooler than late summer in North Carolina.

Rose looked around. "It's gone." She was right. The window had vanished.

"And look." Eli held up the flashlight. The bulb was black and smoky.

Anna took it and gave it a shake. "Must have overheated or something."

"What now?" asked Eli.

Anna shrugged. "Rose, what's the compass say?"

Rose looked at it, then shook it. Both arrows were unhelpfully lazy. She looked anxiously around. "How we gonna get back?"

"Um . . ." Eli began.

Anna saw where this was headed. She was feeling intrepid now and was not about to let a little question like "How do we get home?" stop the adventure before it got started. So she cut across the fear with as much confidence as she could put into her voice. "Now, hold on there, Dexter! Let's not freak quite yet. The window may come back on its own. Let's not worry about it now. I want to explore!"

"Let's at least make sure we know how to get back to this spot in case it does." Eli began kicking together a small pile of rocks.

Anna was reluctantly impressed. "That's pretty good thinking, El. Did you read that in a book?"

Eli blushed. Anna rolled her eyes.

They walked a hundred yards or so in each direction, always coming back to the pile of rocks before setting out again. And after they had gone in all four directions, even Anna had to admit that heaven, if it was heaven, was not a very interesting place—just woods like they had back home.

"Let's go back to the clearing and set up some sort of camp in case the window comes back," said Eli. "The first thing we need is shelter."

Anna snickered.

"Well, it is! Look, just 'cause I read it in a book doesn't mean—"

"Oh, I know," said Anna. "It's just that most people learn about this kind of thing by, you know, actually going camping." Deep down, though, she was a little relieved by Eli's know-how. Teddy had taken them to lots of museums and art shows and once even to a conference on the Ancient Near East (*yawn!*), but wilderness survival was not his idea of a good time.

At the end of the glade where they'd arrived was a large boulder as tall as Rose and as wide as Anna with her arms outstretched. Eli took charge and told them to look for branches, explaining that they would use them to build a lean-to against the rock.

"Okay," said Eli, as she laid the final branch. "Now we have the frame. We need to tear some of those pine branches off and put them on the lean-to to give more protection. And then we need water."

"How about you two finish the shelter," offered Anna, "and I'll look for water."

"Wait!" Eli called. "Make sure you walk straight out of the camp and count your steps, so you don't lose your bearings."

"Okay, okay. But if I walk off a cliff and die because I'm busy counting my steps, it'll be your fault." Anna was ticked off, mostly because she knew Eli was right. She was always right, and that gets annoying! So she walked into the woods, looking back over her shoulder frequently to check her bearings until the camp was out of site. When she had walked out about two hundred steps—who was she kidding, she'd stopped counting at around fifteen—she heard the rush of water. Before she had taken two dozen steps more, she came upon a small stream. It bubbled over the rocks and plashed in small rapids.

"Bingo," she said to herself and bent down to take a drink. It was cold, clear, and delicious.

When she got back to the campsite, the other two had made a regular summer home of the lean-to. They had not only covered it with green pine branches, but Rose had "swept" it clean so that the floor was free of rocks and leaves. Eli was trying to light a fire with a long stick and a piece of flat wood.

"Oh, don't tell me you can start a fire," said Anna incredulously.

"I know how," grunted Eli, without looking up, "but I don't know if I can . . . unless you got a lighter."

"Sorry, I'm trying to quit. All I have is my jackknife."

As if by divine appointment, Rose flounced up. "Here!" She presented Eli with a red book of matches.

Anna was impressed against her will. "You thought to bring matches with you?"

"No, I found them on the ground over there." She pointed to the rock.

"You just found them? How could you just . . . *find* them?" But Eli took the matchbook and opened it. "There's only two matches!"

"And you're welcome."

"Well, save them 'cause you don't want to light it yet," said Anna. "It's not dark."

They gathered some sticks for firewood, and then all went to get a drink from the stream. By the time they had drunk, their concerns about getting home had been pushed aside. They were all starting to feel adventurous. They ended up taking off their shoes and socks and splashing around in the water. They even managed to catch two crayfish, which Anna insisted on roasting for lunch. Rose protested, but Eli agreed with resignation that it would be necessary to "live off the land." Anna tied them into one of her socks to keep them from getting away.

On the way back to camp, they stumbled upon a patch of wild strawberries, which was fortunate as they were now really hungry. While Eli started the fire, Rose took off her jacket and went back to fill it with as many berries as she could, and Anna skewered the crayfish on sticks for roasting. There wasn't much meat on them, but as Rose adamantly refused to touch the "baby lobsters," Eli and Anna each got a whole one.

By the time they were finished eating, it was late afternoon. They went back to the stream. It had grown warmer as the day wore on, so they left their jackets on the bank to mark the place and walked upstream. It was obvious by the rockiness of the shore that the river was only a fraction of the width it had once been. Outside of a small waterfall that chirped and bubbled downstream, it was rather dull.

A most exciting thing, however, happened on their way back to their coats. They had crossed the fall and come down the opposite bank when they came upon an eddy formed by a ring of rocks, and swimming lazily in the little pool was the most beautiful trout. Or salmon. Well, a fish anyway—since none of them had ever been fishing, they weren't certain what kind. But it was longer than Rose's arm.

"It must have gotten stuck in here when the water was higher," said Eli.

"Cool!" cried Anna. "Supper!"

"No!" cried Rose. "Absolutely no! And I'm not eating bugs, and I'm not eating—"

"Oh, come on," said Anna. "You like fish. You just never had to get your own before. You'll be glad for it later."

Finally, under threat of being dunked head first in the river,

Rose agreed to help. They stripped down to their undies and stepped into the cold water.

It was a long process requiring a great deal of thrashing and splashing, but after nearly an hour, they all lay exhausted on the bank—all except the fish, which continued to thrash about on the grass. They would have never gotten it at all except that the fish, in a final bid for freedom, had leapt high out of the water. Rose, standing right in its flight path, had screamed and thrown out both hands, knocking it clean out of the pool onto the bank. Anna dove on it and wrestled it away from the water's edge. Afterward Eli called Rose "Little Nimrod," a name Rose proudly used for the rest of the night, though Anna was sure she didn't know who Nimrod was—because Anna didn't.

It was a long and messy haul back to camp, and when they arrived, they were famished. They were fortunate that it was a large fish. Between their botched attempts at gutting it with Anna's knife, burning the tail black, and Eli's dropping a piece into the fire after singeing her fingers, there was a lot less of it than there might have been. But even so, it was one of the best meals Anna had ever eaten.

Chapter 7

It would be nice to say the girls had a good night's sleep, but they didn't. Their lives had featured some hard knocks, to be sure, but they'd always had a roof and a bed. The idea of sleeping out under the stars always had a romantic appeal to Anna, but the reality proved much less comfortable. The ground was hard and the air chilly. By lying close together in the tiny lean-to under all three of their jackets, they almost managed to stay warm. Eli and Anna had shared a bed for a few years and could do so without bothering each other, but Rose was a fitful and greedy sleeper. Her unconscious bids for the "blankets" kept Eli and Anna awake in alternate turns.

Many hours after the sun went down, Anna was forcefully jostled awake by Eli.

"What the . . . ?" Anna began.

"Get up, look, look!"

Anna sat up bleary-eyed. Rose was out cold, but Eli was sitting by the fire, which she had prodded back to life. She pointed at the sky. One look heavenward and Anna too was awake and out of the shelter. Floating high above them (or maybe not so high) was the largest moon she had ever seen. It was at least a third larger than her own moon, nearly full, and a curious red color.

"Have you ever seen anything like it?" Eli loved astronomy along with . . . well, everything else, and she knew loads of stuff about planets, asteroids, and things. Anna's own knowledge was limited, but that monstrous red circle left her speechless and wondering.

"You know what this means, don't you?" Eli poked the fire timidly with a stick. "We're not on Earth anymore."

"What?"

"Yeah." Eli sat there calmly, but her voice betrayed a sort of wistful excitement. "Haven't you wondered where we are?"

"I guess." Actually she hadn't really thought about it. Now that the subject had been raised, however . . .

"I've been thinking about it," Eli said. "At first I thought maybe we were still in Carolina somewhere—maybe even somewhere close to home, but now . . ." She looked up at the moon again—that great, bloated orb. "That's not our moon. And since the moon always looks the same from anywhere on Earth, it's got to mean we're not on Earth."

"So you do think we're in heaven?" Anna gave a halfhearted laugh.

"No." By the sound of her voice Anna could tell Eli's face had reddened. "Not heaven, but the heavens, maybe. My best guess is Deimos or Phobos."

"Huh?"

"You remember—the Martian moons."

"You think we're on Mars?" said Anna

"No, stupid. Look!" Eli pointed up again. "See how red that is? Just like Mars in pictures. And if we're close enough for it to look like that, then the only thing I can think of is that we're on one of its moons."

"But that's impossible," said Anna.

"Yeah, I know. I thought moons were barren."

But Anna wasn't thinking about the vegetation. She was scandalized by the idea itself. She could not bring herself to believe it. It was impossible. Another planet? It was science fiction. But then, she would have said the same about the window in the wine cellar, and . . .well, here they were.

The realization was so disorienting that neither felt like talking. They just sat, staring at the great crimson sphere in the kind of silence usually reserved for churches. But Anna knew they should sleep and eventually said so. They crawled back in under the jackets and lay with their heads sticking out so they could see the moon.

The fire dwindled again, but they were warm now huddled together, and neither moved or spoke.

Long after she thought Eli had fallen asleep, Anna's mind was still racing. *It just can't be.* She finally dozed and dreamt. In her dream, she saw the black expanse of an eternal ocean, dotted far and wide with insignificant motes of rock, like grains of pollen. She floated among them, thinking, *I am on one of those.* She blew, and they scattered before her like dust.

Chapter 8

Anna was again rudely awakened, but this time by Rose, and it was morning.

"Anna, Anna!" Rose banged her on top of her head. "Eli! Look, look!"

Feeling groggy and sour and not convinced Rose had anything to say important enough to justify waking her, Anna grunted and rolled over. But she felt Eli dutifully stir, and a moment later she was almost trampled by Eli rocketing out of the shelter.

"What the—" complained Anna.

"Holy crud!" Eli cried.

Anna peeked out of one eye.

"You guys were sleeping," said Rose breathlessly, "so I got up quiet as I could. Then I looked, and . . ."

Anna could see a blurry Eli standing next to a blurrier Rose. Both were staring intently at something small and round in Eli's hand. The compass. Suddenly Anna was wide awake too and scrambling out of the shelter.

Sure enough, the needles on the compass had stopped their freewheeling holiday and gone back to work. This time, however, they both were pointing due north (if it really was north) and were lying nearly on top of one another.

"What's it mean?" asked Rose.

"It means there's another window—in that direction." Eli pointed.

"Hurray!" said Rose. "Camping was fun, but I want a Pop-Tart."

"But we don't know how far away it is," Eli said.

"Then we should get a drink," said Anna, "and pick as many berries as we can carry."

After the drink, they washed up, put out the embers of their fire (at Eli's insistence), and made for the berry patch. They filled the pockets of their jackets.

"I wonder what the Nag will say when she sees your coat." Anna watched Rose put a particularly mushy berry into her pocket.

"Meh!" said Rose with a shrug. "I don't care, so long as I don't have to eat another strawberry for a long time! I wonder what Cook's got for breakfast. Actually I just want Cheerios."

When they had a good supply, they consulted the compass again and made in that direction. Rose, carrying the compass, bounced into the lead like a bird dog. The trees grew farther apart and the undergrowth thinned, which they took as a good sign.

After a few minutes of walking, Eli sidled up to Anna and, making sure Rose was too far ahead to hear, said in a low voice, "You know, we're not on a Martian moon."

"No?"

"Nu-uh." Eli pointed upward. "Look at the sun. If this were anywhere near Mars, it would look a lot smaller than that. That's about the same size as our sun."

"Well then, Galileo, where are we?" asked Anna.

"No idea, but—"

But she was cut off by Rose's hollering. "Guys, come quick! Look at this!"

The two girls broke into a trot and caught up with Rose at the tree line. A scrubby landscape descended before them into a broad valley. The wood continued along the top of the highland to their right, but to their left it followed the descent of the land into the valley, fading into indistinct shades of brown and green for a few miles. At that point, like a line drawn in the dirt, all the green stopped, both of the forest on their left and the heath before them. Everything became sand, or what looked to be sand. A vast plain of it stretched all the way to the horizon in three directions. But for the color, it might have been the ocean.

All this they absorbed in a moment and almost unconsciously, for their attention was immediately seized by something else. In the middle of the valley lay a city—a very large city with many buildings. Not large like Chicago, but like an old city—like Jerusalem or Baghdad might have looked long ago. Its original circumference was clearly defined by a circular wall of medieval proportions. But the city had spilled beyond the walls into suburbs, with streets running far in every direction except toward the sand.

Two gigantic boulevards crossed the city in the center, like a cross. In the midst of the town, dominating the landscape, stood two great hills, one on either side of the main road. What looked like a bridge joined the peaks together.

The city was too far away to make out more detail, but it sprawled like a sleeping giant, its nearest part at least a couple miles away. The intervening terrain, descending gradually, was broken up by fields framed with walls of heaped-up rock, and everything had an old and withered look to it. Little thatched-roof houses dotted the landscape.

"There's people," said Eli, dumbfounded. Not that they saw anyone; even in the outlying streets and fields, they saw no movement except for an occasional sheep.

"Is the arrow pointing to the city?" asked Anna.

Rose looked at it for a moment, then shook it as if she wasn't sure.

"Oh, give it here," said Anna impatiently. She made a grab for it, but Eli was quicker. She held it up so they all could see. The horizontal arrow still pointed straight ahead, and, somewhat discouragingly, so did the vertical one.

"No, it doesn't point at the city," said Eli. "The height arrow doesn't point down into the valley at all. It points . . . well . . . out over it." She gestured at the vast sea of sand before them. "Like out there."

"To the desert?" cried Rose.

The full significance of this took a moment to register. Then Anna collapsed onto the grass and said in a voice full of sarcasm, "Of course it does. Right out into the desert! Well now, ain't that just ditty!"

Her sisters sat down beside her, and for a few minutes none of them spoke. What were they supposed to do now? Go down into that strange city? Or more unthinkably, go wandering out into a desert looking for a window that they might or might not be able to see? Suddenly Anna thought that listening to the Nag chew them out over berry-stained coats wouldn't be so bad, if only they could get back for her to do it.

"Oh!" cried Rose, as if she had been pricked with a pin. "Look!" and she pointed.

Anna didn't see anything at first. Then she too started. About thirty yards away, just before the tree line, on a great boulder similar to the one they had camped by the previous night, sat a chubby old man, watching them intently. Realizing he had been seen, he wriggled off the rock, not altogether gracefully, and wad-dled toward them, assisted by a long, ebony-black wooden staff.

From below a bald spot on top of his head, snow-white hair cascaded to the man's shoulders, framing a shiny round face, clean shaven—a boyish face. Shabby, steel-blue robes with black bands at the seams cloaked his portly frame. To Anna, the robes resem-bled those of a wizard—or a college professor—but the man's face and hair made him look more like Ben Franklin or the guy on the oatmeal can.

Startled, none of the girls moved until finally Eli stepped for-ward and, as the man paused, executed a deep, graceful curtsy. Anna's jaw dropped. If this had happened anywhere else, she would have burst out laughing. Eli must have been practicing curtsies privately in her room since the first day she got to Keddy Manor!

"Now, now," said the old man with a wave of his hand, "this isn't court. We needn't stand on such manners here."

Anna liked him instantly.

Eli jerked upright and blushed. Realizing he had embarrassed her, the old man added, "But it isn't every day an old duffer like me is greeted with such graceful respect. It would be scandalous not to respond in kind." He laid his hand upon his heart and bowed deeply to Eli.

"Uh . . . thank you," said Eli. An awkward silence ensued till the man spoke again.

"Now, what shall I make of three young ladies wandering the moor in such strange clothing? First, I might imagine that you're looking for your mother or your—"

"Our mom is dead," said Rose curtly.

Anna stared at her. Rose was usually the sociable one.

The old man looked surprised. "Dead? Oh my, I'm terribly sorry. May I ask how she died?"

It was such an oddly forward question that Rose just stared blankly at him. But Eli, diplomatic to the core, gave a measured reply. "It was a long time ago, and it's not a subject we enjoy talking about, if you don't mind."

"Oh, again, I am sorry," he said, looking genuinely apologetic and laying his hand on his heart. "I did not intend to pry. I can sometimes see people's circumstances. I am a prophet of sorts . . . well, just a bodache, technically, but sometimes I know things. That is, sometimes." He gave a strained laugh. "Though I am not so clear-sighted as in my youth. Oh, in those days, I could have told you your names, your birthday, even your favorite food."

"Ice cream," said Rose, still a little chilly.

"Yes, of course it is. Just what I was about to say." He smiled kindly at Rose. And they all stood there looking at each other as another inelegant moment passed. "Well . . ." He sighed again, looking down at the city. "I suppose I should leave you to your adventure then." And he turned to walk away.

"Wait," said Anna. For better or worse, he was the only one there who knew where he was. "We're sort of . . . well, lost." She looked at Eli, who nodded. "And we could use some help."

The old man paused. "You mean to say you really are here alone?"

Anna nodded.

"I knew it, I knew it!" He looked very pleased with himself. "The moment you stepped out of the woods, I said to myself, 'Now, Whinsom, there are three girls who don't belong here.' Now, don't tell me . . ." He stared hard at them and put one finger to his temple in concentration. "You've come from somewhere else . . . not, eh, even part of this world, I shouldn't wonder."

"Why, yes," said Eli with genuine surprise. "That's it exactly . . . or I think it is."

"I knew it, I knew it." He patted his chest. "I still have it. Well, sometimes at least."

"But doesn't that seem a little strange to you?" Anna could not imagine herself telling some stranger that they were from another world—although she had often seen people at the mall about whom she'd wondered.

"Oh, yes indeed, very strange, to be sure," he said. "Not at all common. But as I said, I am a prophet . . . well, a bodache at least."

"What's a bo-dash?" said Rose.

But Eli interrupted. "Then can you tell us where we are?"

"Oh, I need not be prophet to answer that, my dear." The old man smiled kindly. "This world is called Errus." He gestured widely. "And you are in the kingdom of Garlandium."

"Of what?" Anna frowned.

"But of course, if you are from another world, then you would not have heard of it. Most interesting. One always underestimates the challenges of communicating with persons from other worlds." He shook his head sadly.

"You mean this has happened before?" said Eli.

He eyed her curiously. "Oh, yes, I happen to know that it has. Not often, of course. Almost never, in fact. If it happened too frequently, I should hardly have reason to suggest it. But as it is very rare, it must mean that you are very special."

"Not really," said Anna. "It was more sort of luck—or an accident."

"As if there really were any such thing!" chortled the man. "I do long to hear the story, but it is nearing lunchtime, and as it seems unlikely that you have another engagement, might I invite you to have lunch with me. I have some sandwiches in the wagon, and if it is amenable to you, I would be happy to give you a ride into the city. It is about an hour's ride back to the temple, which would be sufficient time, I think, to hear your tale. And I presume you have some questions as well?"

The idea of a sandwich pulled Anna forward, while her concern about going off with a stranger held her back. But he was offering answers, and she could see that Eli was also weighing his offer. In the end, hunger and the desire for information won out, and the girls found themselves wandering over the grassy hill after the old man.

Chapter 9

Soon they came upon a cart hitched to a small donkey, standing on a lightly trod path.

"Oh!" cried Rose and rushed forward to pat its nose. The donkey accepted her affection like a well-treated animal—neither overly grateful nor disinterested, merely contented, looking at her with soft, liquid eyes. Rose's indulgence, however, meant that she lost her chance to sit on the bench of the cart, which was only wide enough for three. She grudgingly climbed into the back, where she was soon playing in the hay that lined the floor.

When the old man was seated, the donkey turned and looked back at him with baleful eyes. Anna was sure it had frowned.

"Don't worry, Cyreneus," said the old man to the donkey. "I'm sure they are quite light, and it's downhill anyway."

The donkey tilted its head to one side and gave a mulish snort.

"We can't leave them stranded here. It's not good manners."

The donkey snorted again and loosed a disgruntled bray.

"That's the most pitiful excuse I've ever heard! I swear, you lazy thing! Remember that you expressed hearty agreement in coming back here today. There's no use complaining just because we found something more interesting than apples to bring back." The old man held no reins, Anna noticed, and the donkey had no bit or bridle, only the halter that held the cart to it. "One would think you'd forgotten that it was only yesterday that, here in this very place, we—"

"Mister?" said Anna.

"Whinsom, if you please," said the old man as the cart lurched forward.

"Uh . . . Mister Whinsom," she tried again, but the donkey lifted its head and brayed, and she was sure she had just been laughed at. "Do you really think your donkey understands you?" With that, the cart pulled up so suddenly that the girls were nearly thrown from the seat, and from the back came a thud and a pitiful "Ow!" from Rose. The donkey turned and looked at Anna as if it had been insulted.

"Well, I never," said Whinsom, not to Anna, but to the donkey. "You old rascal! As if you haven't already made it perfectly clear what you think of them! Remember, they're not from around here. Get along, you old ass, or I'll rethink my offer of the mash tonight."

Old Cyreneus looked at Whinsom, snorted once more, and the cart jerked forward again. Apparently having forgotten the question, the old man began to whistle. Anna and Eli looked at each other.

"I think it must," whispered Eli.

"Mister." Now it was Rose's turn. She leaned over the back of the seat with her head poking between Anna and Eli's shoulders.

"Whinsom, I must insist."

"What's a bo-dash?"

"What? Do you not have priests in your world?"

The girls were taken aback. They were only "educationally religious." That is, Teddy took a very academic view of religion. They had been to church numerous times, or rather, to numerous churches one time each. And he'd selected each for its educational and experiential value. At one, everyone sang loudly, shouted a lot, and some even ran around the auditorium. At another, no one had spoken much at all except a robed man at the front, and he only in Latin—or was it Greek?

"Sort of," said Anna, thinking of the priest at the Mass, "But they're not called bo-dash . . . es."

"Bodachie is the plural," the priest corrected. "In Garlandium, a bodache is a priest of considerable age and experience. But you mustn't think ill of me. I am not a Merrisian bodache; I am of the Thesian order." And there was a hint of pride in his voice.

Anna could make nothing of the last part of that, so she said nothing. Even Rose only grunted, "Oh," and retracted her head like a turtle into its shell.

"Goodness grief! I have almost forgotten our lunch." The priest looked over his shoulder at Rose. "Dear . . . oh, I don't even know your names. There is a small basket there under the blanket. You'll find several sandwiches in it and a flask." Anna heard Rose shuffling around, and a minute later a few squashy packages were handed forward. They were sandwiches, but not like those the girls were used to. The bread was dense and dark and tasted like dried peas. The meat was strange and gamey. Anna liked it. Eli and Rose were not so fond, but they were all hungry. In return, the girls shared their strawberries with Whinsom, and with Cyreneus as well. The priest offered them a flask of green glass covered in a wicker sleeve. Anna took a sip, but it made her gasp and cough. Eli and Rose declined. The priest apologized profusely, saying he hadn't realized their palates were "so young." Then he offered them water from a skin he carried under his cloak.

"I am sorry to have to ask you each to take but a swallow," he apologized. "After all, it *is* water, and we must not indulge too freely." This puzzled Anna, but the girls all complied. They found the water warm and unpleasant. The priest drank none but immediately put the skin back inside his cloak.

"I know I said I wanted to hear your story, but we'll be in the city in a wee bit, and I shan't be able to hear you over the ruckus. And now I think of it, I should like my brother Cholerish to hear it as well—we're, twins you know," he said with a proud smile. The city had grown gradually larger as they weaved down the hill.

The girls could now see the meandering path was widening and would eventually become the main road through the city center.

Thatched huts were giving way to houses of stone and brick. Cobblestones began rattling under the wagon's wheels.

But they still saw almost no people. Only very occasionally an old woman's head would pop through a window, or a child would run along a side street.

"Where are all the people?" Eli shivered. It was a little eerie.

"Well, there are a great deal fewer people here now than when I was boy," sighed the priest. "But that's not what you mean, of course. Today is the final day of the Merrisian Revelry, and everyone is at the temple celebrating. A lot of horsefeathers, if you ask me."

"But I thought you were a priest," said Rose.

"Of course I am. But as I said, I am not a Merrisian bodache. I am a Thesian."

Rose stared at him blankly.

"Oh, how I forget. In your world you probably still have but a single religion." Anna and Eli exchanged looks but said nothing. "Here, since the beginning men have worshipped Thes, the one true God who made all things, even the celestial emissaries." And he gestured toward the sky. "But about eight hundred years ago, the Merrisian order arose." And here he pointed at the sun, which was now high in the sky. "Yes," he continued sadly. "Over time the emissaries—that is, Merris, Vercandrus, and their five children— were elevated to the chief order, and Thes was nearly forgotten."

"What is a Merris?" asked Rose.

"Merris is she who gives life and warmth to the world." He pointed again to the sun. "Surely you have celestial emissaries in your world too."

"If you mean a sun, yeah," said Anna, "but we don't worship it."

"And quite right. You shouldn't," said the priest. "She is a servant of Thes, and so too her consort, Vercandrus, and their children as well. Thes made them all, and important though they be, they themselves know their place better."

"Do you mean planets or just mythology?" said Eli.

"What's the difference?" said the priest. "The heavenly bodies are but the physical expression of their great spirits. But yes, I do mean the sun and moon and the planets. To each is given a part of creation to judge and care for—to one the sea, to another the land, and so on. But we never ought to have made gods out of servants, even servants so grand as the emissaries."

Anna was about to comment that they had no such nonsense in their own world, when Eli surprised her by saying the exact opposite. "Yes, it's like that in our world too. Mars brings war and Venus brings peace and love."

The priest looked at her with sincere interest. "Young lady, I would hear more of this."

"But people don't really believe that stuff anymore," said Anna, who felt that Eli was beginning to show off a little too much.

"Really!" said the priest excitedly. "So you've actually been able to orchestrate a return to Thes. How marvelous!"

This was going all wrong, thought Anna. How could she explain something so complex as religious diversity to someone who knew only two religious orders? But other things were rapidly consuming their attention. The buildings were growing denser all the time. The city wall was before them, and a great arch with twin gates was looming. For the first time, they also began to hear sounds of commotion and life.

"Behold," said Whinsom with a grand gesture. "The once-great city of Halighyll!"

Chapter 10

It was clear what Whinsom meant by "once-great." Halighyll was a city of splendor, or at least it had been at some earlier time. The buildings were large and many-storied but dilapidated. Everywhere she looked, Anna saw pillars and stone porches, but with holes where blocks had fallen out, crumbled, or been removed. Large frayed tapestries hung out of windows and across archways. Most were faded and dull, but Anna could tell they had once been of rich reds and purples. Everything seemed to have a layer of grime, and an ancient, decrepit drabness clung to every surface—much as she imagined places like *Byzantium* or *Persia*.

The religious aspect of the city was also on display. Hanging over the city gate was a humungous faded yellow banner featuring a woman seated on a throne, with two great trees growing on either side of her, their branches arching together over her. The sun was portrayed rising directly behind her so that its rays formed a crown that encircled her head, and she held her hands apart in a gesture of welcome or embrace.

"Is that Merris?" asked Eli.

"To be sure."

Other celestial emissaries were represented on banners hung up and down the streets—boys and girls, one holding a great diamond; another sitting on a panther-like cat; another holding aloft a hammer; and many others. "Her children," they were told. And finally Vercandrus—a great, bearded titan of a man, brandishing a sword above his head and holding out his other hand in protection toward the viewer. It was all very grand and very dismal at the same time. Anna sniffed. The city even smelled old.

The depressing, semiruined condition of everything was, however, out of step with the people—of whom hundreds, perhaps thousands, yammered in the streets. From the moment the girls clattered through the gates, they were surrounded by a great throng—groups dancing in circles, musicians with stringed instruments and drums, vendors with stalls of fruit and pastries and small mechanical trinkets. There were jugglers, contortionists, and buffoons. And everywhere, people were moving and milling and running about the streets and in and out of doors.

The girls also saw people who appeared to be priests. They wore robes similar to Whinsom's but of different colors. They were the only brightly colored things anywhere—like Christmas ornaments popping in and out of view among the tree branches. Anna saw robes of rich maroon, dark blue, and canary yellow. Though mingled throughout the crowd, they were also curiously separate. People drew back from them and bowed as they passed. But no one bowed to Whinsom; he was met with looks of curiosity, confusion, and even dismay.

Eli had noticed this. "Why do people look at you that way, Whinsom?"

"Hah! They're wondering who I could be—some poor impostor or heretic."

As if on command, the cart halted. A troop of soldiers in rusty mail and helms had surrounded it. Each had a sword strapped to his side, and several carried halberds. They looked rough and callous. Rose ducked down into the cart, peeping out like a rabbit from its hole.

Anna held her breath as a tall, thick man, presumably their captain, stepped up. "Here now, what's this?" He had a droopy handlebar moustache and dark eyes that looked as if they didn't get a lot of sleep. People had drawn back from the wagon but remained out of curiosity. "You best hope you's a priest out of uniform, because if you is impersonating a—"

Whinsom was unruffled. "You must be Dolphus. I heard the garrison was getting a new commander. All settled in, I hope? How was the journey from Garlandvale?"

The captain stood openmouthed for a moment, squinting one eye suspiciously at Whinsom. "You seem to know lots about me, but what I needs to know is what you're doing parading about in a priest's robe. And I ain't never seen one that color before."

Whinsom sighed. Apparently deciding that this fly needed swatting, he stood up in the wagon and thundered, "Nor shall you oft see them much hereafter. I am a bodache in the service of almighty Thes, whose name you impugn by this festival. It is beyond your authority to detain me further." He plopped back down, calm as before. "Get along now, Cyreneus." The donkey brayed loudly, and the soldiers in front of them stepped nervously aside.

"Thes!" Dolphus was wide-eyed. "Gawl! I'd heard about you folk in the Vale, but I never thought I'd actually see one." But he did not stop them, and the wagon clattered on. When Anna looked over her shoulder a minute later, the soldiers were still standing in the street, watching them. Dolphus had removed his helm and was scratching his scalp.

Whinsom leaned over to them as if imparting a great secret. "It's always the same with the new ones. They've never seen Thesian colors before, and I have to break them in. He's actually more informed than most. Many who come to Halighyll have never even heard of Thes. In fact, I and my brother are the only two of the order left now that old Robey is gone."

They were now in the shadow of the two great hills, which the girls could see formed, together, the base of a single complicated temple site with ascending stairs and buildings built right into the hillsides, and with a great stone structure atop each one. The two peaks were joined by a great bridge, and they could see people celebrating on the peak of the arch, throwing streamers and flow-ers down on the streets below.

"This—" the priest pointed upward—"is the temple of Merris, monstrosity that it is."

"Is that where we're going?" shouted Rose from the back. A vendor with snow-white hair had thrust some sort of baked good into her hand, and she was munching happily.

"No, no. We're going to a much humbler place than this."

Even in its griminess, the Merrisian temple was impressive—court after pillared court encircling each hill up to the pinnacle, where rested massive stone temples reminiscent of the Parthenon but with spires. The girls stared awestruck as they passed under it. After this, the crowd began to thin. Celebrants still danced and congregated at every corner and in the street, but fewer vendors and carts blocked their way.

Anna knew exactly when they reached the center of the city, for a great circular colonnade like a roundabout presented itself where the two main roads intersected. Here the festivities were redoubled, and the whole of the intersection was filled with "wretched jollification," as Whinsom called it. But he bobbed his head and hummed along to the music. Anna got the impression that he very much enjoyed "jollification," and she wondered what made it "wretched."

They slowly wound their way around the revelers, continu-ing north on the same road past the junction. But here the girls learned a bit more of the strange ways of that country. At each of the four corners where the roads entered the city center stood a stone arch with a marble statue upon it. A thick column holding a fifth statue stood at the circle center.

"They are the five children of Merris and Vercandrus," shouted Whinsom. The statues were all very stylized—children in size and proportion but with oddly adult features and positions, like those very old paintings of the baby Jesus with his halo. All were fac-ing the Merrisian temple with some gesture of acknowledgment.

Anna's attention was drawn to the statue of a girl riding a fish and holding a goblet aloft with both hands.

"What's with the fish?"

"That is Therra. She is the emissary of the sea, and the fish is her consort. The emissaries each have many representations within creation—symbols of their sphere of governance."

"It's just like ancient Rome," said Eli.

"And just as stupid!" said Anna.

"That's the spirit!" Whinsom clapped her on the back. "But do not deprecate the emissaries just because all these ignorami have misunderstood them. They too are creatures of Thes, and it is only when Thes is forgotten that their proper place in the cosmic order becomes confused."

They progressed up the road toward the northern edge of the city, and the crowds continued to thin until they came to neighborhoods of relative quiet. Even shops were closed as proprietors attended the revelry. Another hill rose before them with a smaller collection of buildings on it and a single thin tower projecting from the apex of the hill. They were clearly making for it.

"Behold, the temple of Vercandrus!" The priest smacked his lips in sarcasm.

"But I thought we were going to your own temple," said Anna.

"Oh, we are. That is the temple of Thes as well. When the new cultus arose, it celebrated Merris *and* Vercandrus together. It possessed at least that much truth and dignity. They built the Merrisian temple first, but when it came time to build one for Vercandrus, they had run out of money. So they just renamed the Thesian temple and added a few Vercandrian bobbles, like that fallacious tower there. Preposterous!"

The road became a wide bridge spanning a chasm, deep like a quarry and encircling the hill like a moat. The bottom was dry and cracked as though it had once held water. The cart rattled forward again, and the girls strained to look over the edge into the ravine.

"Do you ever put water in it?" asked Rose.

"Dear child, the reservoir has not held water for nearly eight hundred years!"

"That's about the same time the new religion . . . uh, happened," said Eli.

"You are a sensible creature, aren't you? But that history is very sketchy, and most believe that the Flow of Segancurs, which ran across the desert into Halighyll to fill this very moat, is just a myth. But you must be exhausted with all these new things. No more stories until you've rested and been refreshed."

They passed the remaining minutes of the journey in silence. And as the cart clattered under a final arch into the temple compound, Anna was not surprised to see a huge statue on the arch. But it was not a nameless piece of marble now. She recognized the great bearded giant, Vercandrus, looking fatherly and protective with his powerful chest bared and his strong arm holding aloft a sword. He was flanked by wild boars with long tusks. An unexpectedly heavy realization pressed down upon her. There was one great difference between this and Rome. The Roman gods were part of her world. Even though she detested them, they were part of her story. But she had no share in this history. She was an utter stranger here, and nothing of it, not even its gods, belonged to her.

Chapter 11

The priests of Vercandrus wore coarse brown robes like Franciscan friars. Anna thought it a somber color that matched their demeanor. Whinsom told them that these priests did not interrupt their fasts and disputations for things like the revelry. She saw several of them in the courtyard in a knot, arguing vigorously, but she could not understand their disagreement. More gathered in antechambers, and still more crowded the corridors of the temple. All wore the same dour face, all had clean-shaven heads, and all were men. Eli asked whether women could be priests—a question so curious to Whinsom that he pulled up short.

"What? Why shouldn't they be priests? Well, now," he mused, "Vercandrus's paternal nature seems to attract more men than women, which is natural, I suppose, but there are a few. The order of Merris is much the reverse, as you might expect, and the orders of their children are quite mixed. Each priestly candidate perceives himself or herself called to the service of the emissary that is most sympathetic to his or her own nature. As a Thesian, I, of course, did not have to make such a narrow choice." And he gave a pious little bow and an impious little grin.

It was also clear that the priesthood of Vercandrus thought very little of Whinsom. "Personally," he whispered as they walked down a long portico filled with morose brown-clad priests, who muttered and pointed, "for as few as they are, I find the ladies of Vercandrus a welcome reprieve from the men. These little boys can be so tedious and argumentative." Whinsom, with his bright and airy personality, clearly shared none of the monks' tendency toward sobriety and solitude. "And I absolutely refuse to wear brown," he said with a wink.

They passed through a large auditorium filled with priests listening to a lecturer, who seemed much exercised about the difference between "logical and essential predicates in reference to the nature of absolute being." Whinsom merely rolled his eyes. Anna wondered if the temple were also part university. Several passages later, Whinsom swung open a door and gestured them through it. It turned out to be his own quarters, which he shared with his brother Cholerish. It was simple but warmly appointed with a fireplace and shelves upon shelves of books. The floor was stone, but the rug was thick; the windows were curtainless but made of a cloudy powder-blue glass; and although the walls were bare rock, numerous hangings adorned them. Small mechanical devices whirled on small tables, and the smell of tea filled the air.

A thin voice called from another room, "Is that you, Whin? I didn't expect you back so soon. Do you want a cup of—"

The speaker came into the room, carrying a tray with a steaming pot on it. His hair was gray-white like Whinsom's, but if they were twins, you would not know it to look at them. Whinsom was merry and round like a ball; Cholerish was straight and thin like a pencil. His face was gaunt and hawkish, with the bright, penetrating eyes of an eagle, and his hair was wiry, disheveled, and projected from his head as though he had lost a battle with a light socket. And even though he had not been smiling when he entered the room, his face still managed to fall when he saw the girls. He stopped in his tracks and stared. His right eye was the slightest bit lazy and tended to wander off to the side as though looking for something on its own. "It's Mad-Eye Moody!" whispered Rose. Anna elbowed her but couldn't help agreeing that he looked at least like a mad scientist.

The counterfeit Auror opened his mouth, closed it again, then decided to speak after all. "Have you nothing better to do, brother, than bring home foreign riffraff? Am I to be subjected to daily intrusions by—"

"Come, come, Chol," said Whinsom in a sing-songy, taunting voice. "I think these young ladies have a story that you will want to hear."

"You said that yesterday too." Cholerish set the tray down on a table, shoving several books aside to make room for it. He disappeared down the little hallway from which he had come, muttering under his breath.

Whinsom looked at them sheepishly. "He is right, you know. I have a great weakness for a good story." Eli had already begun to edge toward the bookshelves. Anna rolled her eyes.

"Oh, by all means, dear, have a look. I would bet you have not heard of many of the titles you'll find here." Anna hadn't thought of that. She too went to the nearest shelf and pulled down a random book. It was titled *Errulogia and Astrologia Omnibus: That is, the properties of the generative elemental natures and of the heavenly emissaries and their relations as they exist in perfect order and by degree* by Dr. Gerundius Bask, First Order of Berducca-scientia.

She lost interest in the rest and turned instead to the tapestry. It looked initially like a series of concentric circles. Well, not circles—more like ovals. Then she noticed that the large yellow circle in the center was labeled Merris.

It's a map of the planets, Anna thought. Each of the ovals was in fact a planetary orbit, and somewhere along each path she saw a little colored circle with a label. From the center orbit out, the labels read Berducca, Therra, Avonia, Errus, and, after a long gap, Vercandrus, which was a substantially larger dot approaching the size of the sun. She also noticed that the planet labeled Errus was enclosed by an exaggerated ellipse of its own. This lunar orbit had its own reddish dot labeled Lemerrus.

"Excellent astronomy," said Whinsom softly over her shoulder, "but a very uninspiring religion." Anna had always been the kind of person who, if she could see it, could understand it. And now she did. Oh, not the mythology part. That she still thought silly. But the reality that she was outside her own world settled over her again—and the recognition that no amount of travel in any direction could take her home. Outside of that small window the compass stubbornly pointed to, no hope existed of Anna's ever seeing Earth or her own father again.

Chapter 12

Cholerish returned with another tray bearing three more cups. Whinsom pulled chairs together into a rough circle, then poured the tea into the cups and handed them to the girls. Even Rose was extra careful and spilled not a drop.

Cholerish sighed resignedly. "Now let's hear what it is that has so captivated my poor brother that he has dragged you from whatever comfortable beds you were sleeping in last night to have thin tea with two moldy old bodachie. And do not skimp on the details, for though I am nowhere near as gullible as my brother, I enjoy a story just as much."

The priests settled into their chairs with a fugue of grunts and sighs. Whinsom pulled out a pipe and commenced stuffing weed into the bowl like Gandalf himself. Neither said anything, but both stared hard at the girls—Whinsom with a grin and Cholerish with a grimace.

Eli never could endure this sort of silence. "So, uh . . . I didn't see any statues of Thes," she said.

"There are none," spat Cholerish. "How should one depict the Maker of all things—as a creature? What then would be the point?"

Eli deflated in her chair and turned red. Rose, however, who was always more aware of her own curiosity than of any social awkwardness, took up the question. "Then how do you know what he looks like?"

"Thes is not a man," said Whinsom patiently.

"You mean he's a girl?" said Rose, with something between shock and admiration.

"No, no!" snapped Cholerish. "Stop being so simple. Thes is . . . just Thes. You don't use pronouns for the Holy. *He, she, it*—pah! Pronouns are the least respectful form of address. Crass verbal shorthand, all of them! Merris, Vercandrus, their children, the longaevi, and we ourselves are all creatures of Thes. But Thes is . . . Thes. Next they'll be telling us, Whin, that Thes should have case endings and even—" he shuddered—"plurals."

"Yes," Whinsom sighed, "we have divine plurals aplenty already. But enough of this. I have waited too long to hear your story, young ladies. If I am forced to wait another moment, I shall burst."

"It's kind of long," said Eli.

"All the better," said Whinsom.

So the girls took it in turns to tell the story of the loss of their mother, their father's melancholy, the move to Keddy Manor, Miss Heavernaggie, the compass, and all that had happened to date. It took much longer than it should have, for Rose kept jumping in to clarify what Miss Heavernaggie was wearing at the time, or which item on her plate had been least palatable, or the fact that Teddy always wore socks to bed. Both priests listened without interrupting, and the longer they went on, the larger Whinsom's smile and Cholerish's grimace became. When the girls had finally finished, neither priest said anything for a long time.

"I don't like it," said Cholerish at last.

"Of course not," said Whinsom, his smile not faltering in the least. "But you have to admit—it is fascinating."

"*That* at least." Cholerish rolled his eyes.

Whinsom leaned in toward Rose, looking very grandfatherly. "I must ask you—and I certainly understand if you don't wish to—but I should very much like to see this compass of yours."

Anna saw Eli start and fidget and knew what she was thinking. Since the compass was their only means of getting home, it was probably unwise to be trotting it out before strangers. But before either of them could say anything, it was in the priest's hand.

Whinsom rolled it over in his palm. Cholerish leaned in to scrutinize. Their heads came close as they examined it, saying not a word. After a moment, Cholerish got up and took it out of Whinsom's hand. Whinsom didn't protest but followed him to a table in the corner, on which sat a complicated mechanism of many lenses on two movable arms, possessing a host of knobs and wheels. Cholerish placed the compass in the central dish, Whinsom flipped a switch on the table, and a bright white light directly over the table popped on—to the girls' surprise, for they had not seen such conveniences yet in the temple. But the surprises kept coming.

Cholerish swung the armful of lenses over the dish and began fiddling with the knobs. He and Whinsom peered at the compass through the various lenses for several minutes, flipping from lens to lens and occasionally trading places, always in silence. Then Whinsom flipped another switch, and a blue light replaced the white one. Every few minutes the lenses or the light changed—blue then yellow then amber—then in various combinations. Using little tools, the priests scratched and tapped the compass at various angles. They hit it with tuning forks under the different lights and bent to listen to the tone. Now and again one would look at the other and either nod or shake his head. For those minutes, it was easy to believe they were twins. They seemed to know each other's mind thoroughly.

When the flipping, plunking, and tapping was finished, Whinsom placed the compass back in Rose's hand. Then the priests sat down again without a word and stared at the girls as before.

"Well," began Eli hesitantly, "do you know what it is?"

"Not exactly," said Cholerish, "but I think we know far more about it than you do."

"True enough, Chol," Whinsom said, "but I think she would rather have us tell her *what* we know, not simply *that* we know. My dears, I believe you already understand what the compass *does*. It is a device for locating a certain chink or opening between the worlds. As for how it does so, that . . . we will need to contemplate a bit. I do not recognize the mechanism, and it does not conform to any law of scientia I am aware of. But I do believe we know where it came from. We are quite certain that it is dwarf-made."

"What-made?" said Anna. She was sure she had misheard him.

"Dwarf-made," repeated Cholerish with no more wonder than if he had said General Electric.

"Are you saying that dwarves made this? Like . . . uh . . . little people?" said Eli hesitantly.

"What other kind of dwarf is there?" snapped Cholerish.

The girls looked at each other in amazement.

"What comes next—questions about whether they live underground or enjoy prospecting for gold?"

"You mean dwarves . . . like real dwarves, not just, uh, short . . . little people." Anna knew that the words coming out made no sense, but it's what came.

The priests stared at her blankly.

"It's just that in our world," said Eli, "we have short, uh, humans, but not real dwarves. Except in stories," she was quick to add.

Now the surprised looks shifted to the priests. Cholerish leaned forward, skepticism etched into every line of his withered face. "You mean to tell me your world does not produce dwarves?"

Eli seemed fuddled by the question. "I don't . . . well, no."

"What of the rest of the Berduccan gnomi?" demanded Cholerish.

Eli shrank away. "I . . . I don't think . . . I mean . . ."

"And what of the longaevi in general—the Avonian sylphi, or the Therran undini, or—"

"Enough, Chol," interrupted Whinsom calmly. "Can't you see she doesn't understand?" He turned to Eli. "My dear, do not let my brother press you about such things. I'm sure your world has all the longaevi that Thes deems appropriate to it. But perhaps, Chol, the longaevi have become even more scarce in their world than they have in ours." Anna sat there dumbly. She followed the verbs all right, but the nouns meant nothing to her.

"Perhaps," said Cholerish a little sulkily. "But it doesn't change the fact that they possess a very ancient dwarf-made relic. It ought to be studied." Anna's heart leapt with fear. "Or better, we should make an expedition to the Aracadian Mountains to find a dwarf and determine the compass's origin. There are Rokan traders in Halighyll for the revelry; we could hire one cheaply—"

"*I* think," said Whinsom pleasantly, raising his eyebrows, "a different expedition is in order for our three young adventurers. The Aracadians are west, whereas their little guide is telling them to go north. And if the desert is their destination, then their timing is quite fortuitous— perhaps even . . . providential."

Cholerish's jaw dropped. "You can't mean—"

Whinsom smiled and nodded. "Lambient."

"But that delirious pseudo-scientist doesn't even believe in what he's looking for!"

"All the more reason he may be willing to help. He has a perfect combination of ambition and distraction to give them transport without being too concerned with their affairs."

"But Whin—"

"Now, now, you of all people know the hazards of interfering in such complicated affairs when we are so unsure of our own footing." Whinsom gave his brother a hard look. "Were it up to me, I would send them east toward Erintenda or even Garland-vale itself. I have reason to think it would be the more helpful journey. But it is not up to you or me, brother, to decide on their behalf. They must be free to act upon their own values. I'm sorry, ladies, that we cannot be of more help. This is *your* adventure, and it is clear that Thes desires *you* to have it. You do not need two has-beens mucking it up with their own agendas. But I believe we can help you by putting you in touch with a certain scientist—an explorer, you might say—who is traveling in your general direction. I cannot say you will find him as conscientious a host as, say, my brother, but you may fare better with others in his company. I must tell you, though, the journey will be a dangerous one. No one has attempted to cross the great Flats for fifty years, and no one who has attempted in the last three hundred has managed to survive. But not to worry," he said with a casual wave of the hand. "This time is sure to be different."

Anna opened her mouth, but no words came out.

Chapter 13

Whinsom rose to his feet, but the girls remained seated in stunned silence. Eli found her voice first. "But to go into the desert . . . it seems so . . . well, isn't there another way?"

"Another way to do what?" asked Cholerish.

"Well . . . to get home."

"Why?" The priest gave his brother a sidelong scowl. "What's so important that you have to get back for?" The question was so blunt that for a moment the girls sat there blinking back at him without an answer.

Rose eventually whispered, "There's Daddy."

"Why should you assume he would still be there?"

"What? Where did Daddy go?" Panic rose in Rose's voice, and she spun like a weathervane in a gale, first to Eli, then to Anna, as if her sisters would know what had happened to their father.

The priest gave a cackle of laughter. "Surely you don't think time runs at the same pace in all worlds?"

"I don't?"

"There is absolutely no reason to think that time flows at the same rate in this world as in yours."

"You mean like Narnia?" asked Eli.

The priest stared at her blankly.

Anna rolled her eyes. "Like he's gonna know what Narnia is, doofus!" Then she addressed the priests. "Look, we have stories where we come from of people who go from one world to another, and no matter how long they stay there, no time has passed when they get back, so—"

Cholerish burst in. "What a preposterously ludicrous idea! What do they teach in the schools where you come from? Time must pass in both worlds at its assigned speed. It cannot stand still in one world while whirling on willy-nilly in the other. At whatever speed it moves in a given world, it must be a constant!"

"What about relativity?" mumbled Eli, but the priests fared no better with Einstein than with Aslan.

Cholerish continued, "Whatever the ratio of difference is, it will be constant. If an hour here equals a year in your world, then it will always be so."

Now Eli took up Rose's fearful look. "But that would mean we've been here for almost twenty years back home!" Fear punched Anna in the chest. That would make father . . . she tried to do the math but realized she didn't know how old he'd been when they stepped through the portal. But at the rate Cholerish had suggested, Dad would be old—maybe even dead. All three girls came to the same realization at the same moment and moved closer together, reaching for each other's hands.

"Now, now," said Whinsom in a voice intended to comfort. "It's not so bad as that. Admit it, Chol—we have no way of knowing. It could be the reverse. A hundred years here could be only a few seconds of their time. The only way to know is to go back and find out." And he again turned hard, persuasive eyes upon his brother, who stared back with the same intensity for a full minute before sighing loudly.

"If that is what they're determined to do, then, yes, they must follow the compass," Cholerish harrumphed, fixing an angry eye on his brother.

"I think we should try to get home as quickly as possible, then," said Eli.

"Of course you should," said Whinsom casually. "It's quite natural that you should want to get home to your father—and your older brothers, perhaps?"

Cholerish burst into guffaws of laughter and sat back down. "Oh, Whin, you haven't been telling them that, have you?"

"Why shouldn't they have older brothers? It's not out of the realm of possibility that—"

"Please tell my brother," said Cholerish, "that you do not have older brothers—even if you do. I have borne long enough his insufferable notion that he is a prophet. I cannot remember the last of his 'prophecies' that were within a hemisphere of being correct."

"I'm sorry, but we really don't." Eli's voice was full of apology.

"Nevertheless, all things are possible," said Whinsom with a wink.

"How could we get older brothers when we don't have any now?" asked Rose.

"My dear, you and I are very poor judges of what is possible for Thes," he said thoughtfully.

"Oh, good grief!" Anna felt the conversation was veering toward the absurd. "Look, are you sure there's no other way? Isn't there another window, or should we wait for another one to open or something?"

The priests exchanged looks, and after a moment Whinsom nodded. "Go ahead, Chol. She did ask."

Cholerish looked intently at the girls, but because of his lazy eye, Anna couldn't tell if he was looking at her or Eli. "Yours is a question that Thesian and Merrisian metaphysicians have debated for many generations. We know that worlds other than our own exist. And we know that windows exist between them—under certain conditions. But they do not seem to be visible to the naked eye, or at least no one has ever seen one. Both legends and independent deductions suggest that devices exist or could be made that would reveal them—devices, perhaps, such as you have in your pocket, young lady. But they would require material from both worlds, and . . . I presume you see the problem of construct-ing one?"

Eli did. Anna did not. Cholerish began rummaging on a nearby table for a scrap of paper as Whinsom explained the problem of having to get the material out of another world in order to build a device that would allow you to get there in the first place.

Anna then mentioned the "chicken and the egg" example, which was apparently new to both of the priests, and they praised her ingenuity. Eli grimaced at being upstaged. Rose still looked puzzled, but by then Cholerish was ready with a quill. He drew two circles on the paper—two circles touching at one edge. "You see, some theories argue that worlds intersect at a point like this but remain distinct by the pressure of the touching 'edges'—like two drops of mercurium that touch but lack the energy to merge. But other theories argue that the worlds all exist in the same space." And flipping the paper over, he drew two more circles, one roughly on top of the other. "We believe both pictures are true, but your particular need determines which of the models is more appropriate."

Here he looked at Whinsom, who flipped the paper back over and continued. "In your case, the first is more important. Your world intersects with ours at such a point, and in this model there can be only one such junction without the worlds merging. But the point can change position under certain circumstances."

"What sort of circumstances?" asked Eli.

"It is likely," said Cholerish, "that the metaphysical tension at the point of connection is strong enough to sustain itself until it is disturbed, say by someone blundering through it." And he eyed them curiously. "If your compass is the sort of device we believe it is, it not only tells you how to find the window but also reveals it—that is, makes it visible."

"So even without the compass, someone might wander through a window like that and not even see it?" asked Anna in wonder.

"That is unlikely," said Whinsom. "I suppose it is theoretically possible, but the rarity of such events would suggest that only the presence of the compass makes the windows permeable." And he looked at his brother as though his questions were not merely theoretical. "But it is an interesting question: How might a person breach the window if they did not possess the compass?"

"It would involve great peril, I imagine, but I cannot guess what sort," sighed Cholerish with a shrug.

"So do be sure you take good care of that little artifact," said Whinsom, pointing at Rose's coat pocket. "It is certain to be your only way home. But we are wasting time. Come, we must take you to Professor Lambient." He stood.

"Professor? Pah!" gasped Cholerish, also rising. "I thought he was expelled from the Avonian Academy of Scientia."

"Brother, there are those titles we possess by the consent of our peers and those we possess by virtue of our work. It would be most ironic for a Thesian priest to forget the difference."

At this, Cholerish's grimace wavered a bit, and he said no more against the professor.

Chapter 14

The priests led Anna, Rose, and Eli down long corridors that grew increasingly ancient and disused as they progressed into the hill. Eventually they seemed to pass out of the world of humanity altogether. They were in the old temple of Thes near the hill's center. Dim orange pinpoints of light dangled from bare wires overhead at wide intervals.

"Watch your step, ladies. We couldn't get the Lemerrian engineers to run the current this far for just the two of us." Whinsom pointed at one of the tiny lights.

"So we did it ourselves," said Cholerish.

"Do not forget, brother, who it was gave us the materials."

"Only so he could . . ." began Cholerish and then clamped his teeth together so tightly that his jaw cracked. Anna gathered that the nameless patron was the same mysterious professor they were going to meet.

At a place where the dim corridor continued straight ahead, a large archway opened to the left. The light was considerably brighter inside.

Cholerish bade them farewell here and entered the room—"to study a very old and influential prophecy by a *real* prophet," he said, with a critical look at Whinsom.

Whinsom shook his head. "Oh, Chol, you know it by heart. There's nothing new to see in there. Come with us. Vercandrus will be rising soon. It should be lovely outside the walls."

"Persistence is the one virtue that produces all others," Cholerish replied. He held up a finger in emphasis and disappeared.

Whinsom sighed. "My poor brother. He's still convinced he can puzzle out that faded bit of stone that hasn't been legible for a millennia. I too went through a phase in my youth when I obsessed over it—every Thesian does—but he's managed to make a career of it. I am constantly after him to get out and do other things. If I wasn't, he'd sleep in there and forget to eat. Ah, well. It is his one joy in life, and I suppose it does no harm to let him obsess." He smiled sympathetically and continued down the corridor.

They eventually emerged from the hill. Anna breathed deeply and gratefully of the fresh air. The northern wall of the city was directly in front of them. Evening was coming on fast, and the first stars were already visible. A bridge identical to the one by which they had entered the temple recrossed the moat. The ditch was wider here and the bridge longer, and it met the wall with some architectural complication they could not quite make out.

The bridge forked in two before the wall. To the left, a stair ascended to battlements and turrets at the top of the wall; to the right, the girls could see a small door in the city wall. But the structure immediately before them, around which the two paths of the bridge wrapped, was so compelling that the girls stopped and stared at it.

It took Whinsom a moment to realize he was walking alone. He turned around, saw them gawking. "Ah, so you've noticed the Amplabium. Impressive, isn't it?" But he didn't sound impressed.

"What is it?" asked Rose, in the tone of one who does not believe the question has an answer.

Staring back at them from the wall was a two-story-tall stone fish head. It looked as if it had been swimming through the wall and got stuck with just its head showing on this side. Its gaping mouth—ten feet across—was open, and if there had been more light, Anna was sure she could have seen right through the city wall into the desert. The stone was cracked and weathered smooth all over, like the Sphinx. At one time it had been adorned by many other smaller stone statues on shelves encircling the head—animals and people probably, but the shelves were all empty or contained only broken fragments of feet or hooves. It looked as though it had been very grand in its day . . . but that day must have been hundreds of years ago, thousands even.

"How old is it?" asked Eli.

"No one knows." Whinsom shrugged. "But it's older than the city wall, for sure. Perhaps even as old as the temple of Thes, which according to legend was the birthplace of men in this world. If we understand our history properly, the last drop of water fell from the Amplabium eight hundred years ago. Most people believe that was the cause of the Ever-War."

"The what?" asked Anna.

Whinsom shook his head. "Oh dear, how I presume upon you. There is a man in Professor Lambient's company who will be able to enlighten you on that subject in his own illimitable way. But the pith of the legend is thus: In the far north in Azhiona, deep within the Alappunda Mountains, once flowed a mythical spring or well. Vizuritundu, it was called. From it issued the great Flow of Segancurs, which flooded across the desert and poured forth from the Amplabium to fill the temple moat. That was in the final days of Garlandium's golden age. Many changes were already at work in the world at that time, and were by this hastened, for the Flow's failure was one of the 'evidences' that gave rise to the Merrisian cultus." Whinsom's tone had changed to that of a well-rehearsed lecture. He seemed now like an absentminded professor standing in front of his class, whose mind is considering deep mysteries but whose mouth, out of long habit, continues to pour forth knowledge. Once again Anna had the terrible feeling of being lost in a history of which she had no part. The utter foreignness of Whinsom's world, its problems and its ways, left her breathless.

"But come along." Whinsom snapped out of his reverie. "A pleasant surprise awaits you outside the walls." When they had passed through the little door in the city wall and out onto the level ground, a cool breeze met them. It felt delicious on their faces after the closeness of the city. The sun was down, and full twilight was upon them. Whinsom pointed to the northwestern sky, and Anna gasped. There, shimmering on the horizon, was a glowing disk in the sky a little smaller than a dime held at arm's length. Anna had never seen anything like it on Earth—smaller than the moon but way too big to be a star.

"What is it?" asked Rose.

"That, my dear, is Vercandrus. He is visible nearly all night in this season over the desert."

"Is it really that close?" asked Eli.

"No, not really," said Whinsom with a laugh, "but he is that big. He is actually several times the size of Errus and even as far away as he is, sailors in Landembrost speak of the Vercandrian tides, rare but most treacherous."

They walked down what was presumably a path, but it varied little from the rest of the ground, which was sparsely covered by clumps of coarse grass. They could see the point where the scrub ended and the sand began about a quarter mile away, and everything was very flat. It grew darker, and Anna became nervous. She didn't like walking blind. She felt Rose's hand slide into hers. She gripped it firmly, telling herself it was for Rose's sake, but felt relieved all the same to have something to hold onto. A few minutes later they heard a great boom some way ahead of them, and the ground shook.

"Mustn't mind that," said Whinsom in an attempt at reassurance. "Probably just another of Lambient's experiments . . . um . . . going off."

Anna was about to ask what he meant when Eli shrieked and jumped sideways into her.

"What the . . . ?" said Anna and then heard the sound of beating wings.

A moment later a small but distinct voice sounded out of the darkness above them. "Eh, Whin? Whatcha got for us tonight? Younglings, eh?"

"Ah, Finch," said Whinsom into the dark. "Please tell the good professor that I've some guests that he very much ought to meet."

"Righto," said the voice. "Looks like a tastier lot than the last bunch, too." And the sound of wings faded.

Anna froze. Eli grabbed her free hand, and Rose yanked on the other as if trying to pull it off.

"Now you cut that out, Finch, or I'll trim your wings while you sleep," called Whinsom at the retreating whatever-it-was. He turned to the girls and said kindly, "You mustn't mind Finch. He's such a scamp. He couldn't know you're . . . well, he's just so . . . now see here, ladies, I have *not* brought you out here to feed you to the fairies." He sounded sincere, and Anna felt Rose's death grip lessen slightly.

Eli was still unsure. "Mr. Whinsom, you're saying that was a bird?"

"A bird?" Whinsom was intrigued. "Do you mean to say the birds in your world have achieved human speech?"

"Of course not!" Anna experienced a surge of sudden anger. "Have they here?"

"I beg your pardon?"

"That thing! What was that thing?"

"That? That was just Finch, the fairy," said Whinsom, with a matter-of-factness appropriate to conversations about the neighbor's cat. "Oh, but I forget—you probably have little experience with the fairies in your world. Even so, you mustn't take Finch seriously. He would give a drowning man a glass of water and think it funny."

Realizing that their only options were to follow Whinsom or to turn back, Anna decided to trust him and stepped forward. Her sisters followed suit. After a few paces, Eli let go of her hand.

A few minutes later, another boom rocked the night. This time it was so close that the girls put their hands over their ears. It was followed by the sound of glass shattering and shouting.

"Here we are," said Whinsom, trying to sound casual. "Just let me see if he's, uh, at home." They were standing before a windowless building whose shape and size they could not fathom in the dark. Whinsom made a motion, and a foghorn sounded. The shouting inside continued, as did the screeching of metal on metal, the splintering of wood, and other disquieting sounds.

"I suppose I'll just try the door then," said Whinsom.

A moment later, the girls were confronted with chaos in miniature. Black shadows flitted to and fro amid the orange glow of leaping flames—flames like a fire burning out of control. Somewhere, a large metal something crashed to the floor, and more glass broke. Water dripped from the ceiling and pooled at their feet, mixed with an oily black fluid. And from the depths of the building, echoing above the mayhem, the sound of vigorous cursing reached their ears. Whinsom sighed resignedly. "Oh, dear," he muttered. "Not again."

BOOK 3

The Great Flats

Who can understand the heroic spirit of those six souls aboard the SkyCricket? What courage, what vision it takes to point at what everyone else calls impossible—at what is certain death—and say, "This I shall do!" Even the shocking events of the decades that followed cannot dim the SkyCricket's glory. Even with how it turned out, that expedition deserves to be sung about so long as Merris shines; its heroes cracked the tragic nut; they laid bare the bones of the story that was to come!

> DR. SONJI RAZHAMANÌAH, *An Attempted History of the Halighyllian Prophecies and Their Fulfillment*, Vol. 4: *The History of the Ever-War and Its Consequences*, 167v.

Chapter 15

As it turned out, the girls' first impression of Professor Lambient's laboratory was not entirely accurate. An experiment had indeed "gone off" and resulted in a rather vigorous fire, but the professor's assistants were clearly used to such incidents, and their response was impressive. They did not panic. They just ran to various lockers, and in two minutes, hoses were blasting water. In ten, the flaming piles were reduced to soggy ashes. Everything was drenched. Even the girls, still standing on the threshold, were damp from the steam and overspray.

Whinsom led them through the bedlam of overturned workbenches and broken machines to where a large block of a man was standing over a conglomeration of tangled wreckage, hands on his hips, grumbling to himself.

"Ahem." Whinsom cleared his throat. The man turned quickly, surprised. Lambient was big—not portly like Whinsom, but strong and thick and solid, like a blacksmith. Although he was not as old as Whinsom, his frowzy hair was already graying. Sweat glistened on his red face, and drops of moisture occasionally dripped off his walrus moustache onto his chest.

"Whinsom!" he boomed, his face brightening. He threw his arms out and enveloped the priest in a great bear hug.

"Just tell me it wasn't your 'dynamic cylinder' again," gasped Whinsom, separating himself with effort.

"Oh, yes," said the professor slowly, falling back, his eyes turning toward the pile of blackened metal in front of him. "And I'll be swoggled if I didn't almost have it this time." He wiped his face with a soiled handkerchief.

A great brown dog of no particular breed (or perhaps a whole bunch of breeds) bounded up and put his paws on the priest's chest, licking his face with enthusiasm. "Yes, yes, Sazerac, enough!" Whinsom cried, pushing the dog back to the floor.

Sazerac turned then to explore the new smells and thrust his nose into Anna's chest with such force that she fell back a step. She was generally good with animals, so she grabbed the canine's head and attempted to love him into submission with coos and baby talk. But the dog pulled away from her and sat with his head tilted, eyeing her curiously. She got the impression that she had offended him, and this sense increased when Rose took her turn to pat the dog's head.

"Well, hello there, Sazerac. It's nice to meet you," Rose said with utmost politeness, as if talking to an adult. The dog warmed to this immediately and even showed all his teeth in greeting.

"Oh, look," cried Rose, "a smile! You're just as smart as Winn Dixie, aren't you?" The dog's tail gave the floor a hearty thumping of agreement, although Anna was pretty certain that he had no idea what a Winn Dixie was. She was a little put out by her sister's success. But then the dog turned to Whinsom and gave a series of staccato barks.

"Yes," said Professor Lambient, "I too am wondering who these young ladies are and why they're trailing a stodgy curmudgeon like you, Whinsom."

"I sent Finch on ahead to announce them, but you appear to have had your hands full." Whinsom gestured about the steamy room. "Why don't you just give up on sealed combustion? It seems so dangerous, and surely you have other means of—"

"Oh, why don't you give up on Thes, you old religious has-been?" answered the professor with a mix of sarcasm and good humor. "The cylinder *will* work! I just have to find some way to cool the machine as it burns the fuel."

"Was anything, uh, important damaged?" said the priest.

"What? No, not that. The Cricket's already out in the field. *That* would have been a devastating loss, but no. All we lost here was our latest cylinder. Or should I say cylinders. There are two now, and they alternate." He moved his fists up and down in contrary rhythm, as if he were milking a cow.

"Excuse me," said Eli, "but are you talking about pistons?"

The professor looked at her blankly.

"An engine, a gasoline-burning engine? Or 'petrol,' maybe—made from oil?"

The professor gaped at her. "Whinsom!" He turned to the priest, his moustache quivering. "You've been talking! Who else have you told?"

"I assure you that whatever the young lady is talking about, she has reached the conclusion entirely on her own. But it sounds like you might profit from a conversation with her." Whinsom nodded toward the far end of the shop.

"Quite right," said the professor, extending his hand to Eli. "Miss, if you have knowledge of such things, I would be in your debt."

Eli blushed before taking his hand. He led her carefully through the workshop and out through a door. Anna grabbed Rose's hand and trotted behind them, feeling left out. They entered an office or apartment—it was hard to tell which. It was littered with desks and cots but was otherwise sparsely furnished. The walls were filled with complicated drawings and schematics on large, yellowish paper. Notes were scribbled over every inch of the paper in an illegible hand. Paper sheets were tacked onto others, sometimes forming paper chains that showed no regard for where the wall ended and the floor began.

Sazerac picked his way amid the papers with a care completely out of character with his exuberant nature. He flopped down at the foot of a cot and watched her. When Rose accidently sent a sheet flying with a careless step, the professor cried out and ran to set it straight again. Then he gently frog-marched her through the labyrinth to a clear space where several cushionless couches were arranged around a low, circular table—a conference table, Anna gathered.

He gestured for the girls to sit and took a seat opposite them. He stared at Eli with wonder and waited for her to speak. Eli looked at Anna, blushed, shrugged, and said, "Where we come from, engines like the one you're trying to build have become very complex, but it wasn't always so."

By the time Eli had made a few introductory comments about the history of the internal combustion engine, Rose figured out the topic and upstaged her sister, prattling on about cars with air conditioning and windshield wipers as Professor Lambient listened in rapt silence. Eli attempted to regain her alpha status with a description of a diesel train, but the train's scale and weight were so much greater than the professor's frame of reference that he was more impressed by Rose's description of a school bus. And when Rose complained about rush hour in Chicago, his eyes went as wide as hubcaps.

Anna was deciding whether she wanted to make her own bid for center stage or simply enjoy Rose's besting of Eli when she felt a tap on her shoulder.

"If I know Lambient," Whinsom whispered, grinning, "this could take a while. May I borrow you for a moment, my dear?" And he nodded back toward the shop. She stood and followed him. The professor was too enrapt to notice, and Eli and Rose were entirely consumed with one-upping each other.

Chapter 16

Whinsom led Anna back into the workshop and pulled the office door closed behind her. The one or two assistants who still hung about mopping up, righting tables, and sweeping up glass ignored them.

"Perhaps now you understand the other reason why I have brought you to Lambient," Whinsom said. "Not only is he going in your direction, but he shows little interest in your, uh . . . personal details. Only his work. He may never even think to ask you. It is a most convenient myopia. If you wish to tell him your unusual story, feel free, but you at least have the choice. A time may come when you will need to part from his company. And he may or may not try to stop you, for he has very little sense of what a girl like yourself can and cannot do." He stared hard at her as though trying to read her mind—or perhaps make her understand something without saying it.

Anna still wondered why he had called her away from the others.

After a moment of silence, the priest reached into a pocket on his robe and pulled out something that he held in a tightly closed fist. "Am I right in thinking, young Anna, that you are the second-born daughter?"

Before she could answer, a beat of wings next to her head made her jump.

"Sorry, Whin," said Finch, who had descended from the rafters and landed on the floor next to him. "Couldn't get to Doc before his wee crate popped off."

Anna found herself staring so hard that her eyes hurt. If Finch was a fairy, he was like no fairy she had ever imagined. Oh, he was small, but not exactly tiny—about the size of a Barbie doll, with a boyish face and a shock of yellow-white hair. And he did have wings, but the likeness to Tinkerbell ended there. His chest and arms were bare, save for a thin band of gold above each bicep. He was thick and well-muscled and wore black leather knickers and boots. Most unexpectedly, his wings were not the wispy translucent wings of a dragonfly but were shaped more like a bird's. They might even have been feathered—Anna couldn't tell—and they folded close to his back just like bird wings. Each wing had a large yellow circle painted on its underside. Finch reminded Anna of a cross between a World War II fighter plane and an old cartoon superhero—Hawkman, perhaps.

The priest quickly stuffed whatever it was he held back into his pocket and waved his now empty hand cordially. "Tut, tut, it couldn't be helped. No harm done. But I would ask you to join him in the next room. I'll need to talk to all of you in a moment."

"Uh-huh." Finch looked at Anna inquisitively and grinned. "Look, missy, whatever he tells you, do the very opposite. Ask him what happened to the last—"

"Finch!" Whinsom looked mortified. "You cannot possibly know what an ass you are making of yourself."

"Sure I do! In here I work with some of the biggest—"

"Enough, you scallywag! Please, give us one moment of peace."

The fairy clicked his heels. "Aye-aye, Cap'n, but don't be too long. His majesty wants to—" he gave a long whistle, accompanied by a swirl of his index finger—"before moonrise. Toodles, missy." He gave Whinsom a dramatic salute and goose-stepped into the study. His face with its impish grin was the last thing to disappear through the door.

"Honestly," sighed Whinsom, shaking his head, "how can I

possibly say what I was going to say after that? Oh, well, you'll find out soon enough to take everything Finch says with a touch of reserve." He retrieved the mystery object from his pocket and looked hard at Anna.

It took her a moment to realize that he was still waiting for an answer to his question. "Oh, um, yes, I was born second."

"I thought so," he said gratified. "I can still see some things." Anna was unimpressed, thinking this not so much clairvoyance as a stating of the obvious. Whinsom seemed to change his mind several times, but eventually inhaled with deliberation and extended his hand to her. "I think *you* ought to have this."

She hesitated.

"Come, come," he said, shaking his hand before her, "before I change my mind. You've come this far. I've no doubt you will run the entire course."

She extended her hand, and something fell into it—something hard, small, and angular on a chain like a pendant. It caught the light and flashed as it fell.

"Although I am sure you would find most interesting the story of how this little artifact came recently into my possession, I cannot tell you now. But given Lambient's particular quest, I do not doubt it will be of immense value."

Anna peered at the object in her hand: a small metal lump on a chain, flat, about a half-inch thick and roughly triangular— like a wide tortilla chip with a bite taken out of the tip. What she noticed most, though, was its unusual heaviness and gray plainness. It was secured to the dull pewter chain by two metal wires running around it.

"I added the chain myself," said Whinsom proudly.

"What is it?" she asked.

"I am not entirely sure. But I have reason to believe that so long as you hang on to it, you will not die of thirst. What else you might die of I cannot tell, but not that."

This was hardly comforting to Anna. "What do I do with it?"

"I am not sure of that either," said Whinsom a little sheepishly, but he brightened immediately. "I can tell you this much. It is a relic related to Therra, the sea goddess." And he pointed at the object.

Anna rolled it over in her hand and saw a faint marking on the one side, like a letter or a rune consisting of two lines forming an arc and an angle. The arc opened upward and intersected the downward-facing angle at the tip, forming what to her looked like a cup.

"That is her sign—the goblet. And I can think of no better emissary to accompany you into the Flats than Therra."

"Better than Thes?" It was out before she thought.

Whinsom looked a little hurt. "Now, now, don't talk like one of the Merrisians. Therra is Thes's servant, entrusted with the sea and water. She serves Thes best when she is about that task. So keep her close. I have every confidence that when you have the need, you will figure her out."

"But why me? Eli's the one who likes figuring things—"

"No!" Whinsom was adamant. "In this sort of thing, one's order of birth is often important. Again, I cannot now explain the theology behind this, but I am convinced you are the one who should have it. You will just have to . . . trust me."

Anna grinned. "Even if Finch says otherwise?"

"Especially then."

He led her back to the door and then stopped her. "I would suggest that you keep it hidden until you need it," he said, taking the amulet back and placing the chain over her head.

"Even from Eli and Rose?"

"Oh, no, certainly tell them, but it would be most inconvenient if Professor Lambient saw it. He might try to examine it, and . . . well . . ." He gestured toward the blackened shop. Anna grinned and put the amulet inside her shirt.

They entered the study just as Rose was describing an airplane, although her arms were absurdly flapping up and down like a bird.

The professor was nearly falling out of his seat in shock and awe. "Whinsom, do you realize what this means?"

Whinsom ignored the question and fixed the professor in a stern gaze. "Ambrosius, I must speak with you. I did not bring these young ladies to you so they could enlighten you with new ways of burning your shop down. I need to talk to you about . . . the trip." And without waiting for a response, he strode through the room and out a door in the far wall. Professor Lambient looked dumbfounded.

Whinsom's head reappeared. "Finch, Sazerac, you'd best come too. This involves you as much as the professor." The fairy swooped down from a shelf, and the dog rose and trotted out, casting a glance over his shoulder at the professor.

"I . . . uh," stammered the scientist, obviously torn. "It seems I'm being . . . well, I suppose a moment wouldn't—"

"Lambient!"

"Right, right. Coming, Whinsom." He pointed a crooked finger at Rose. "And you—don't move. I want to know more about this ary-o-planer machine." He followed Whinsom out of the room, and the door closed behind him.

Immediately, Anna took out the amulet and showed Eli and Rose. Rose pulled the compass out of her jacket pocket, and they compared them. Rose was the first to notice that the symbol on the amulet also appeared in the tiny runes inscribed on the bronze band of the compass. Eli seemed a little huffy, and Anna wondered if she were jealous at being the only one without a pretty trinket. Partly this annoyed Anna, and partly it made her feel smug. But before she could decide on the appropriate means of needling her sister about it, they heard raised voices coming from the other room, mixed with a series of barks. These continued for some time, then stopped just before the whole group trooped back into the room.

"It is agreed, with one dissenting vote—" here Whinsom glared at Sazerac, whose tail shot up and whose canine face glowered at the priest—"that you three are to join the professor's quest for the lost well."

"And most heartily welcome you are, ladies," said Lambient, opening his arms as if desiring a hug. But the girls just looked uncertainly at one another. "Well, then," stammered Lambient, clearly disappointed with the reception. "Finch, would you be so kind as to go and inform Dashonae of the change of plans? He's winding up the Cricket."

"Righto, your majesty," said the fairy, leaping up and flapping out a high window.

"Finch! Don't call me that!"

Whinsom brushed his hands down the front of his robes, as if his palms were dusty. "Now with these arrangements made, ladies, I believe it is time for me to retire. I leave you in good hands."

Sazerac gave an odd bark, which to Anna sounded oddly sarcastic.

"Well," said Whinsom, taken aback, "I did mean Lambient's good hands, but of course I meant Thes as well . . . or primarily . . . oh, bother."

The professor broke out into belly laughter. "He's got you, Whin. Admit it when you're beaten and leave gracefully. I shall take as tender care of these flowers as if they were my own children."

"That—" Whinsom thrust a finger into Lambient's face—"is exactly what I wish to avoid. How is poor Augustus anyway?"

"Oh," the professor grinned sheepishly, "the ogre just got in a lucky shot, that's all. The bone-mender said he'll be up and around in no time."

"Uh-huh," said Whinsom, turning to the girls. "I cannot help you more than I have." He looked hard at Anna. "But I have great confidence that you will find your way back home." He moved toward the door. "Until we meet again."

Eli leaped to her feet. "Thank you, Whinsom. You've been so helpful." And she hugged him.

The priest embraced her awkwardly in return. "Oh! There,

there, child. It was nothing," he fumbled. And when Rose followed suit, he blushed.

Anna, who was not about to hug anyone she was not related to, and even then only on a holiday, held out her hand. "Thanks for everything."

Ten minutes later they were following Lambient and Sazerac out the door of the shop into the cool night.

Chapter 17

"Back there . . ." began Eli hesitantly as they wandered a worn path toward the hazy line of gray that was the desert. She faltered.

"Speak, child," said the professor over his shoulder. "Don't be shy. We shall all know each other better than we desire before we are done, I should think." And he jammed his thumbs into his belt and laughed at the sky.

"Did your dog actually speak to Whinsom? He seemed to understand it."

"*My* dog?" The professor was puzzled. "You mean Sazerac?"

"Yes, of course."

"He's not my dog."

"Then whose is he?" asked Rose.

"He's his own," said Lambient, puzzled. "He is my assistant in this venture. And a better one I've never had. Sazerac, tell them."

Sazerac barked enthusiastically.

"I couldn't have said it better myself," said Lambient.

"Wait a minute," said Anna. "He didn't say anything. He just barked." She had been walking next to the dog with her hand on his back, but at this comment, he pulled away with a suddenness that made Anna think she had hurt his feelings again.

"Of course he just barked!" The professor turned and looked at them, his great moustache twitching. "He is a dog. What would you expect him to do, sing an aria?"

"So you understand what he's saying?" asked Eli, full of wonder. "And he understands you?"

Sazerac barked again, clearly irritated.

"I could not agree more," said Lambient, "Of all the rude and insensitive . . . his accent isn't that—"

"No, no, please!" Eli pleaded. "We mean no offense. It's just that where we come from—"

"What did he just say?" cried Rose, realizing that something wondrous was afoot.

The dog and the inventor exchanged looks of confusion mixed with no small bit of irritation.

"He wonders why you insist on speaking about him as if he isn't even here. The indignity of it! What sort of ignorant ingrates has Whinsom saddled me with?" He sputtered with something approaching anger.

"Please, if you'd just let us explain," Eli tried again. "We didn't mean to ignore him. We're just not used to it. The dogs where we come from don't speak." She paused a moment, thinking. "Or at least if they do, we can't understand them."

After a moment the dog barked again. This time sympathetically.

"Yes indeed," said Lambient, also softening. "And here we thought them so advanced, aeroplanes and automooboobles, and yet they cannot understand something as simple as canineish." He shook his head.

The walk in the dark continued, and no one said anything for a time. As Anna pondered the speech of dogs, she was again overcome with that strangeness of breathing foreign air and walking on foreign soil. What sort of world was this—where animals talked but you couldn't understand them? Vercandrus was well up in the night sky, and so clear he actually illuminated things around Anna—her sisters, the great hulking professor, and his four-footed "assistant."

A thousand other stars had joined the great sky-father. Anna looked upon them in a double wonder. These were not her stars— the stars of her own world. But then again, having grown up in the city, she realized that even the stars of her own world were strangers to her. She decided that when she got home, she was going to learn some constellations—*if* she got home.

The ground changed under her feet. It crunched. She was now walking on the coarse sand of the desert. Before her stretched that unending sea of thirst—a world of utter sameness stretching to the horizon—dry, dead. But at that place where heaven met earth afar off, the desert ended, and a glorious new world began. As she looked up at the pulsing starlight that now stretched from horizon to horizon, she felt suddenly different—as though something from those stars was coming down to her, as though she were being spoken to in a language she did not yet understand. She had a sudden flash of memory—something her dad had once said about how medieval people looked at the night sky. They spoke of it as full of mighty spirits that sent their "sweet influence" down to humanity. When *she* looked up, she had only ever seen outer space—vast emptiness. But now, as she felt this something from the sky kneading her soul, she wondered if the ancient people had known better. Was it just space, or was it really the *heavens*? Her hand went unconsciously to the amulet she wore around her neck. She felt a deep shudder in her soul—almost a premonition—that she and these living heavens were linked in some strange way, but it was dim, so dim.

Eli was apparently thinking similarly deep thoughts. "So is Vercandrus king over the stars as well as the other planets?" She said it dreamily, as if lost in her own contemplations

Anna, wishing her sister could just endure silence, resented the intrusion. *What a stupid question*, she thought.

But the professor only sighed deeply and said, "Missy, you should know from the start I don't believe in Vercandrus or Merris or the rest."

"So you believe in Thes, like Whinsom," said Eli, still lost in the overhead view.

The professor turned sharply, and Eli found his great walrus face an inch from her own. "Now, listen to me, missy." He waggled

BOOK 3: THE GREAT FLATS

his finger in her face. "If you've been listening to Whinsom and Cholerish, you've probably got it in your head that all the people of Garlandium are religious fanatics. Most people don't have any use for all those stories. Most only go to the revelry for the food and dance. Those two old addle-headed mystics just don't get out so much as they ought. Rattling around in that old temple like a set of lopsided dice, they think that all there is to life are those old prophecies that nobody remembers. They think *everybody's* as all-fired concerned about the gods as they are.

"Merris, Thes—it makes no difference to me which planet you think is bending over to smite you. If you've got something important to do, you gotta get up off your back end and do it, gods or no gods. And if the gods get in your way . . ." He snapped his fingers in her face. "So I suggest you just put all that mumbo jumbo out of your heads for now. When we get out in the desert, I'll give you a real astronomy lesson."

A familiar flurry of wings whirled above them.

"Ah, Finch, have you made the arrangements?" said the professor.

"Absotively, possolutely, your grace," came the reply from somewhere above them.

"Very good. Now if you could please tell Dashonae to break out the safety harnesses on the Cricket. I want to depart within the hour."

"Sixty clicks, then into the sticks, got it," sang out the fairy and flew off.

Anna and Eli exchanged glances. A cricket that needed a safety harness?

Chapter 18

Anna looked over her shoulder. They were perhaps a half mile out in the desert now, and the walls of Halighyll had lost their dominance behind them. A mild, dry warmth sprang up as the sand gave back the heat it had collected during the day. But Anna's interest in what lay behind was short lived. Suddenly and without warning, the sky before them lit up in a cascade of dull bluish light, accompanied by an electric humming not unlike a giant bug zapper, but louder. So loud, in fact, that the professor had to raise his voice to be heard.

"There she is, my merry ladies. The technological wonder of Errus, and our ticket across the Flats. I give you . . . the SkyCricket." And he threw both hands out in front of him in a dramatic tah-dah gesture.

There indeed, illuminated by several banks of spotlights, was a . . . a something. At first Anna thought it was a great ship standing on its stern with its prow pointed toward the heavens. But there were complications. Steel booms lay along the sides in awkward configurations. At the base, four cylinders, each taller than Anna and as wide as she could spread her arms, connected to the ship. Fuel tanks, maybe? But then, other metal cylinders were strapped along the sides of the ship, like propane tanks on a barbecue. And the underside of the ship had a curious shimmer, unlike metal, more like cloth or silk.

The dominant feature at the moment, however, was a huge

metal wheel, studded like a clockwork gear or the wheel in the game show *Wheel of Fortune*, protruding from the side of the ship near the ground. From it extended long, thick ropes connected to the harness of two great Clydesdale-like horses with hairy hooves. These strained against the ropes, and as they did, the metal wheel turned minutely. There was a loud, metallic click, and the ship appeared to have been ratcheted a tiny bit closer to the ground.

A figure in a hooded cloak stood before the horses, speaking encouragingly to them. The horses pulled again, but this time the wheel did not move. "Sorry, professor. It's no good," the man called in a clear, strong voice. "They say they can't make the next pin."

"How many rounds did they make?" Professor Lambient shouted back, hurrying toward them.

"Twelve rounds, ten pins," came the reply.

"Boys," he yelled to the horses, "I'll throw on an extra twenty of oats—good ones—if you can draw it two more pins." Lambient bent to Rose and said, "That'll give us an even thirteen rounds. And thirteen is a very lucky number."

Rose looked at Anna with wide eyes. Anna just shrugged. So numbers were different in this world too—what of it?

The two horses drew their heads together for a moment, exchanging whinnies and head shakes. Then, as if reaching an agreement, they threw themselves against the harness again. The girls were close enough now to watch. The lines stretched and groaned. The great wheel on the craft creaked around an inch, then two—but then it stopped. The horses were flecked with sweat and clearly tired, but they poured all their remaining strength into the pull. The wheel trundled round another inch, and there was another loud metallic click.

The horses relaxed a moment, breathing heavily. Then they heaved again. This time Lambient added his great frame to the effort, grabbing one of several lines stretched out in the sand alongside the horses. Wrapping it around his middle, he leaned backward like the anchor in a tug-o-war. The wheel trembled, but did not move.

Now the other man threw back his hood, revealing luxurious hair that cascaded around his shoulders. He grabbed a second line and slung it across his back. Both men strained with the horses. Even in the blue light, Anna could see that the professor's face was red and puffy with exertion, and beads of sweat erupted on the other man's forehead. The wheel rotated an inch, then slid back to the eleventh pin.

Though she had no idea what this effort was about, something like a duty clarified itself in Anna's mind. These were going to be her comrades. They were going into the desert together. Whatever they were doing, it was her business too.

"Come on," she said and ran forward to grab another line. The other two hesitated. Eli looked down at her porcelain hands; Rose was simply too caught up in the spectacle to move. "Don't just stand there gawking like birds! That thing ain't gonna move by itself!" She began pulling for all she was worth. This broke the spell on Rose. She ran to Anna's aid. Eli trudged hesitantly forward, but once a line was in her hands, she too pulled as hard as she could.

The struggle seemed to last forever. Anna pulled so hard that the blood rushed into her head. Lambient gave a great groan, and the horses grunted and blew their lips hard. The edges of Anna's vision began to blur, and she was sure she couldn't last another second when, like a church bell, a solid click rang out.

Lambient collapsed onto his bottom in the sand, and Anna fell to her knees beside him. The other man straightened slowly and with difficulty, and the horses' heads drooped low. Suddenly the professor let out a great "Ha-ha!"—loud and deep from the belly. He clapped Anna on the back so hard she belly-flopped in the sand. He lifted his hands high in triumph and laughed with gusto, nodding his head at each of them and pointing at the ship. His laugh was so grand, so infectious, that Rose began to snicker, then Eli, then they were all laughing. The horses threw back their heads, whinnied, and stomped their hooves.

"Now then," cried Professor Lambient, shaking his fist at the glowing disc in the sky, "let's see the almighty Vercandrus do that even on his best day!"

Chapter 19

The other fellow was a knight named Dashonae, who bowed low to the girls. Once he had cast aside his cloak, it was easy to believe he was a knight. A long straight sword hung at his side, and every muscular bump across his chest and midriff was clearly visible through his coarsely woven undershirt ("ripped" was the word that came to Anna's mind). He was young, clean shaven, and very good looking, with high cheekbones and a straight, thin nose. Eli attempted to return his bow with a curtsy—deeper than the last. It was her undoing. She lost her balance and fell on her backside in the sand. The knight controlled himself admirably, but the tiniest grin tweaked the corner of his mouth as he helped her to her feet. Anna rolled her eyes and wondered if she could make her own first impression separately.

But there was no time for further pleasantries. The horses had been paid and were wandering back toward the city with several sacks of oats slung over their backs, and the scientist was itching to be skybound. He herded the girls toward the ship, saying, "Yes, yes, how cozy when young people chat, but niceties can wait till we're aloft."

Eli hung back, staring upward at what looked more and more like a boat standing on its stern. Lambient explained that all the effort had been necessary to tighten the four "launch springs." The large cylinders Anna had thought fuel tanks were actually casings that held huge metal springs—"of my own design," added the professor, grinning.

"Once we're all strapped in, I'll throw the lever and . . ." He threw his hand into the sky to simulate a launch. Anna felt Eli stiffen. "Let's prep for launch." He rubbed his hands together greedily before mounting a metal ladder affixed to the ship. Actually, it lay flat along the starboard deck, but since the ship pointed straight up, the ladder ascended to a small, round door in the side of the cabin. If the ship were setting properly on the ground, it would have featured a good-sized deck you could walk about on, like the whaling ship from *Moby Dick*, but since everything currently pointed up, the decks were all just vertical surfaces like walls. "Off we go," the professor added gleefully and climbed the ladder.

He reached the top of the ladder and swung open the door of the cabin. His hinder parts disappeared through the hatch, but Eli remained fixed, staring at the ladder.

Anna gave her a shove. "Get going."

"But I don't think—"

"All the better. Don't think. Just climb." Anna was now feeling adventurous and resented her sister's hesitations.

Eli hoisted herself up. Anna put her hand on a rung of the ladder and followed. But when Eli reached the porthole, she looked down at Anna with wide eyes.

"What?" said Anna impatiently.

"You do realize what he's going to do to us, don't you?" Her eyes were wild.

"Yeah, he's going to launch us like the shuttle."

"But not on a rocket. On a boat . . . with springs!"

"Yeah, big ones."

"Don't you get it? It doesn't matter how big they are. You can't get something this heavy off the ground with just springs. And even if he does, we'll just fall out of the sky again. "

Anna gritted her teeth. "So at least we'll bounce when we crash. Now are you getting in or are you getting down?"

"There's got to be another—"

"There is no other way. Look, you want to find the window and get home? Then climb through the stupid hole. You want to spend the rest of your life here? Then go back to Whinsom. I'm sure he can make you a nun." She knew she was being harder on Eli than she needed to. Eli would go through with it. She just thought about things too much. But sometimes you have to just bite your lip and jump.

"What's going on up there?" called Rose from the ground. Eli was shaking violently, but she put her hands on the porthole and clambered in.

When Anna reached the entrance, she looked around her and was amazed how being a scant twenty feet off the ground could change your perspective. As she considered the distance to the ground, it did seem entirely probable that they would crash to their deaths a few seconds after takeoff. The whole machine did seem as if it came out of a bad science fiction movie. Lambient seemed confident, but she had seen his lab.

On the ground, Sir Dashonae had removed the great metal gear and was stowing it against the portside desk under stout leather straps. Sazerac sat beside him, staring up at Anna. He looked her in the eyes for a moment, then lowered his head, shook it from side to side resignedly, and trotted around the ship.

"What?" Rose was still looking up at her.

"Nothing," said Anna and climbed in.

Chapter 20

Being in the SkyCricket did feel a little like being in a space shuttle. The seats all faced up so that you had to climb into them and lie on your back, looking upward out a large oval window. The pilot's chair sported a host of levers, switches, gauges, and dials. The whole cabin was roughly barrel shaped, with small, round windows on the sides. But any likeness to a spaceship ended there, for it was also weirdly Victorian. The interior was dressed out in mahogany or cherry. Carved flowers and beveled woodwork ornamented the corners and edges, and the floor was covered in a plush red carpet. A framed painting of the night sky hung on one wall, and various brass navigational devices—compasses, sextants, and the like—were displayed in a glass-covered case on the other. Tasseled curtains hung on the round windows, and the chairs featured thick velvet cushioning. Even the needles on the gauges were fancy, like tiny brass fleurs-de-lis. And the whole thing hung curiously askew, as if it were intended to hang earthward but for the moment had been turned on its side.

Eli was horrified. "Doesn't all this just make the ship heavier?"

"Missy—" the professor leaned over her in a paternal fashion—"there's more to science than function. The universe is a beautiful thing, and you've got to show it the proper respect. You wouldn't suggest we go on so great an adventure in some tin-plated shipping crate, would you?" Eli slowly shook her head, more confusion than agreement. "That's right, of course you wouldn't. Why, it would be better to crash to the ground in a respectable ship than to fly all the way to Lemerrus and back in some sterilized bottle. Now, you just have yourself a seat, and let old Ambrosius show you how science was meant to be done."

Old Ambrosius insisted on strapping each of them into their seat personally, and the seats featured straps in abundance—ankles, thighs, and a four-point harness across the chest. Arms went into sleeves across the chest, like a mummy's. To top it off, a strap went over the forehead, complete with a rubber mouthpiece. Rose didn't want to have all the straps fastened, especially the one going over the forehead. And she absolutely refused the mouthpiece.

"Now there, missy," said the professor gently. "When the Cricket leaps, you might well leave your teeth behind anyway, but there's no need to tempt fate. Trust me on this, and wear the dental." Rose consented with a grimace.

With all of the professor's distracted babbling about this or that special decorative touch he had added to the interior, it took about twenty minutes to get them all strapped in. Then another twenty for the professor to turn all his gears and check his array of levers and gauges. Shortly after Lambient was seated, Dashonae climbed in, carrying Sazerac on his shoulders. He strapped the dog onto a couch designed just for him at the rear of the cabin. Dashonae sealed the door and took his seat next to the professor at the controls. Finch was nowhere to be seen.

Anna could barely turn her head, but she could hear Eli muttering something next to her about physics, weight ratios, and other things. Anna's heart pounded with excitement or fear or both, and she wished her sister would shut up and let her enjoy it.

Both Lambient and his copilot, Dashonae, left their arms free to work the controls. Anna expected to hear the sound of an engine warming up, or a turbine turning like in an airplane, or even the hum of a computer. But silence prevailed. Only Lambient's chair gave off rubbery squeaks as he leaned this way and that, tapping gauges and fiddling with dials, and he talked softly to himself and occasionally to the knight.

Anna was wishing they would hurry up and do whatever it was they were going to do; she had developed an itch on her nose and had no way of scratching it. But all thoughts of this disappeared in a moment as Lambient called back, "Okay, we're ready. The wind is perfect. Prepare for launch in ten . . . nine . . . eight . . ."

Anna had no memory of the final numbers. She did not know if the scream she heard was Eli or herself. She had a hazy memory of Lambient heaving back on a great wooden lever, but then everything went dark.

Her eyes fluttered lazily. She had apparently blacked out, but not, she thought, for very long. The great springs had done their work, for the ship had careened upward at breakneck speed and reached the top of that terrible arc as Eli had predicted. Now Anna, experiencing a falling sensation in her stomach, began to reevaluate her sister's hesitation. She forced her eyes open just in time to see Lambient pull a big oblong lever on the console. From her imperfect view out the front window, she saw a great white cloud burst forth from the bow of the ship—a sort of parachute or sail. It billowed up before them, expanding. The terrible falling sensation was growing worse, but just as she began to be frightened, the sail came full, and the ship gave a great forward jerk.

Dashonae had not been idle either. At the top of the launch arch he began to spin a number of faucet-like handles in front of him. Each handle, when opened, produced a great hiss from somewhere. The falling sensation eased.

Finally Lambient grabbed a great set of handlebars above his head and pulled down with a mighty grunt. Anna could hear cables uncoiling and gears turning, and the whole feel of the ship's weight changed. She could turn her head just enough to see out the starboard window. A great boom had swung away from the ship, and another sail, like a wing, had unfurled. It seemed that Lambient knew a little something about not crashing after all.

The ship was nearly level now, and the perilous sense of falling had disappeared. It would have been just like being in a jet except for the quiet. She could hear the air rushing past and wind billowing in the forward sail. It was more like a sailing ship than an airplane.

Except . . . *oh!* The ship fell several feet in a pocket of turbulence, and Anna's heart bounced off the roof of her mouth.

A moment later Lambient was out of his chair and nearly dancing a jig in the tight aisle between the seats. He sang in a loud voice, "They laughed at me! Those little flea-minded Avonians! Kick me out of their academy, will they? Well, I'm closer to Avonia now than they will ever be! Ha, ha!"

Without warning, the ship pitched forward and threw him to the floor.

"Perhaps," suggested the knight, "we should break out the harnesses?"

"Quite," said the professor, wiping a little fresh blood from his smiling lips.

Chapter 21

By "harnesses," the knight meant an actual vest worn over one's clothes. It had rings in various places whereby one could secure him- or herself by a metal cable to any number of matching metal eyelets throughout the ship. This was particularly important outside on the main deck, for the ship pitched up and down or back and forth occasionally in the wind. Unless you were secured to a bench or rail, one of these sudden movements might well toss you over the edge, and unlike on a real boat, you wouldn't hit water.

Thus outfitted, within a half hour of launch Anna and her sisters found themselves seated on one of the ornately carved wooden benches on the main deck, safely secured and staring at Lemerrus, the lately risen moon just above the horizon. Dashonae was inside, trying to coax the acrophobic Sazerac out onto the deck. Lambient had a seat mid-deck behind what looked like a ship's wheel. He had prepared two control centers so the ship could be steered from either inside or outside the cabin. "No point in missing all this beautiful nighttime air because of a little necessity like steering," he said.

By "steering" he really meant just keeping aloft, for he had only slightly more control of the ship than a person trying to walk a cat around the block on a leash. Now the girls could better see the mechanics of the SkyCricket. It was, as it had appeared, a great sail that Lambient had deployed, and it billowed out ahead of the ship like a parachute, dragging the ship through the air at a respectable clip. The superheated air over the desert formed unusually strong and consistent updrafts and winds, often nearing gale force in the higher atmosphere. The sail thus provided both upward and forward movement.

Eli shook her head, still arguing that it was impossible that such a large craft should be kept aloft by just a sail, and she was resolute even when Lambient pointed out the "wing" sails projecting from either side. But finally even she had to credit the professor's ingenuity when he pointed out the many metal tanks strapped to the sides of the ship. A metal hose ran from each beneath the ship to a great gas bag filled with "helum" (Anna assumed he meant helium). This great balloon reduced the ship's weight significantly. They had jettisoned the empty canisters after launch, but a dozen remained for emergencies.

Just then the cabin door opened and out stepped the knight, shaking his head. "He said he'd have none of it. Honestly, Lambient, I can't figure out why he even came if he's just going to hole up in that cabin for the next two days."

"Yes, the poor thing." The professor laughed. "Seems that the more legs you have, the more you like to have them on the ground."

"I still say you should hook him up with his own wings!" It was Finch. He was standing on the roof of the cabin, leaning back into the wind with superb balance and no harness. "Then when you nosedive this crate, he can fly the rest of the way on his own."

"Now, there's no room for pessimists aboard my ship, Finch," cried Lambient. "Any more talk like that, and you'll walk the plank."

"Aye, aye, Cap'n." The fairy made a show of walking to the stern edge of the cabin, stepping off, and disappearing into the thin air.

"He's a crazy thing." The knight sat down next to Anna, connected his safety strap, and smiled. The wind blew his hair straight out, giving him more the appearance of a warrior god than a human soldier.

"Are you a real knight?" asked Rose.

He inclined his head in a suggestion of a bow. "Sir Theodore au Dashonae, of the Therran order, first class, at your service."

"Theodore? That's our dad's name too." Rose was amazed that there could be anything in common between a brave knight and her bookish father. "But everyone calls him Teddy."

"Teddy?" said the knight, with a slightly upturned nose.

"Teddy, Sir Teddy, Sir Teddy is ready," the fairy sang out, this time from the prow of the ship. They could just make out his form in the dark, dancing on the boom.

"You will not call me that!" shouted the knight.

Once again the fairy dove off the side, still singing. "Sir Teddy is ready to get into his beddy."

"I've always wondered," said Lambient, ignoring the fairy, "why you took the Therran oath. That's more of a marine order. I would have thought the Vercandrian order would have better suited someone this far from the sea."

"Yes, yes," said the knight with a bored wave of the hand, "but Vercandrian knights are so brutish. All you need to get into that order is to be over-wide in the shoulders. No, my devotion to Therra is sincere." And he spoke the name with the sort of reverence that gave Anna no doubts that he believed in Therra the way Whinsom believed in Thes. "My father is a merchant, running trade ships between Eddiggen and Landembrost. So well known is he that he is even permitted to cross the Sands in Landembrost and enter the Azhionian Citadel." This visibly impressed Lambient, but it meant nothing to Anna. "When my youth was nearly over, I embarked upon a voyage with him to the Trinity Isles to check our copper holdings there. A day out of Landembrost, we were taken by a gale. I was lost overboard, and I clung for a day and a night to a piece of driftwood. As the sun rose that morning and I approached the very end of my strength, I vowed that if Therra rescued me from the deep, I would dedicate my life to her service."

"And did she?" asked Rose full of wonder.

"No doofus, he drowned!" said Anna. "He's here, isn't he?"

The knight laughed. "Your sister is correct. I was spotted by an Azhionian trader within the hour and rescued."

"And they picked you up?" asked Lambient with an odd satisfaction.

"Yes, what is said of Azhionian cruelty in Garlandium is certainly true. But on the sea, even the Ever-War's effects are tempered."

"What is the Ever-War?" asked Eli. "Whinsom mentioned it but didn't tell us what it was."

The knight sighed. "The people of Garlandium and those in the northern country of Azhiona (although they call themselves the Azhwana) have been at war for over eight hundred years."

"A *sort* of war," added the scientist with a cynical laugh.

"Do not be deceived, Lambient. The hundred-year truce has lasted only because the Flats have grown so wide that they cannot be crossed on horseback. But I have seen the looks in the Azhionian traders' faces in Landembrost. I have beheld their guard upon the northern walls of the Citadel. They are by very nature a savage and warlike people. Their soldiers swarm like ants, and their archers are the most fell in all the world. They are quickly provoked and slowly appeased. In Landembrost, they have been known to slay lost Garlandian children who strayed across the Sands into their half of the city. If an army could be transported across the desert in strength then, believe me, Lambient, there would be much bloodshed in Garlandvale and much rejoicing in Arzhembala." And he began to recount a host of atrocities committed in past centuries by the Azhionian armies. Anna shuddered. They sounded like a truly cruel and terrible people.

Lambient let him go for nearly ten minutes before interrupting. "Be honest though, Dashonae. And you're a knight, so your honor forbids you to lie. Isn't it true that if your mighty king in Garlandvale found a way across the desert first, he'd be more than ready to make preemptive war on Azhiona?"

"My king? Is he not yours as well?"

"I'm a scientist. My loyalties are to the truth, not to some ridic-ulous grudge out of the dawn of mythology."

"Wait—wait a minute!" Eli's face had gone pale. "Azhiona is in the north?"

"Yes." Dashonae still glared at Lambient. "What of it?"

"Doesn't that mean we're going toward it?"

"Better than that, missy," replied Lambient, still holding the knight with a quizzical eye. "We're landing right on her border and marching through a whole province of the country."

"But," Eli stammered, "what if they attack us?"

The scientist and the knight turned in unison and looked at Eli—Lambient in surprise, Dashonae with a hurt expression.

"Missy," said Lambient, pointing at Dashonae, "what do you think I brought him for?"

Chapter 22

Anna did not pass an agreeable night. For all of his forethought, the professor had not made adequate provisions for sleeping, perhaps because he did so little of it himself. Sazerac was the only one who had anything like a bed, and the girls knew enough not to ask if they could use it. So they ended up back in their chairs, which did recline nearly flat—"for landing," was Lambient's ominous observation. Lambient and the knight said they would sleep on deck so as to take turns steering the ship.

Anna still slept better than Eli, who found the idea of being in the middle of a long-standing war more immediately troubling than did either Rose or Anna. Anna just shrugged. *Like before, what's the alternative?* Before going to sleep, they put their heads together and looked at the compass. It still pointed north, but a bit more to the west than their current heading. Eli asked to see Anna's amulet again, and they talked through their adventures. As Anna climbed into her chair, she glanced back and saw Sazerac awake on his couch, looking at her with his soft liquid eyes. *Drat,* thought Anna with a yawn, *I forgot about him.* Who would have ever thought to worry about an eavesdropping dog? But since he didn't move or *say* anything, she thought that perhaps he didn't understand as much as the others gave him credit for.

It was so late when they finally got to sleep that they missed the sunrise the next morning. In fact, at their altitude, the sun had been up for several hours when they tumbled onto the deck to find

Dashonae at the wheel and Lambient turning fitfully on one of the benches. He bounced up immediately when he saw them.

"Ah, ladies!" He pointed out a tray of food. They breakfasted on cold biscuits, tinned meats, and coffee. It didn't appeal much to Anna, but she was ravenous. Even Rose didn't complain.

The girls sat on the forward bench to see what could be seen. And it was not much. Level sand in every direction—a never-ending monotony of beige. From the wheel, Dashonae told them they were already farther out into the Flats than anyone in recent memory had gone. "So even if we don't make it, Lambient, it looks as if you've already got the record." Lambient bellowed with laughter, but Eli put her head in her hands. The cool night air had been replaced by an increasing warmth from the morning sun. Anna began to feel a warmish prickle on the back of her neck.

Eli spun slowly in a circle, surveying the horizon. "I thought we were going north."

"We are," the inventor replied.

"But then shouldn't . . ." Eli spun slowly again in obvious confusion. "But that would make *that* the west," and she pointed toward the rising sun.

"Sure enough."

"But the sun rises in the east!"

The inventor and the knight looked at each other with raised eyebrows. The knight added with gentle condescension, "Now that's all right. Why don't you just stow those jackets? You won't be needing them where you're going."

"But we'll need them again after we get through the desert," insisted Eli.

"What on earth for?" said Lambient.

"You just said we're going north," said Eli, whose confusion was growing by the moment.

"Yes, but what of that?" Dashonae replied.

"But won't it get colder?"

"Yes, but not for several thousand miles." The professor sat up and looked at Eli with interest. "Don't tell me where you come from the equator is cold."

"Of course not," said Eli, pointing stubbornly behind them to the south. "But the equator's that way, and . . . and the sun should be . . . over there." She pointed east again.

No one said anything, but the men exchanged looks of pity.

"Poor girl," said the professor. "Heat-addled already."

"I am not!" said Eli defiantly. "The equator is south. It's always south! And the sun . . ."

At that moment Anna had an epiphany. She saw the solution to the puzzle—or two puzzles really. She saw it sooner than her sister did—a rare feat. And she reveled in the moment. She had no interest in saying anything. It was too rich, too beautiful. Let Eli "I learn everything I know from books" Hoover squirm. She sat back with her hands behind her head and felt the warmth on her face—warmth that would only grow, just as it should if one goes north out of a country in the *southern* hemisphere. *Like South America*, she thought.

She stared at the morning sun, rising gloriously in the west—just as it should in a world that rotated in the opposite direction from the Earth. *Just like one of our own planets*, she thought, but couldn't remember which one.

She was only vaguely aware of Lambient giving a tedious lecture about the nature of hemispheres and planetary rotation. But she was pleasantly conscious of her sister's frequent protests. Eli had realized only a moment too late these basic differences between this world and her own. She was now interrupting desperately, trying to make them see that she was not an idiot. Yes, she understood the concept of hemispheres very well, thank you, and knew just as well that a planet rotated on its axis. But the professor had warmed to his lecture and droned on anyway, further driving Eli to protest. And so it went for some time.

But eventually the issue became dull even to Lambient, and he said he was going in to stow the breakfast things. Dashonae repeated his advice about the coats, but then, realizing it would take them some time to get their jackets out from under the harnesses, said he would go help the professor clean up the meal.

Anna had her coat off except for one arm when she heard the sound, a small, glassy *clink* behind her on the deck. She spun around, fearing the worst. Sure enough, Rose had her own jacket partially off, and out of its pocket, the compass—their only means of ever returning home—had fallen and was now rolling, rolling, rolling . . . toward the edge of the deck.

No!

Anna dove for it, but her harness tightened just as her hand was about to close on the precious sphere. It hit the curb of the deck, bounced up into the slipstream, and was gone.

The three sisters stared in silent horror at the place it had gone over. They were stranded. No window, no going home.

Rose burst into tears.

Eli's face had gone ashen.

Anna felt sick enough to throw up and lacked the strength even to rise.

Suddenly, small wings fluttered up over the side. Finch the fairy landed next to the frozen Anna—holding the compass.

"Finch!" Anna cried. She wanted to hug him but had no idea how to do it. He stood before her looking like Atlas with the world on his shoulders. "You caught it!"

"Caught it?" he cried. "It nearly bonked me into next week. I was just flying along under the ship—'cause it's cooler, you know, in the shade—when this thing comes along, and *whammie*, Finch is seeing stars."

Eli rushed forward. "Oh, thank you, Finch. Thank you so much! Now can we have it back?"

Anna groaned inside. *She has no subtlety.*

The fairy looked at them suspiciously and then at the compass. "What is this, anyway?"

Anna's mind raced. "It's a toy. It's Rose's." She held out her hand and looked him hard in the eye.

The fairy turned the globe over in his hands. It was bigger than his head. He looked back at her and smirked. Anna knew that her bluff had been called one second before it happened. In a flurry of wings he cast himself off the side again.

"No!" cried Eli and Anna together, both throwing their hands out in desperation to stop him. But he was gone.

"No, no, no," Eli continued to moan.

Rose's face was buried in her hands again. She was still sobbing. "Sorry, so sorry . . ."

Anna sat up, trembling all over. A terrible and eternal minute passed, and none of them could move. It was over—again.

Then they heard a voice from the other side of the ship.

"I guess it's one very special toy." The fairy was standing on the rigging on the opposite side of the ship, still holding the compass.

"Finch!" all three cried again. Anna was suddenly filled with rage. She stood and approached the fairy with clenched fists.

"Now, now," said the fairy with a mixture of threat and curious humor. He held the compass up and over the side.

Anna froze. "Okay, okay, what do you want?"

The fairy smiled. "You're young, but you're quicker than Lambient at the important things."

Anna fought to speak evenly. "What do you want?"

"I want the truth. I'm a fairy, I am. I know dwarf work when I see it—nasty little moles, they are. And I want to know what this is, and how it happened to come into your possession, and what you plan to do with it."

Anna looked at Eli, who sat in an immovable heap of panic on the deck. She sighed. *No choice but to tell him*, she thought. So she did.

The fairy stood wide-eyed, taking in the brief account of how they had come to Garlandium and how they hoped to get back home. When she was done, he wore a strange look—not disbelief or wonder but something else she didn't recognize.

"And you plan to take this dwarf trash with you when you leave?"

Anna nodded, but before she could say anything the cabin door swung open, and Lambient lumbered out onto the deck, wiping his hands on a towel. He stopped, realizing something was up, and looked from Rose's tear-streaked face to Finch and his orb.

"What's going on here? Finch, what is that?" His moustache quivered with curiosity. The fairy looked from Anna to the professor and back to Anna. She held her breath.

"The little girl dropped her toy." He flew over and dropped the compass in Rose's hand. Rose quickly shoved it into her pocket.

"Shame on you, Finch. Stealing toys from children. I would have expected better from you!" And he settled his great bulk into the navigator's seat with a grunt and wiped his brow.

Finch smiled knowingly at Anna. "Sorry to disappoint, your highness, but I've always had an attraction to . . . foreign objects. Say, did I really miss breakfast?"

Chapter 23

The hours dragged on. The day grew hotter; the sun grew brighter. The ship continued its relentless northward trek, dragged by the white sail. By early afternoon the girls were sweltering on the deck, but there was nowhere else to go; the cabin was even hotter.

"I wish we had air conditioning," said Rose, leaning over the side to watch the shadow of the ship racing along the desert sands far below.

Anna was sitting next to her, watching Dashonae at the helm and thinking that adventures were highly overrated, when suddenly a snort of laughter exploded from her without her consent. She had just realized that, while she understood why she and her sisters had to take this mad voyage, she really had no idea why the men were going. Everything had happened so quickly. It was hard to believe they had only been two days in this strange world.

"Dashonae, where exactly are we going?"

"Now that depends on who you ask." The knight stroked his now stubbly chin. "In this case, the end seems to depend a bit upon one's starting place. I can't speak for Lambient. His goals are, uh . . . complicated. But as for me, this is a pilgrimage."

"What do you mean?" asked Anna.

"I know it must seem odd that a knight committed to the service of the sea goddess should sign up for a trip into the driest place in the world, but Vizuritundu is one of Therra's most sacred places."

"Fizzi-what?" asked Rose.

"Vee-ZUR-ee-TOON-doo," repeated the knight carefully. "As I learned the story, in the ancient time when the gods still walked among men, a conflict arose between Therra and her sister, Berducca, over who was of greatest repute. In a fit of rage, Therra rose from the water and heaved her great trident at Berducca, where she stood upon a high peak of the Alappunda Mountains. She missed her sister, but where the trident struck, a great flow of water burst forth. The waters that surged from it became the great Flow of Segancurs, the very stream that once fed the Amplabium in Halighyll and caused the desert to bloom. This source of life came to be called Therra's Well in the southern lands and Vizuritundu in the Azhionian tongue.

"In wrath, Berducca responded in kind by cleaving out a great hollow of rock from the mountaintop and casting the boulders into the sea. They became the Trinity Isles, whose coral reefs have ever been one of the richest places for marine life in all of Errus. And so it was that in this grievous exchange, two dead places of the world were given life. And so peace was made between them, for they realized that they—the sea and the earth—needed one another for their mutual prospering."

"So it's this well—Vizuri-whatnot—we're looking for?" asked Anna.

"The very same. It is a holy quest to find the site of the ancient well. For it is certain that the trident must still stand upright at its center. I wish to kneel before it and do my obeisance to Therra, who preserved my life."

"Pshaw!" spat the professor, emerging from the cabin. "That is about the wildest collection of mythical rubbish I've ever heard."

"As I mentioned," said Dashonae through gritted teeth, "the professor has his own thoughts."

The girls looked at the professor.

"The Amplabium certainly had a source of water long ago. That is not in question. But to claim that it came all the way from the Alappunda Mountains is absurd—"

"But," interrupted the knight with a smug look, "the Flats of Kavue were not always as wide as they are now. The desert has grown wider. Remember, open war between Azhiona and Garlandium was once waged across it. How do you explain this, Professor?"

"Come, come, simple knight, I freely admit the evidence that the Flats are growing wider at a faster rate than they should. The same is true of the snowy Wastes in the south. What of it? Expanding and contracting desertification is nothing more than a geological cycle."

"No!" The knight was adamant. "It is not. Kavue grows wider because the Azhionians destroyed Vizuritundu eight centuries ago in an attempt to lay siege to Halighyll. It was the original cause of the Ever-War. The responsibility of the never-ending thirst of Halighyll lies solely at their feet!"

"Oh, for the love of . . ." The professor clasped a hand to his forehead in exasperation. "You're describing neither history nor science nor even reason. This is pure mythology. I tell you, no such well could have ever existed, and therefore the Azhionians could not have stopped it up, and therefore the whole legend of the Ever-War is just that—a legend, a story perpetrated by nobles to enrich their coffers at the expense of real exploration and scientific advancement! Do you realize your noble king would not put a single dynar in my pocket to fund this expedition? If it weren't for—"

But the knight was now shouting. "That's because you are a heretical scientist, who lacks any respect for the gods, and—"

It may have actually come to blows if Eli's soft voice had not managed to cut through. "Excuse me, professor."

The tension broke, and both paused to look at her. "What is it, missy?"

"I'm wondering what you hope to accomplish. If you don't believe the well even exists, why are you doing all this?"

"That's just it. I'm out to prove that it doesn't," he replied smugly.

Dashonae put his head in his hands and groaned.

"But with all due respect—" Eli spoke with a calm so complete that even Anna was impressed—"how would you prove that? To prove that something like this *doesn't* exist, you'd have to go everywhere and look everyplace."

"True enough," he replied cheerfully. "But everywhere I look is one more place that it wasn't!"

"I tell you, he's mad!" cried the knight, storming to the cabin, but as he threw the door open, the sound of Sazerac's furious barking was heard.

"Now what's got into him?" said Lambient, rising.

"Lambient!" cried Dashonae from the door. "Look!" The professor looked southward, where the knight was pointing. "He saw it from the windows. He's been trying to get our attention these ten minutes."

On the horizon behind them, a great tan haze was building up like a thundercloud, growing larger by the second.

A moment later Finch landed on the cabin top. "Time to watch your backsies, boys. Looks like Kavue's whipped up a wee wind for you."

Anna realized in a heartbeat that the wall of wind and sand was not just getting taller but nearer. That was scary enough, but she was not really terrified until Lambient put his hand on Dashonae's shoulder and said, "If you really believe Therra can help, my dear knight, now's the time to ask."

Chapter 24

"Quick!" cried Lambient, holding the cabin door open. "Inside, everyone! Chairs flat, straps on. Not a moment to lose." The girls scrambled for the door.

Sazerac wriggled back into his harness, but he couldn't fasten the buckles. As panicked as she was, Anna had enough sense to rush to the stern and fasten his straps first. As she turned to her own seat, she was stunned to hear the dog say, "Thank you," as clear as any human could have said it—though much more *doggy*. She stopped, wondering if she had imagined it. The dog was looking her in the eye and, yes, he was smiling.

"You're welcome?" she stammered. The door flew open, and Lambient and Dashonae tumbled in.

"To your seats!" Lambient cried. "It's almost upon us." Anna jumped onto her chair—more like a couch now—and strapped her legs down. Eli had finished helping Rose and was clambering into her own chair.

The professor and the knight were in their seats with only their chest straps fastened. Dashonae was furiously turning cranks, tightening cables, venting gas. Lambient was sitting still in the chair with his eyes closed, holding the wheel so tightly that his knuckles were white.

Anna lay down and had just fastened the chest strap when it hit. A howl went up all around her, like a freight train in a tunnel, and the light changed from amber to dusk to nearly midnight in about three seconds. The Cricket leapt upward and forward like a boat in a hurricane—and from there on, it was pandemonium. One moment, Anna was lying on her right side; the next, the bottom dropped out and she was free-falling; then the vessel would pitch left and press her into her seat as the Cricket shot upward. Once she was sure she was completely upside down. All sense of direction was obliterated in that dusky dark.

The heat! Oh, the heat! She thought it could get no hotter, but it did. Her blood throbbed in her swollen veins, her hair was drenched in sweat, and she panted, tasting a strange, metallic dust on her tongue. It choked her, and she gagged. The straps rubbed her legs raw as she slid back and forth on the chair. Vaguely she heard Lambient coughing out orders over the screaming siren— "Tighten starboard wing!" "Contract sail by twenty!" And she knew deep down that it was all over. She would die staring at the decorative tin plating of the cabin ceiling.

And yet the dusky terror droned on, not yet ready to kill her.

She had never prayed before, and it occurred to her, as such things often do in moments of great terror, that she did not even know whom to pray to—Merris? Thes? Jesus? Buddha? Was there a Jesus in this world? Was there a Merris in hers? It seemed to her that everything depended on her getting it right. But she did not know whether any religion was true or false; she did not know if there were any gods or a God. Then she remembered the amulet pressing painfully into her breast. And without knowing why or even choosing the words, a simple, absurd thought passed through her mind: *Therra . . . ?*

The next moment, she was sorry she had thought it. A great creaking and tearing sound echoed around the cabin, and the ship jolted hard to the left. She felt a persistent port-side pull, and she began to feel dizzy, as though the ship were describing hard circles. It was descending—and fast.

Lambient and Dashonae fought the storm for nearly twenty

minutes. But wood and metal have their limits. Inevitably, a critical component buckled, some cable snapped, and the crew of the noble SkyCricket found themselves in a semicontrolled free fall. For the girls, strapped on their backs, there was nothing to do but stare at the ceiling and wait for the end.

After another ten minutes of circling, falling, rolling, and recovering, Lambient yelled something about landing gear. Anna didn't catch the details, but she knew what it meant. She had enough presence of mind to keep her tongue well clear of her teeth.

Unlike the launch, Anna remembered every hideous detail of the landing in hi-def and slow mo. There was a terrific crunch that she thought would break her in half—then they were airborne again. Another whole minute passed before the second touchdown. This one wasn't quite as hard, more of a bounce, but she knew her shoulder blades, elbows, and heels would be bruised. A few more seconds and then they hit for the third and final time—and a great rasping came from below, as if the bottom of the ship was being torn away as the merciless wind dragged it across the sand. Would the whole hull give way and suck them all out into the storm? Was this what the space shuttle astronauts felt like just before . . .

But none of her worst imaginings materialized. For another eternity—or every bit of ten minutes, at least—Anna could feel the ship being blown forward and hear the strange rasping noise. Then the roar outside seemed to lessen. Was it a little lighter in the cabin? Yes, the howl was now a loud whine—not a train, just a lawnmower. Then, almost instantly, it was silent. The sense of movement ceased.

They were at rest.

Anna's head spun, and she felt a little nauseated. She could hear Rose sobbing quietly behind her and Lambient exhale in exhaustion. Sazerac whined tentatively from the backseat. She treasured these sounds—small, common, precious, the sounds of life. They did not come from some strange and foreign world not her own. They were familiar, friendly, welcoming.

Anna lay there, feeling an overwhelming sense of gratitude.

She smiled, she exhaled—and then she laughed.

Chapter 25

"So far as I can tell," said Lambient—he was standing on the deck of the Cricket, holding his compass and some other device Anna didn't recognize—"we've been blown off course. But I won't be able to tell how far until the stars come out tonight."

All in all, Anna was amazed at how well they'd weathered the storm. She stood with her sisters on the sizzling sand, looking up at the professor. It was slightly cooler in the shadow of the ship, which stood now a few feet off the ground. Apparently Lambient had thought of nearly everything, even landing, and had built long, retracting, ski-like appendages into the hull, precisely engineered to run on sand the way a sleigh runs on snow. There was even a sophisticated shock-absorbing system, which explained why they had not splintered in pieces when they hit.

Nevertheless, Lambient and Dashonae had already exchanged terse words about their unexpected survival, Lambient crediting his engineering and piloting expertise and Dashonae attributing it all to Therra's protection. Since there seemed to be no middle ground between them, Anna lost interest and fell to examining their surroundings.

Bleak was an understatement. Desert to the left, right, front, and back. Above, a bowl of pale, apathetic blue stretching from horizon to horizon in every direction, filled with the blazing late-afternoon sun. The heat and light were so oppressive that it hurt to look at the horizon, it hurt to touch the sand with your bare skin, it hurt to move or stand still or sit down. Anna had never experienced such a dry, passionless, unrelenting torment as this prickling dance the sun did on her skin whenever she stepped out of the ship's meager shade.

The two men meandered around the ship surveying the damage. The starboard wing had splintered about a third of the way down its length and the sail hung limp and tattered. Two helum tanks had been torn loose, and the water cask in the stern had literally exploded in the landing. The remaining moisture that still dripped from planks and rigging now fell into a bucket sitting under the ship.

In the plus column, the main sail had survived more or less intact. At least, no holes had been torn in it, and the frayed edges could be mended. The girls were put to this task immediately with a spool of thick string and several needles the size of chopsticks. Most remarkably, the helum bag under the ship had also sustained no damage in the landing.

They attempted to retract the landing gear but found that one of the pulleys for it had snapped, so it had to be left down.

"That's going to create a terrible drag at launch," sighed Lambient.

"You're going to try to launch again?" Eli cried out in surprise, but melted immediately into sullen silence. Yes, she too realized that this was their only hope.

So the professor and the knight began to prepare the ship for launch. The wing booms were collapsed and reconnected to their deployment springs; the main sail was carefully repacked into its forward hatch. Finally, Dashonae extended the small hydraulic under the bow of the ship that would ratchet it back up onto its stern into launch position. They worked tirelessly at this for what little of the afternoon remained, all the while throwing sidelong glances at the heavens as though hoping for a rescue. But that was impossible, and Anna could not figure out why they kept looking toward the sky.

As daylight began to wane, the ship fell with a heavy thud onto its launch springs. It now pointed straight up as they had first seen it.

They shared a meager meal and the last of the water rations. The girls were very thirsty but had decided together that the professor and the knight needed the scant remains of the water more than they. The men rejected this utterly, and they had to compromise, each of the girls taking one long drink and giving the rest back. Sazerac too took one small drink and refused any more. Finch alone had to be rationed, for he would have drunk the remainder dry despite his small size.

Rose thought it was cruel to refuse water to someone as diminutively "cute" as Finch. Finch, of course, agreed. But Dashonae made some cryptic comment about his not needing a lot of water, being an Avonian sylph and not a Therran undine. Anna was going to ask him what he meant, but Lambient conscripted them to gather up all the broken wood fragments from the ship lying around the desert.

"What for?" said Anna, wiping the sweat out of her eyes. "It's not like we'll need a fire."

"Now you just wait, missy," replied Lambient. "The desert is only hot during the day. You'll be plenty glad for a fire when Merris goes down."

They gathered the few fragments they could find, but there weren't many—the wild scattering wind had made sure that once something was loose from the ship, it would land miles distant. To get an adequate supply, they had to strip the ornamental woodwork from the ship. Lambient wept as they tore loose various pieces of the beautiful trim, and Eli tried not to look smug. "It will really lighten the ship," she whispered to Anna as they dumped armloads of richly stained cherry and mahogany on the woodpile. Anna rolled her eyes.

To save the professor further indignities, Anna thought she might wander farther away from the ship looking for stray bits, but when she suggested it, Sazerac began to bark furiously. And the men agreed, insisting she stay close.

"What for? It's not like I can get lost," she shot back. They were a hundred miles from anything, and she could probably see the ship from a mile away. "I'm not a little kid." She was hot and short tempered, and she had survived the sand hurricane just as they had. This was no time for them to go paternal on her. But the men just looked at each other with that same apprehensive look.

"It's not you," said Dashonae gently and lowered his voice solemnly. "We don't know what may have come out of the storm." He rose and went out into the sun again to dig a shallow pit for the fire.

"Out of the storm! *We* came out of the storm! What else could possibly have survived that storm?" She did not know why, but she was feeling an uncontrollable urge to get some distance between her and the others. It was as if a heavy weight hung about her neck. And her mind, made fuzzy by the heat, could not sort out the source or purpose of the impulse, but she wanted to go out into the desert a ways to . . . to . . . she didn't know. But she felt she had to.

"Oh, missy," said Lambient with an equal hush in his voice, "surely you know the first principle of science: 'Where'er there is disturbance in the earth, the elementals give longaevi birth.'"

"What is long-ivy?" asked Eli.

The scientist and the knight looked at each other in wonder.

But Sazerac gave a series of barks amid his heavy panting, to which Lambient nodded. "Oh, yes, of course. I do remember Whinsom saying that. But theirs must be a dysfunctional land indeed to have had no contact with the longaevi at all." He paused for a moment collecting his thoughts before pointing a rotund index finger at Finch, who was basking in the sun on the prow of the ship and sulking over his meager water ration. "*He* is longaevi. The dwarf is longaevi, and so too the fire salamander, the mermaid, the nymph, the giant, the kraken, and all the other man-ifestations of the four elements."

"Four elements?" Eli sat up with excited understanding. "You mean the basic elements? Like earth, air, fire, and water."

"Ah, so you do have some understanding of these things. Yes, each of the basic elements stands in a harmonic resonance to a series of life forms—earth to the dwarf, air to the fairy, and so on. Whenever a disturbance in the symmetry of the elements occurs—like that windstorm or an earthquake or forest fire—then the conditions are prime for the spawning of longaevi."

"From where?" asked Eli. Anna recognized the incredulous look her sister always got when she thought someone was pulling her leg.

"Aren't you listening, missy? From the disturbance. It gives birth to the longaevi. Finch himself is the result of a windstorm over the lowlands of Eddigen sixty-three years ago this spring."

Eli began to laugh. "But that . . . that's spontaneous generation. Making living things out of nothing. It's just . . . just so . . ."

If he did not understand why she was laughing, the professor looked pleased nevertheless. "Now you've got it, missy. A funny phrase for it, to be sure, but very much to the point. The rele-vant longaevi are generated spontaneously from various elemental disturbances."

"But that's not science. It's alchemy, it's science fiction," scoffed Eli, determined not to be gotten the best of.

Lambient was offended. "Madam, I do not pretend to under-stand the mixed-up nature of your country, but I assure you, this is a most fundamental principle on which many other sciences depend. It is utterly scientific, and I could refer you to a number of sources wherein the various processes are mapped out."

"But it just isn't possible." But her certainty had been shaken.

"How then do you explain Finch?" Of all the arguments the professor might have presented (and Anna guessed he could have buried her sister under a mountain of them), this simple question left Eli's mouth hanging open. Anna felt a little guilty over the pang of pleasure that coursed through her at Eli's predicament, and she knew she ought to try to drum up a bit of sympathy. She even managed a little when she considered that it must be hard to always have been the smartest kid in the room, only to find all one's knowledge irrelevant, unimpressive, or just plain out of sync with the whole world.

But it was Rose, having only the most cursory comprehension of the topic under discussion, who saved Eli from having to answer. "Doesn't he have a mother, then?"

Now it was Lambient's turn to laugh. "What a sweet and innocent thing you are!" he cooed. "Of course he doesn't." Then he bent and said in an indulgent whisper, "Perhaps that's why he's so troublesome." Rose found this funny, and they laughed together. "No, no, they have no parents, and even their siblings from the same event are seldom found together. They soon drift apart. Well, that's true of the various sylphi like Finch, and the vulcani also. Some of the gnomi and the undini are quite communal—or once were."

"But he has not yet told you the full story of the longaevi," said Dashonae, joining them in the lengthening shadow of the Sky-Cricket. "Their birth is superintended by the gods."

"Now, we are about to leave the world of science, and enter this scienty-fiction thing you mentioned." Lambient said it in a hoarse whisper, clearly meaning it to be overheard. He waved his arm superciliously to the knight, bidding him continue, leaned back against the launch-spring housing, and folded his arms in grim satisfaction.

The pious Dashonae ignored him. "The professor is correct that what he describes *is* a fundamental principle of the various sciences. But he has failed to give you the most important cause of the whole process. Each of the houses of the longaevi are governed by one of Merris's children. The sylphi like Finch are under the authority of Avonia, goddess of the air, just as the undini are Therra's charges.

"And the dwarves?" asked Rose.

"All such gnomi are given to Berducca, the goddess of the deep earth and all things old and ponderous."

Eli had rallied a bit and now ventured a cautious, "That leaves fire?"

"Yes, the vulcani, such as the salamanders, are under Lemerrus, god of labor and of fire. Speaking of which . . ." He pointed at the pile of firewood and began to hoist himself up the ladder into the ship. The sun was far westerly now, beginning to turn red. Anna even imagined that it was not quite as hot as before.

"What about Thes?" Anna realized he hadn't mentioned the god Whinsom was most interested in.

"Thes?" The knight's eyebrow went up. "Oh, you mean the two priests in Halighyll. I know what they say about Thes, but I believe the word at best refers to the combined operations of all the emissaries in the world . . . at best. There is no such being. There can't be."

"We agree on that at least. Now tell them the dirty little secret," called Lambient after the knight, who gave only an exasperated grunt as he climbed the last few rungs to the cabin door. "See, Merris has five children, according to his mythology," said the professor. "Errus, who represents this here planet, has no connection to any elemental or longaevi. So it's a case of too many holes and too few pegs." He laughed to himself. "What rubbish!"

Once again Anna felt that strange longing to have a walk in the desert apart from the others. But when she said so to Lambient, his response was quick and firm: "No! You'd be easy prey out there without Dashonae and myself to protect you."

"But even with what you said," said Anna, feeling hot and bothered, "why be so afraid of a bunch of Finches? He's a pain, but I think I could handle him if I had to."

Lambient laughed again. "As simple as your sister, are you?

Two problems there. First, Finch is far stronger than you. All the longaevi bear a sympathetic energy with the events that generated them. If you and Finch had a fight, he could just carry you up into the heavens and drop you like a stone." He gave a whistle like a falling bomb. "What's more, why assume that Finch is the worst a windstorm can drag up? There are worse things than fairies. And I don't just mean imps, who make Finch look like a saint." His voice fell to a hush again. "A storm that big probably created more than a couple of . . . well, other things too." Then he rallied. "But enough of that. Dashonae! The sun's almost down. How about that fire?"

Yes, the sun was setting. Its direct heat was significantly less now, but the sand still had plenty to spare. Anna felt restless; her legs itched to move, and she could hardly sit still. She was dry and thirsty and weary, but not the least bit sleepy.

A single bright star broke through the darkening sky. Her head snapped back instinctively to look at it. Lambient noticed and pointed. "Look, there's Therra now. She's often the first out in this season."

Therra, Anna thought, and the longing to wander increased. The starry planet twinkled and beckoned. Anna's hand went unconsciously to the amulet she wore around her neck. It felt unusually heavy, gravid with a meaning she could not identify.

Chapter 26

Within minutes of Merris's descent, a wind with a hint of chill swept through the little campsite. Though welcome, its benefit was tempered by the steady stream of heat still rising from the sands. The two men and the dog jumped at every sound and jerked to look over their shoulder every time a breeze touched them. Anna found this odd after the courage both had shown in the face of the storm.

They laid out plans for the next day's work, for without water, the options were either launch or die of thirst in the desert. But this raised the issue of how to tighten the launch springs. "We'll just have to do what we can and hope for the best," said Lambient with enthusiasm.

Eli squeaked a little but said nothing.

Lambient took star readings and was astounded to find that they had come much farther than he had expected by that time. But not in the direction he had planned. His map showed a dotted line running roughly northeast from Halighyll to the sparsely detailed region labeled Azhiona. The map, though very old and wrinkled, showed northern Azhiona as a vast forested country only half the size of Garlandium, with few details save a large river running through the middle and a single dot, labeled Arzhembala, in the far north at the river's delta.

Jutting out into the Flats by many miles was a sort of peninsula of green forest. It was the shortest route from Halighyll as the crow flew, and it had been the scientist's intention to fly as the crow.

And now where were they? "Here!" Lambient stabbed his finger into the map. They had been blown northwest by many miles. This was not as bad as it might have been. They were far closer to the Alappunda mountain range, where the legendary well had been. Lambient believed they might be able to touch down right at the foot of the mountains, where they met the Azhionian jungles. This meant a lot less trekking through Azhionian territory. But the professor had little knowledge of what lay in that part of Azhiona, which bore the nondescript label "Balungorah."

"If we can launch before lunch tomorrow, we may be able to land by nightfall," he said.

With this small hope in everyone's heart, they retired. Lambient, Sazerac, and the knight said they would take turns watching the fire. Anna thought this was just to keep it from going out, but then Dashonae explained. "Even small fires have been known to generate salamanders. The foundry in Farwell, which lies at the foot of the Aracadian Mountains of Garlandium, has a garrison of soldiers who patrol the furnaces day and night to deal with, um, threats." Knowing this, Anna didn't know whether to sleep with her back to the fire or the desert. But eventually all were asleep, Lambient with a snore that matched his bulk.

Anna awoke with a start as if to some great noise. She lay on her sandy mat, listening. The fire had burned low, and she figured whoever was on duty had dozed off. It was chilly. She looked upward and saw great Lemerrus, the moon, pouring down his strange red light. It was so different from the white moonlight she was used to back home. The stories she had been absorbing since she arrived in Errus began to congeal in her mind in a way that made her wonder if she were not still asleep and only dreaming. Red Lemerrus, the god of labor and of fire, the moon. Images of foundry fires, ruddy-faced guards, and lithe salamander bodies in the flame; they spoke to her in wild hissing voices, but she did not understand them.

She turned her attention to another point of light. A star—no, a planet. Therra. *My dear Therra*. Now, that was strange; where did that thought come from? But a breeze blew, and she smelled salty sea air. Fish danced before her eyes, but they had faces. They sang and waved their arms—they were mermaids. Cheerful sailors on ships sang the praises of Therra with foaming goblets in their hands. Goblets, goblets . . .

She sat straight up and knew with an almost religious certainty that she was not dreaming. She looked up. Therra was bright on the eastern horizon and would be out of sight in a half hour. That same longing that had hounded her all day returned with a power that surprised her. Drawn, beckoned, forced—she didn't know which, but, unable to resist, she rose and walked eastward out of the camp, Therra before her, smiling on her from the heavens, calling her to come and see. The amulet grew unnaturally cold against her breast. She padded across the sands for perhaps a hundred paces, never taking her eyes off the winking star.

Without warning, she fell to her knees. The amulet had grown so heavy that she could hardly raise her head. The chain cut into the back of her neck, and she felt afraid. The amulet seemed to strain against the inside of her shirt, wanting to be free, to be out in the salty night air. *Salty?* No time to think about it. She struggled to remove the chain. It took all her strength to lift it over her head. The amulet grew heavier by the second.

Unable to hold it any longer, she dropped it on the sand and watched in disbelief as it disappeared. It made a sort of splash on the ground and simply parted the grains of sand as though they really were water. Then it was gone.

An inexplicable panic filled her, and she began to dig. She could not lose it; it was her only hope, her only—

Her fingertip hit something hard. The hole she had dug was perhaps a foot deep, and she scrabbled in the hole like a dog after a bone. Then she jumped back. Her hand came out of the hole *muddy*. She peered in the moonlight and saw her amulet lying neatly arranged in the bottom of the hole in a puddle of moisture.

She seized it and threw the chain around her neck. It had become light again.

She dug again. After only a few minutes work, she found herself with both hands plunging into a small pool of water at the bottom of the hole. It bubbled up like a spring. She bent her head and tasted. It was good—not hot or even tepid but cool and clear and clean, as if from a mountain spring. She jumped to her feet and ran back to the camp, yelling at the top of her lungs.

Chapter 27

"Impossible!" cried Lambient. Hands on his hips, he stared incredulously at Anna's small, moonlit hole, which had filled with water that was now forming small rivulets in every direction across the flat sand.

"Some scientist," said Dashonae with humor, water dripping from his chin as he drank. "Doesn't believe his own eyes."

"I don't doubt what I'm seeing, Sir Teddy, but I am quite certain that the sun baked every drop of water out of these sands hundreds of years ago. And so I mean that there is no natural explanation for what my eyes are witnessing."

Sazerac barked in response. To Anna's utter surprise, not only did Dashonae laugh, but Rose began to giggle too.

"On the nose," laughed the knight. "What do you say to that, dear professor? How does a scientist deal with a *super*-natural explanation?"

The professor only harrumphed and trooped back to the ship to gather the water skins and canteens.

By the time they had filled every vessel that would hold water, the sky was growing gray in the west. No hope of going back to sleep, for an immense amount of work had to be done. The girls were set to stowing the water, then Eli and Rose were instructed on how to combine the helum from partially depleted tanks. Anna came behind them with a wrench, loosening the empty tanks and tossing them to the ground.

"We have to make the ship as light as possible now," said

Lambient, much to Eli's relief. The decorative paneling was stripped from the interior walls and the carpet pulled up from the floor.

"It would have been easier if we'd done this while the ship was setting flat," grunted Eli as she straddled a seat-back uncomfortably. But they had the easier work. The two men were preparing the ship for launch. Even Sazerac did his share by picking up discarded junk and dragging it away from the ship. Only Finch was nowhere to be seen.

"Of course he's not around," said Lambient. "There's work to be done."

By the time all was accomplished, the ship had been stripped of several hundred pounds of material. Now she fully looked the part of the shipwreck. The sandstorm had scoured her hull raw, and her insides now matched. Anna felt a little sad for the ship as she watched Dashonae connecting the large spring-tightening gear. Lambient had already laid out a number of cables in the sand.

"Well," he said to the girls with a not-quite-so-cheerful smile, "Now all we have to do is give a little tug on these lines and . . ." He made the same ascending gesture he had made when they had first seen the Cricket.

The first two rounds of the wheel Dashonae made just by grabbing one of the handles on the gear and turning it. By the completion of the second turn, it was too tight for him to move on his own. Lambient picked up a line, pulled, and brought it past the third and nearly completed the fourth. With both men pulling, they completed the fourth, the fifth, and half of the sixth. And with everyone but the AWOL Finch pulling as hard as they could, they made it to seven rounds, nine pins.

Lambient threw his cable down in the sand with a huff, pulled a stylus out of his pocket, and began scribbling in the sand. Sazerac came over and looked at the equations he was doodling. Lambient whispered to himself as he wrote, and every so often he cast a glance at the ship or the girls or the pile of wreckage. A couple of times Sazerac barked, and Lambient would reply with a terse, "I know, I know," or "I was about to do that," and even once with "Oh, yes, I missed that." Eli sidled up to the pair and looked down with interest. Anna saw her sister's face drop as she realized the math was beyond her and used unfamiliar symbols.

After several minutes, Lambient sighed. "It's no good, ladies. The calculations are full of guesswork to be sure, but I'm quite certain that we can't get her off the ground without nine turns at least. And I'm sure we can't achieve sailing altitude without ten and a half."

"What will we do then?" said Eli in a voice that threatened full-blown panic.

Lambient cast his eyes up and down the ship again. "Hmm, the railing will take most of the morning to remove, but it probably weighs—"

At that moment a shadow passed over the sun. Although it was already quite warm, a chill passed through Anna. She saw Dashonae leap to his feet and grab his sword. Then for a moment everything went into silent slow motion. The chill came over her again, and she saw Lambient looking at her with wide, fearful eyes and outstretched arms. Then something collided with her and knocked her backward onto the sand.

A great flurry of weight was atop her chest, and hot pain seared through her left shoulder. She opened her eyes but could see nothing because she was looking directly into the sun. A black shadow bobbed before her eyes, occasionally blocking the sun, but she was too dizzy to make out anything clearly. Then her hearing returned, and she heard the beat of wings, shouts, screams, and a loud, screeching noise that reminded her vaguely of old Godzilla movies. But she still could not get up.

Then into her blurred vision a face descended—human-shaped but with great projections like horns or oversized ears. Blinded by the sun, she could make out no more than a twisted mouth with pointed teeth that snapped inches from her nose. The creature, whatever it was, exhaled into her face. The sweetness of its breath surprised Anna—and now she could no longer hear the others, was no longer lying on her back on the desert floor. She was flying! Wisps of cloud encircled her. Her mind had been dragged upward and was now floating in the heavens, free, without hindrances. The world spread out before her all the way to a darkening crescent of horizon far away. It was glorious.

A single star winked in the heavens. She knew she was seeing Avonia, goddess of the air. The star descended toward her. No, not a star—a woman beautiful beyond description. She looked familiar, but Anna could not tell where she had seen the face before. The vision held out both hands to Anna, but as it came near, the face contorted. No! This was no goddess—it was a demon, a banshee! Wild hair flew about her head as if in a gale, hollow eyes burned with malevolence, the outstretched hands grew wrinkled, and the nails became long and pointed—bird-like. The mouth opened, and a great scream of rage poured down on Anna as the hands closed about her throat.

Then she heard a wolfish growl, and she knew she was still lying on hot sand. Somewhere above her, another collision occurred. Hands that really had been around her throat were torn away as Sazerac threw himself into the creature—all teeth and claws. Suddenly the shadow was gone, and the hallucination, vision, whatever it was, evaporated. The sun seared Anna's eyes again. She rolled onto her knees coughing, gulping at the hot air.

She looked up, and the first thing she saw was Dashonae running at her with sword drawn. The sword swung around his head and down in a circle as he prepared to leap. Their eyes met, and he uttered a single syllable, "Down!"

She was not sure she understood, but she rolled flat onto her back again. He was upon her, up, and over her in a single move. She heard the sword whizz by inches from her ear as it swung upward. She followed his shadow as he passed across the sun, landing gracefully with both feet on the ground with the sword above his head. Then down it came in an arc. There was a confused screech and a thud, and Dashonae was gone out of her view again as though he had never been there.

She sat up and looked. He was behind her now, running in another direction. Next to her on the ground lay a limp form. It was like an ugly parody of Finch, if Finch had been six feet tall and hairless, with great, leathery wings like a bat and hands like claws. As for its face, it had none. The head was gone.

Anna found it hard to think. Her head seemed full of pudding, and her ears still rang. But Sazerac was nudging her to her feet, and she understood him. "Come!" And she did. They ran together toward the ship, Anna stumbling in her wooziness but gently guided by the dog.

Another shadow passed overhead. Anna could make more sense now out of what was going on. They had been attacked by whatever Lambient and Dashonae had so feared the night before. Lambient was standing at the foot of the ship's ladder shouting, "Come on, missy. You mayn't be so lucky with the other skerzak." She put her foot unsteadily on the ladder and began climbing as Lambient bent to grab Sazerac. Glancing around, she saw a sight that cleared her mind instantly and filled it with horror.

Dashonae was running in a circle, his sword drawn, and descending on him was another one of those things—a skerzak, Lambient had called it. It did look very much like a muddy-colored Finch, but bigger, and naked, and it howled unearthly as it closed in on the knight. Dashonae fell to his belly at the exact moment when its claws should have raked his back open. He rolled, jabbed, and tore a long gash in one of the skerzak's bat-wings. It spun out of control and crashed into the sand ahead of him, screaming with rage. He was up in a second and running back toward the ship, yelling, "Go, go!"

Now Anna was inside and climbing into her seat. Rose was crying, and Eli was moaning, "We can't launch. You said we can't—" Lambient came through the hatch and nearly threw Sazerac at her.

She understood, and the two of them tumbled backward to the dog's couch. She hurriedly threw on the dog's straps, wondering what the point was because she knew Eli was right. They could not launch with only seven odd rounds on the springs. But as she finished and turned to climb back to her own seat, she looked out the window and saw a sight she would remember the rest of her life.

Out where the shadow of the ship ended in dazzling noon sun, Dashonae was waving his sword gracefully, keeping the now grounded skerzak out of arm's reach, but the heat was clearly taking its toll on the knight. The gargoyle-like creature, which Anna now saw did indeed have great oversized ears like the elves in old storybooks, snapped its sharp teeth angrily and continued thrusting its hands in under the sword movements, trying to get at him. Then it made contact. Its leathery hand closed on the sword blade as it swung. The impact cost the creature a finger or two, but it also ripped the sword from the knight's hand. She heard it clang against the hull of the ship.

The knight was helpless now, and the skerzak doubly enraged. It sputtered something angrily which the knight seemed to understand, but Anna could not hear. The creature leaped, the knight ducked, and when he rolled back to his feet, he held one of the spring-gear cables in his hand. The skerzak leaped again, flapping its lamed wings wildly to get above him. It did and fell crushingly on top of him as the first one had on Anna. They rolled and wrestled tooth and nail for a moment before the skerzak screamed and leapt up. Dashonae's belt knife was lodged in the back of its shoulder. The knight began to run, but to Anna's horror, he ran away from the ship. The creature could not reach the knife handle, but, further angered, began loping after the knight. After only a few steps, however, it was pulled off its feet again, although Anna could not see what had done it.

When it stumbled upright again, Anna saw that, in addition to the knife, the knight had managed to wrap the spring-gear cable around its neck like a noose. This had drawn tight and nearly strangled the creature. But it still wanted Dashonae, who had approached it again, and was shouting something at it, taunting it. It strained and pulled, but the knight remained just out of its reach. Anna felt the ship shudder as the creature pulled with all its longaevish strength against the cable. She felt the spring gear ticking around like a clock and the ship shuddering as it was cranked click by click closer to the earth.

Sensing mortal danger but not understanding it, the creature was ignoring Dashonae now and pulling as hard as it could against the cable like an animal in a snare. The gear continued to turn, and the springs continued to tighten.

Now Dashonae was climbing through the cabin door, sword in hand, crying, "There's your eleven turns, Lambient. Now launch, or he'll pull the ship over!" As if to prove his point, the ship shuddered, and the sound of splintering wood echoed through the cabin from somewhere below. Anna was in her seat in a heartbeat and throwing on the straps. She rammed the dental into her mouth and lay her arms across her chest just as Lambient cried, "Two . . . one . . . go!" And the blackness took her again.

Chapter 28

The second launch of the SkyCricket made the first one seem like a balloon ride at the fair. When Anna regained consciousness, the ship was shuddering all around her. It listed to starboard and bounced up and down so wildly that even with the dental protector, her jaw ached.

They were not exactly falling. She could see the mass of white sail before them, so she decided they had made it through the launch arc and were now fighting to stay airborne. Lambient and Dashonae were madly throwing switches and pulling levers and shouting at one another.

After several minutes of jostling and stomach drops, the ship began to level out. And in a few more, they were floating in a relative calm. Lambient exhaled wearily and fell forward in his harness, his arms at his sides. Dashonae too was panting but still making small adjustments to the helum distribution. Anna didn't dare move until the professor turned and flashed a tired smile at the girls. "I think the worst of it is behind us now. I'm going out to look at the damage."

"No." Dashonae grabbed his arm. "You sit and keep the ship straight. I'll go out. It may have managed to . . ." He nodded somberly at Lambient. But if he meant to keep his meaning from the girls, it didn't work. It was obvious that the creature might still be aboard or even tethered to the ship by the spring cable, like a fly on a hair. Rose squeaked in her chair. Anna unstrapped her forehead and removed the dental so she could look out the window.

She was prepared for a hideous face to appear against the pane, like in that old *Twilight Zone* episode she'd once seen. But all that met her eyes was blue, cloudless sky.

The knight put on his deck harness and went out with sword drawn. Anna saw him pass carefully by the window, the wind throwing his long hair around his face. And then they sat in an awful silence for several minutes. Lambient fiddled with the helum knobs as he waited.

Then the door flew open, and the knight reentered. "No sign of it. The rope was around its neck, so it was probably killed when we launched."

Eli shuddered. "But then the rope will still be—"

"No. And that's the bad news. Looks like the point that gave was the spring-gear. The whole assembly has been ripped away."

Lambient sat silent for a moment. "That's it, then. This was our final launch. Without the winding gear, there's no way to tighten the launch springs. We have to make it on this flight."

"You mean we might *not* make it?" said Rose, as though it had only just now occurred to her that the venture stood a chance of failure.

"No, no." Lambient was characteristically optimistic. "I think we will, no doubt. But let's get out on the deck and look around. It's a bit stuffy in here." Lambient stayed in his chair until Dashonae got to the exterior controls. Then he and the girls carefully crawled out of the cabin. The first blast of air in Anna's face gave her a sense of heady height and speed. Feeling a little sick to her stomach, she staggered to the nearest bench and tried not to look down while attaching her harness.

"Look!" cried Rose after a minute. She was pointing over the port side. Everyone gathered at the railing. Anna looked a little unwillingly. Far toward the western horizon, a dark streak in the desert wound its way southward like a thin brown ribbon. It must have been huge if they could see it from this distance.

"What is it?" asked Anna, interest overcoming her queasiness.

"Proof," said Dashonae in a soft, reverent voice.

"Paah!" said Lambient.

"What?" Anna was confused.

"It is the remains of the Flow," said the knight, still overawed.

"The what?" *Why must he always dribble the information out in pieces?*

"The Flow of Segancurs, the path the ancient river traveled across the Flats. The memory of it remains upon the sand even after all these centuries. If the Flow existed, then so must the well that supplied it!"

"We don't know what that is," said Lambient, although with not quite his usual bravado.

Dashonae rounded on him. "You cannot deny it, Lambient. It is the Flow. What else could it be?"

Lambient said nothing. Anna could see a bead of sweat on his forehead.

"You mean," interrupted Eli, rescuing Lambient from his uncomfortable place, "that is where the water ran from the mountains all the way to Halighyll?"

"Yes," said the knight. His voice became quiet. "It is said that the water from Vizuritundu flowed under the mountains for a long way until it burst forth upon the desert at the Geat of Segancurs, where it flowed in a mighty torrent toward Halighyll and the Amplabium."

"I'm sorry to say that even if the Geat exists, we won't see it," said Lambient, "We wouldn't have even seen this . . . whatever it is, if the storm had not blown us so far westward."

"Praise Therra for her grace, then," cried the knight.

"Praise Therra?" Lambient's temper rose. "For nearly killing us in that storm? You might as well thank Avonia for sending the skerzak! I'm getting lunch." And he worked his way back toward the cabin, slamming the door shut behind him.

The knight remained unmoved in his reverie staring at the dark line near the horizon.

"Dashonae," said Anna softly to him. She did not want her sisters to hear. The knight did not respond, but she continued anyway. "When that thing—the skerzak—attacked me, I saw . . . or at least I thought I saw . . ." She could not get it out. She tried again. "What does Avonia, uh, look like?"

"She is said to be the fairest of the daughters of Merris. Why do you ask?"

"It's just that when that thing attacked me, I thought I saw . . ."

He looked at her with his powder blue eyes—eyes that seemed to be looking not at her but through her. "Whatever you saw, it was a lie."

"What?" She had not expected that.

"Yes. The skerzak lie, just like Finch, but more maliciously. After all, they too are Avonian sylphi. Do not tell me what you saw. It is blasphemous. The skerzak lie about the very goddess who draws them forth from the storm. Nothing is more reprehensible than a creature who maligns the god who gives it life. Whatever you saw, do not let it discourage you. If you could not believe before, you have there in the sand all the proof you need that the old legends are true. So believe now, and in the believing you will understand."

His face had gone strange. Even in the bright desert sun, it seemed to glow with an unearthly light. It was as though she was listening to a man under a spell—one that made him not less of a man but more of one. In that moment, he was more like Dashonae—more clearly his own self—than at any other time since she had met him. It was this face, at this moment, that Anna would always remember when she thought of Dashonae. He cast his gaze back over the desert and would say no more. Anna inched away from him, feeling as if she were intruding on something holy, something untouchable. She felt suddenly hollow and empty, as though she were again on the outside looking in.

I don't know what to believe, she thought.

Chapter 29

A dark green mass loomed on the horizon directly before them and extended eastward as far as they could see. The southern edge of the Alappunda Mountains dominated the western view. Piles upon piles of rock ascended, climaxing in breathtaking pinnacles devoid of snow. Although they were still miles off, it felt as if they were about to plow the bow of the ship right into those peaks. The desert was gradually losing its hold on them. The end of their journey approached.

The sun was nearly spent as well. Merris hovered on the horizon, and the desert floor far below was probably already witnessing sunset. The air had gone from hot to warm to deliciously cool. Finch had even showed up once, just to prove he still knew where they were. Lambient had excoriated him for abandoning them to the skerzak. Finch had shrugged and told the professor not to pick fights with bullies. Then he zipped off, saying he would see them "when they crashed."

They had experienced no trouble throughout the afternoon. But now a debate bounced around the deck, and the girls watched with a mixture of fascination and fear.

"Sazerac's right! He's done the calculations!" said Lambient in a heated voice. "The thermals will disappear when we reach the forest. We'll drop like a stone. We must land before we reach them."

"You can't know that!" said the knight. "We have been guided this far. Therra will not abandon us at the Azhionian border."

"It's bad enough that you actually believe that." Lambient was nearly shouting. "But at least get your gods straight! Therra is a sea goddess and has no say up here!"

"She is wherever I am, for I am hers. She is faithful and will defend us even against Avonia's ill will."

"That's it!" said the professor with a wave of the hand. "No more! I can't take it. This is *my* ship, and she will come down when and where I say." And he began his predictable stormy march to the cabin.

"And was it *your* say that landed *your* ship back there in the desert?" the knight spat. "Did *your* ship obey you in the face of Avonia's fury? Is your science stronger even than the gods?"

Lambient's shoulders sagged. He turned slowly back to the knight with a sad face. "Dashonae, we must not do this. Who knows what we have yet before us? It may be that the gods *and* the sciences will both forsake us before we are done, and all we will have in that moment is each other. Let us be friends. You may have your faith. It may be that what you call the gods is nothing more than what I call the laws of nature. So be it. But let us not fight."

The knight thought for a moment. "You are right, Lambient, in all things save one. It *is* your ship, we must not fracture our fellowship, and you likewise may have your science. But know this, professor. What you call science is not the gods but only your word for describing their operations in the world. Vizuritundu exists, and Therra will guide us to it."

"Fair enough, gentle knight," said Lambient. "Now if you will excuse me, I must prepare the ship for what landing can be made." And he entered the cabin.

The girls continued to look after him for a moment before Dashonae said, "You heard the captain. To your seats. We'll be landing shortly."

They tumbled into the cabin and strapped themselves in. Lambient and Sazerac were already in place, and soon Dashonae joined them. This descent was so gentle compared to their last one that Anna didn't even realize they were coming down until just before they hit the sand.

The first trouble didn't arise until they actually touched down. It was every bit as jarring as their last landing, but they didn't bounce. Anna heard a terrible cracking sound under her, and felt the ship dip on the starboard side.

Lambient yelled over the skidding sound of the sand under the skis. "Not to worry! The landing gear has jammed, but it's already done its work."

Anna wasn't comforted, for a moment later the sound of splintering wood and bending metal rattled the ship and the whole thing fell onto its starboard hull. Lambient pulled a lever, and the white cloud of sail barely visible outside in the failing light disappeared altogether. "Just cutting the sail loose, not to worry," Lambient shouted.

Wish he had given us a commentary last time, thought Anna ruefully. So they came to rest on a single ski, for the starboard one had torn away, and a few moments later when they climbed out of the ship, well bruised, they could see pieces of it littering the desert for a hundred yards behind them.

Anna wanted to kiss the ground. On the last landing, she had been so scared and numb it had taken her an hour even to be sure she had stopped moving. This time she was fully ready to appreciate how close they had come to disintegrating. The helum bag had been torn completely from the underside of the ship and only shreds remained. The starboard boom had likewise been ripped away when the ski failed, and the main hull supports were fractured in several places. Everywhere metal helum tubing hissed away its remaining life. She did not have to be a scientist to know they were grounded for good. But in their favor, the forests of Azhiona stood before them less than a quarter mile off. In the gathering dark they seemed foreboding after the openness of the desert, and yet for the same reason they offered a sort of comforting return to the familiar.

Lambient produced rucksacks from a bin and gave one to each person, which they loaded down with canned goods, matches, bedrolls, and other supplies. Each took a skin of water and a belt knife (Dashonae too, for he had lost his in the skirmish with the skerzak).

Being thus prepared to venture into the unknown, Lambient paused for a moment before the broken form of his beloved Sky-Cricket. No one, not even Dashonae, said anything to him. More than one tear fell from his cheek as he placed his hand on the weather-beaten hull. "She was a good ship, a faithful ship . . . a beautiful . . . beautiful . . ." He broke off in a sob.

Unable to contain himself even at such an emotional moment, Dashonae said, "We will commend her soul to Therra's eternal memory."

Anna winced, expecting another fight, but Lambient only sniffed and said, "Yes, that would be nice, thank you." He opened his arms to the knight, and they embraced while Lambient sobbed on Dashonae's shoulder. The knight comforted him and shed tears of sympathy. Anna and Eli exchanged looks of bewilderment. Here were two of the strongest, bravest, and most manly men they had ever met, weeping in each other's arms like children. Until now, Anna would have scoffed at such a tearful display, mistaking it for weakness, but this moment cured her of that misunderstanding forever. She knew that weak men cried, it was true. They cried out of weakness, cowardice, or shame. But now she understood that strong men cry as well—but their tears reveal their nobility and strength.

Eli's eyes were wet, and Rose already had a tear streaming down each cheek. Anna looked from the two men to the broken hulk before her, thought of what they had been through, thought of the beating the ship had taken to keep them safe. The thought gathered strength in her mind, and before she knew it, a tear had leaked unbidden from her left eye. Then the right eye found one as well and sent it gliding down to her chin. Instinctively, all five humans gathered in a big, weepy group hug. Sazerac sat in their midst, baying like a wolf at the crimson moon in a voice that expressed as much as the human tears.

"Enough of this foolishness," said Lambient finally, wiping his eyes. "She did no more than she was meant to do. Now it's time for us to do the same." He broke from the group and marched toward the trees. *Not even a backward glance at his life's greatest achievement,* thought Anna. She wondered if she would be able to walk away from her own accomplishments with such ease.

Chapter 30

They set up a meager camp amid the trees at the edge of the Azhionian forests. A small but encouraging fire burned. It was cool and comfortable amid the trees, a pleasant change from the withering heat of the desert. But the darkness beyond the glow of the fire was absolute. No stars shone down through the leafy canopy; no red light from Lemerrus would reach them tonight.

Lambient and Dashonae opened a bottle of something that made Anna cough when she tasted it. Anna knew about drunkenness from pirate movies but had never seen anybody actually upend a bottle in person, much less pass it back and forth and chase it down with a second bottle. It certainly wasn't something Dad did. Eli looked unsettled by it, but Rose just giggled as the men grew gradually less coherent and more wobbly.

They drank with the gusto of men celebrating an achievement. Anna's mind had been so focused on the different emergencies that she had forgotten what they had just accomplished, a feat no one else in four centuries had succeeded at. They had crossed the Flats of Kavue. Whatever dangers Azhiona harbored, the professor and the knight seemed without concern tonight.

Sazerac took a single swig from the bottle and curled up and went to sleep, grateful just to be back on the ground. The rest of the party was about to fade away as well when Finch showed up and demanded a share in the libations.

"Wha' for?" said a groggy Lambient, "Wha'djyou do?"

"You have no idea what I did," said Finch, stamping the ground.

"While you were all messing about with your little flying matchbox, I flew forward and back, searching the skies."

"Oh, let him be," said Dashonae, handing him the bottle with a shaky hand. "He pulled his weight."

The joke, if it was a joke, took a moment to work its way into Lambient's dulled mind. "His weight? Ho, ho . . . his weight!" He began to snicker, then to laugh, then to bellow. The knight joined him, and for a half a minute the two roared with laughter. Rose giggled, but more at the sight than the joke. Eli just grimaced in a very Naggie-like way.

The fairy stamped his foot again with impatience. "It's always like this. I do important work, and you never appreciate it. I've carried your messages, I've been your errand boy, but you've never let me so much as turn a screw on one of your projects. I think I've earned the chance to do something important."

Lambient sobered his face as well as he was able. "Fair 'nough, Finchie, old boy. What djyou wanna do?"

Without missing a beat, the fairy shot back, "I want to stand watch tonight."

Caught completely off guard, the two men stared at him in silence for a full ten seconds before erupting into an encore of laughter.

"Fine!" Even in the firelight Anna could see the fairy's cheeks pink with anger. "Just say it. Say you don't trust me."

The two men looked at each other and then, arm in arm, leaned forward and shouted in unison, "We don't trust you!" then broke into another round of laughter. Finally Dashonae said to Lambient, "Seriously, Ambrosius, I'm in no condition to sit up. I know my limits, and you don't look any better."

The professor stroked his moustache. "All righty, Finch. You wanna job? You can keep watch while Dashonae and I sleep off our good cheer. But you know where we are, right?" And he pointed around at the trees dramatically.

"I know, I know," said the fairy impatiently. "You can trust me."

"No," replied Lambient with a shake of his finger, "I cannot. When I wake up tomorrow safe in my bedroll, then I shall trust you." And as if a sacred pact had been struck, the knight and the inventor collapsed on their mats and were snoring in minutes. It all happened so suddenly and carelessly that Anna was seized with a sense of inexplicable dread. The girls snuggled close together on their mats. They were not cold, but cuddling felt more secure. The last thing Anna saw as she closed her eyes was the little fairy standing resolutely in the firelight with his hands on his hips, looking very important.

∽

Anna didn't know what time it was, but it was very dark when she was dragged from her bed by strong arms. Before she was awake enough even to cry out, a gag was stuffed in her mouth, her hands were wrenched behind her and tied, and her ankles were bound in one swift movement. She heard her sisters' muffled cries as they too were overcome in their sleep by unknown assailants.

She was hoisted over a massive and sweaty shoulder like a sack of potatoes and carried away from the camp. The fire winked in and out of the trees for a few moments and then was lost. All was dark. Sazerac was barking furiously in the distance, but within a minute that stopped as well. The only sound remaining was the heavy breathing of the massive form that bore her. She didn't know if her sisters were near or even alive. She could not move or cry out. She was afraid, but more than that, she was angry. After all the terrors they'd survived, it was stupid, even absurd, to be taken so easily. Her fear-addled mind held onto a single thought—a mental picture of her strangling the life out of one wretchedly unreliable fairy.

BOOK 4

The Teeth of Azhwana

Oh war, so great and terrible you were,
Raging 'cross the desert and the years.
Choose the explanation you prefer.
Who first turned that crank of bloody gears?
Was Southern pride the cause of all the tears,
Or had Northern arrogance its share?
In the end the dead have ceased to care.

> FRANKO RAZHAMANÌAH, from
> "Senseless" in *The Ballads of the Ever-War.*

Chapter 31

The strangest part of that midnight journey, which lasted an hour if it was a minute, was that Anna was not sure it was a human shoulder over which she was slung. Her captor's breathing sounded human; its gait felt human; even its musky perspiration smelled human. But Anna had been in that world long enough to realize that not all things that seemed human were in fact so. Finch was roughly, albeit diminutively, proportioned like a human, as were the skerzak, in a grotesque way. She'd heard of dwarves and giants, both of which she assumed were roughly human shaped. She did not find it hard to believe that stranger humanoid creatures might lurk in remote forests such as these.

It took her awhile to realize that, while they were still in the forest, her bearer was no longer ducking under branches. He moved smoothly, as though on a well-worn path or even a road. But she still could not see anything in the darkness. It was torture bouncing up and down on that shoulder, unable to move any of her limbs. But the worst was her neck. It was stiff from holding her head up, yet every time she relaxed, her nose banged painfully against her abductor's sweaty back. If the creature carrying her was human, it was in great physical condition, for while its breathing was slightly more labored than when the journey started, its pace had not slackened a step. It seemed as if it could continue in that same swift silence indefinitely.

But eventually they broke from the forest. Anna knew this because suddenly there was light all around them—not light from the sky but from directly in front of them. She could see several things. First, they had indeed been on a path. The forest rose behind them, and they had just emerged from it through a large, ornamented gate. Second, the two legs that had been crisscrossing her line of vision *were* human legs, covered in black, soft-soled leather boots. Third, craning her neck up, she saw several more men come out of the forest through the gate behind her. They were heavily muscled and cleanly shaven, swarthy, with black designs painted or tattooed on their bare arms. They wore smooth leather caps that fastened under their chins, and they bore swords, bows, and long knives. Over the shoulders of the man directly behind them dangled a pair of sneakered feet that looked like Rose's. Anna felt welcome relief course through her. It appeared that their abductors wanted them alive—for now.

Anna had been vaguely expecting a jungle village with grass huts and a roaring fire in the middle. Instead, before her lay a whole city. Nothing so big and fusty as Halighyll but cleaner and more open. The buildings were lower, seldom more than two stories, and so many trees stood around that it looked as though the city had been built around the forest instead of the forest being cleared for the city. Ivy and other vines grew and flowered on stone walls. The smell would have been fresh and delightful had not Anna been working hard for the last hour at *not* smelling the man who carried her.

Halighyll had felt old and depressing, as though history had forgotten it and its people. But this place seemed like a vigorous adolescent—precocious and daring, on the verge of something. No other people were about, which was not surprising since it was still the middle of the night. Even so, the city was ablaze with electric lights—not clumsily strung as in Halighyll but designed into the buildings and pillars. Was this really the barbaric and primitive Azhiona which Dashonae had spoken of throughout the trip? Anna's imagination had prepared her for cannibalism and bones through noses, not this clean metropolis. Then again, it did not sound as though anyone in Garlandium knew much of what lay north of the Flats. Perhaps this was a different people, some third tribe or nation.

After passing through various arches, gardens, and public spaces, the captive train finally stopped. Anna was hoisted down from her captor's shoulders and set on wobbly feet before a wide set of marble steps that led up to a brightly lit palace. Eli and Rose were dumped onto their feet next to her. They looked at Anna with panic in their eyes but could not speak as they too were gagged.

One of the soldiers bent before each of them and cut the cords around their feet. "March," came a thick, deep voice from behind. Anna turned to see who had spoken but was jabbed in the ribs by something hard. "Ah, ah! Do exactly what you are told and less harm will befall you."

She desperately wanted to know if any of the others had been captured. But she did the only thing she could do—she marched up the steps toward the great wooden doors, which swung open automatically, like the doors at the grocery store. The three girls stepped across the threshold into a great hall, dimly lit. The bright lights outside cast three shadows before them on the stone floor. Anna could see nothing in the relative darkness ahead. Then her eye caught a light moving afar off, a small flame descending a staircase at the other end of the hall. The light reached their level and began to come toward them. The girls shrank back toward the threshold but were blocked by large arms.

One of the soldiers came forward with a casual air of authority and pulled the black skullcap from his bald head. "Tell my lazy brother that we've caught something unexpected." The man's accent was unfamiliar. He had the most complicated tattoo on his right arm of any of the soldiers, so Anna assumed he was in charge.

"Your royal brother has gone to bed, as have all his loyal citizens," came the reply. It was a female voice, rich and clear but filled with sarcasm.

"Pah," the soldier spat. "'Loyal citizens.' I think not. I have urgent business with the onderkoning."

"So you've dealt with our little birdie, have you?" A woman stepped forward into the light of the door, Anna thought she was the most beautiful woman she had ever seen—tall, willowy, with silky chocolate skin, high cheekbones, and dark, piercing eyes. Her long black hair was piled high on her head in curls so intricate that it must have taken a score of hairdressers hours to arrange them. And she wore a bright red dressing gown fringed with gold brocade.

"No, not that. Not yet. Something more important," said the soldier. And grabbing Anna's wrist, he pulled her forward.

"What? You've taken to importing southern children? My, my, Ragundiae, I didn't realize your tastes were so extravagant."

"Guard your tongue, Ahvorazhie," the soldier said. "My honor is above reproach—unlike yours—and I don't care who your father is." The soldier was incensed, and Anna got the impression that the lady enjoyed goading him.

"My father is exactly the one you should be concerned about, ever since he gave me to your brother and made you a simple tara." Her bright red lips parted in a malicious smile, but she turned and walked away, calling back over her shoulder, "I shall go wake the onderkoning for you, but he won't take kindly to being disturbed by a mere tara."

They all stood in silence while her light ascended the staircase and then winked out as a door closed. The man called Ragundiae clenched his fists and ground his teeth in agitation.

"Tara," said one of the soldiers, "why do you let the princess speak to you this way? You are more worthy to be onderkoning than your brother. We all think so." And grunts of assent followed.

Ragundiae turned and struck the soldier on the cheek, not hard, but enough to show displeasure. "Do not forget your loyalties, Djerack. You and I have both sworn allegiance to the koning. He has shown favor on my house by giving his daughter to my brother and making him onderkoning of the whole of Balungorah province. So he has our allegiance as well. You will not speak like this again in my presence, any of you."

"Aye, tara!" shouted a dozen voices.

The light reappeared on the second level, and Ahvorazhie's sweet voice echoed down to them. "His royal highness, the Onderkoning Tengomaniah, will see you now in the council chamber. Try not to keep him up too late. He's so cranky when he doesn't get his sleep." She let out a musical laugh and retired.

Ragundiae stormed off into the darkness, mumbling things Anna could not hear. They were thrust forward into the relative dark. Dim lights slowly brightened, and Anna looked around her at a great hall with marble floors and many pillars and arches. A vaulted ceiling sloped from three directions to a single point. Every inch of the ceiling was covered in complex paintings of people and strange creatures, eating or fighting or dying. It was like the Sistine Chapel but far more wild and exotic.

A great set of double doors stood before them, but the tara, which Anna guessed was some kind of rank like a captain, led them to a smaller door on the right. They entered a large room, unappointed but for a long table with chairs around it. The chair at the head sat on a platform a few inches off the floor, slightly elevating anyone who sat in it above all others.

The girls were seated in three chairs situated against the wall. But Anna leaped to her feet again when three bundles—two large and one small—were dumped on the floor before them. Lambient, Dashonae, and Sazerac! Fear welled up in her, for they did not move. Then she heard a soft snore coming from one of the bundles. Lambient, far from hurt, was sound asleep!

Ragundiae prowled the room like a cat, muttering to himself. His soldiers, twelve of them, stood stiffly and silently against the walls. But when Dashonae groaned, one of them leapt forward with a syringe in his hand.

"Back," said the tara. "We will want him awake before long."

The door in the far wall swung open and in walked a sleepy-looking man in a purple robe with a small crown sitting cockeyed on his head. He was a full head shorter than Ragundiae but clearly his brother. He threw himself into the elevated chair and rubbed his eyes.

"Ahvorazhie tells me you have not yet found the impundulu," he said in a voice thick with sleep and displeasure.

"No, my brother, but greater things than this are afoot—"

"Then why have you waked me?" the onderkoning yawned. "You were under orders not to return until it had been destroyed."

"Kavue has been breached."

"What?" Tengomaniah sat up in his chair, losing every trace of weariness. The tara stepped back and pointed at the form of the unconscious knight. The onderkoning rose slowly, staring as if at a nightmare. "How?"

"On a machine that floats on the air. Had we not been patrolling for the impundulu, we would not have known, but as it was, we saw them land. We waited until they were asleep before we took them."

Tengomaniah now wore a panicked look. He gathered up his robes in his hands and began to pace the room, a diminutive and fretful replica of his brother. He mumbled to himself, "We must send word to Arzhembala immediately. It could be a vanguard." He looked up. "You!" he said to the first soldier his eye lighted on. "Prepare a message for the koning. Rouse the umemelugha and have him prepare to transmit."

"Settle down, brother," said Ragundiae with disgust. "It is not a prelude to an attack. Or if it is, we have been greatly misled as to Garlandish strength." And he gestured at the three girls.

"Those aren't soldiers," said Tengomaniah in wonder, collapsing back into his chair.

"Of course not, but what they are, I cannot guess."

"Then we'd best ask them."

"My thoughts exactly." The two men turned in unison and looked at Anna. Anna decided then and there that she would never again fault Eli for liking the spotlight—for as the tara drew his knife and stepped toward Anna, she was more than willing to let her sister have it.

Chapter 32

"Now, southern child," said the tara, "tell us what brings you to trespass in the free lands of Azhwana." Anna had been dragged forward and ungagged. The onderkoning had resumed his seat and was watching her petulantly. She cast a nervous look back at Eli, still gagged, who shook her head imperceptibly.

"No!" Tengomaniah banged his fist on the table. "Do not look to her for help. Speak first."

Ragundiae lifted his hand to calm him. "Now, now, brother, there is no need to terrify the child further." Then he spoke very gently to Anna. "You will find us very accommodating to the truth. Lies alone will bring you to grief."

Anna thought hard. She had no intention of telling them about the compass or the window, but they already knew about the Sky-Cricket, and surely Lambient's desert crossing was soon to be famous, so she decided on that. She told them all about Lambient's desire to be the first to cross Kavue and his invention of the ship for that purpose.

"But why then does he travel with a Therran knight?" said Tengomaniah, leaning forward in his chair and pointing a finger. "Admit it, this is a probe to test our defenses. How many more are coming?"

"No!" said Anna, shaking her head violently. "He only came as protection against the Azhionians."

She was not aware of having made a joke, but suddenly everyone was laughing.

"You poor, simple southern child," laughed Ragundiae. Then to his men, "You see how young the lies begin? Even at this tender age she has been taught to fear and hate us. Garlandish deception is matched only by its arrogance. They have landed on our very porch and brought with them for protection this one knight. Do you see the slight, my brothers? They would compare this single knight with the whole of Azhwana's brave men." Laughter died, and Anna felt malicious eyes boring into her from every direction.

She was saved from responding by a voice from the floor. "And it would have been a fine match had you the courage to face me fairly." Dashonae was now awake.

This earned him a kick from Tengomaniah. "Garlandish dog! What say you? You, who have pillaged our lands and killed our people for eight hundred years! The tara ought to have slain you in your sleep rather than allow you to insult your betters."

But again the calmer words of his brother intervened. "It is surely fruitless, knight, to peddle your lies here. Garlandish atrocities are well documented. But since I know it is against your honor to lie, tell me, rather, what you thought of the girl's story?"

"She, at least, speaks the truth," he spat. "Now unbind me, and I shall answer your falsehoods with the true edge of my sword."

Ragundiae let the challenge pass. "So you maintain that this was a purely scientific venture?"

"No," said the knight flatly. At that moment Anna wanted to cry. "Mighty Therra has brought us across Kavue in search of Vizuritundu." Laughter erupted for a second time.

"Mighty Therra!" Ragundiae said with derision. "You see again, my brothers, how deep the Garlandish folly goes. You see how they entrust themselves to children's tales and false gods. Therra, indeed! If Vizuritundu ever existed, its location is now known only to Thes, who knows all."

Eli started, and Anna gasped so loudly that the attention of the men returned to her. "What frightens you now, little one?"

"You said 'Thes,'" she stammered.

"So I did, but what can that holy name mean to a southern infidel?" Eli began to shake her head so violently that the tara ordered her ungagged.

"No, no!" she spluttered. "We know about Thes from the priests in Halighyll."

Guffaws and jeers went up around the room. "You lie!" shouted Tengomaniah, banging his fist on the table again. "Thes has no believers in the south. It is a land given over to the darkness of the false emissaries."

"No," insisted Eli. "There are two priests named Whinsom and Cholerish. They say they are the last, but they believe that Thes stands over all the other gods."

The tara held up his hand for silence, then looked to the bound knight for confirmation.

"She is correct," said Dashonae. "I know the two priests. They misunderstand the holy gods, but they are honest in their belief."

Ragundiae stroked his chin thoughtfully. "Yes, they are misguided, but not so much as the rest of that land. They believe in Thes *and* in the false gods as well. How interesting." Then he turned to his brother, who was still fuming in his chair. "Brother, I suggest we take private counsel on how to proceed."

"Why the delays? We have a clear right to all their heads now. Let us be done with it and back to bed."

"I agree," growled Dashonae. "Take the coward's way out. Finish what began in treachery and sleep—"

"Treachery?" Ragundiae restrained his brother from delivering another kick. "Sleep, yes, but how treachery?" He was actually smiling now as if a joke were in the offing.

"Admit it! Admit that cursed fairy was in league with you." Dashonae writhed in his bonds. "Confess how he sold us out."

"The silly choice of using the sylph as a watchman was not mine." The tara was amused. He snapped his fingers and a soldier came forward carrying a large tray with a silver dome over it. It looked like, and in fact was, a serving dish. He set it down upon the table. The tara lifted the lid, and there, like a tiny child, or more like the main course at a banquet, lay Finch, sound asleep. His leg twitched, and he mumbled in his sleep, "They never trust me, never let me do anything important, but I'm dependable, I am . . ."

Ragundiae waved, and the tray was removed. "The sylph was taken by the same means you were—sleep drugs."

"Enough of this," said Tengomaniah impatiently. "Let us be done with them, for my bed calls to me."

"Do not fret, brother, there will be time enough for your sleep," said Ragundiae dryly. "I do not believe we have yet understood their full designs. I would question the doctor and the canine once they are alert. Djerack!" And a soldier snapped to attention. "Take our visitors to the guest house and—"

"Guest house!" said Tengomaniah in disbelief. "Cast them into the gaol, and let them rot!"

"No, no, brother. We must not forget our manners. These are not brigands. We have here a southern knight of apparent honor, an inventor of great achievement, and some children. We must not add needless fuel to their doubts regarding our chivalry." Then to Djerack, "Take them thence and provide for their comforts. But post double guard. And you have orders to remove by sword any part of them that shows itself out of window or door." And he looked hard at Dashonae to be sure he understood the threat.

The guest house to which they were taken was comfortable and well lit. They were all unbound and provided with a tray of fruits and dried meats, jugs of wine and water, and a plate of rubbery, tortilla-like rice bread. Sazerac awoke minutes after they arrived, but Lambient, who had been dumped on a couch, snored on for the remainder of the night. Dashonae insisted that they all attempt some sleep. He sent the girls into the single bedroom, saying that he and Sazerac would stay in the main room with the professor.

The girls sat together on the immense bed they found there. While they had all been relieved of their belt knives, and Dashonae of his sword, the girls had not otherwise been searched. Whether this was from carelessness or through a sincere belief in their childish innocence, they did not know nor care. They consulted the compass and found it still pointing determinedly in one direction and toward a higher altitude. They examined Anna's amulet, but it was unhelpfully inert. Besides, escape was not possible. Two guards were posted at the front door, two at the back, and two patrolled the perimeter. Plus, where would they go?

None of them felt frightened. So long as options are still available, it is easy to be frightened, but once every alternative has been removed, fear often loses its power. Time becomes the greater enemy. And this was true now. They huddled together in the great bed, waiting. Rose fell asleep eventually, but Eli and Anna lay awake. It was absolutely quiet but for Lambient's muffled snores in the other room. Finally Anna felt Eli breathing slowly. She was asleep. Anna could not help imagining halls far away in which two brothers with heads bent close together decided their fate.

Chapter 33

Anna awoke to bright sunlight streaming through gaps in the curtains. It had a warm cozy midmorning feel to it, like the sunlight on a holiday or a weekend when you've been allowed to sleep as long as you want. She was surprisingly comfortable. She hadn't slept in a bed for several days, and for a moment she didn't quite remember where she was. But this lazy feeling was shattered in a moment by angry voices from the next room. The three girls tumbled out of bed and pushed the bedroom door open.

"But you have no authority or jurisdiction for this!" Lambient was speaking loudly, his great unkempt moustache twitching angrily.

The large form of Tara Ragundiae stood outlined in the door against the bright sunlight. "You have trespassed on the sovereign soil of Azhwana uninvited and bearing arms. We are most certainly within our rights to try you as Garlandish spies."

"You waste your breath, Lambient," said Dashonae from the couch. "Don't forget where you are. There is no law in this land save that which decrees continued war against Garlandium."

"You will find more equitable justice here than at home, knight," said the tara through gritted teeth. "I have heard how you mistreat the Rokan in your midst. And how often in Landembrost have Azhwana children been summarily executed for wandering from their mothers into the Garlandish half of the city?"

The girls exchanged looks of wonder. This was the same story Dashonae had told them, but with the players reversed. Anna knew Dashonae; he had saved their lives. He was no merciless killer. He was noble and brave. But could it be that Ragundiae was also? In that moment Anna's whole notion of friend and enemy was shaken.

"The tribunal shall convene at noon in the grand assembly hall. And I suggest you rehearse a more respectful demeanor. Your lives may depend upon it." With that he left, and the door slammed shut behind him.

The girls ventured cautiously into the room and stopped as Lambient cursed loudly. But turning, he saw them and was immediately contrite. "Oh, missies, I'm sorry. I shouldn't speak so, but I didn't know you were present."

Rose giggled. It was not one tenth of what they heard in a single recess at school, but Anna was moved by the idea that one ought to apologize for crass speech. Naggie had said the same thing on a dozen occasions, but it was different coming from someone she respected.

"What was that all about?" ventured Eli.

"Not much," said the reclining Dashonae languidly. "Only that they're bringing us all before a tribunal of the elders of Ishtagung. That's where we are now. And we all have the privilege of being tried as Garlandian spies."

"But we're not," said Eli.

"That has little to do with it," said Lambient, who was now munching on a yellow gourd fruit from the tray. "We are certainly the first Garlandians to set foot in Azhiona in three hundred years. They have no precedent for such things. I imagine they want to make an example of us. After all, how would the garrison in Halighyll respond if half a dozen Azhionians landed at its doorstep?"

"We'd kill every mother's son of them," muttered Dashonae bitterly.

Lambient gestured helplessly at the knight. "You see, missies, the price of hatred."

"But I don't understand," said Eli. "If no one has crossed the desert in three hundred years, how can there still be a war between the two countries?"

"It is true," sighed Lambient, "that there has not been actual combat between the two nations in many years, and wiser souls are grateful to the widening of the desert of Kavue for that." And he looked hard at Dashonae, who just snorted and lay down. "But a *state* of war has existed for eight centuries between the two nations, and while the hundred-year truce was signed several generations ago for the sake of profitable trade, the two nations are still formally at war. And you can see why." He gestured toward the knight. "There is still much hatred and suspicion on both sides."

It turned out that they did not have to wait long, for the girls had slept late into the morning. So they all ate something, and about the time they finished, they heard boots on the porch. The door opened, and Djerack ordered them out. In daylight, the city was even more magnificent than it had seemed. Fountains, which apparently only ran during the day, bubbled everywhere, and they passed fruit trees at such regular intervals that one could have satisfied hunger even before one's legs got tired of walking.

They finally saw the people of Azhwana. The streets were filled with pedestrians, some carrying bags of groceries or tools. Children ran freely about the streets without fear. They were all dressed in robes or loose-fitting pants of solid bright colors or sometimes stripes. News of their arrival had apparently traveled through the city with lightning speed, for everywhere they went, people stared, small children hid behind their mother's skirts, and occasionally someone jeered. They saw no beggars, no peddlers, and no litter on the streets. Nor were the streets congested like Halighyll during the revelry but were open and easy to traverse. Anna longed to wander freely amid the colors and the sounds.

They were marched back to the palace and up the marble steps. But upon reaching the great hall, they were directed not to the council room but through the great carved doors at the far end. They entered a large room that was part throne room and part courtroom and passed down a center aisle with long, curved rows of seats on either side. A balcony gallery looked down on them as well. The room buzzed with people moving about, finding seats. The room was already half full of men and women dressed in even more brightly colored robes than they had seen outside. They were ornamented with various festoons and embroideries that seemed both decorative and heraldic. Similarly decorated banners hung from every wall. And though she was distracted by much of it, Anna thought she recognized patterns from the banners repeated in the clothing of various persons.

Before them was a great open area shaped roughly like a crescent, where sat five chairs and a single brown cushion on the floor, apparently for Sazerac. In the front, a great rounded stage or dais thrust out into the room. On it sat two thrones and a series of chairs on descending levels. On the two central thrones sat the Onderkoning Tengomaniah and the Princess Ahvorazhie. The princess was robed in a breathtaking violet robe with silver trim, and her hair circled gracefully upward on her head. She wore a silver crown, not circular but spiral in shape. It wound its way in and out of the folds of her hair upward to the summit, where a single purple gem was mounted. Tengomaniah was clothed with equal flair, but the result was less impressive. He was a head shorter than his bride while sitting. His chin rested on his hand, and he yawned periodically. On the level directly below him sat Tara Ragundiae, clothed in a black robe, which lay open to reveal silver mail filled with various painted symbols like military medals or decorations. The other chairs were filled with about a dozen elderly men and women, all clothed in regal finery.

What most caught Anna's attention, after her eyes had adjusted to the profusion of color, was the small podium that sat next to the onderkoning's chair. A red velvet cushion sat on it, and on the cushion a small creature was coiled. It was red also, but such a violent shade as to make the cushion look faded. Small silver lines ran around its back, and Anna could not tell if they were part of its hide or if they had been painted on. But as they sat in the five chairs, a small lizard-like head appeared from the coils, and it rose on four legs, repositioning itself to look at them.

"By Therra's trident," mumbled Dashonae, "they have a salamander."

"Now don't worry about that," replied Lambient in a hoarse whisper, "but do please let *me* do the talking. You'll just get them riled up."

The knight did not respond but continued to stare at the salamander.

Now a soldier in a green cloak with orange feathers on the shoulders, like epaulets, stepped forward and banged the steel butt of a long spear on the marble floor. Everyone went silent as the clang, clang echoed through the room.

"Oyez, oyez! Elders and noble families of Ishtagung and her provinces!" he shouted to the room. "The onderkoning of Balun-gorah and lord sovereign of the city of Ishtagung, his royal high-ness, Prince Tengomaniah, has called forth this tribunal to address the threat posed by these Garlandish spies."

Anna, who sat next to Dashonae, felt him stiffen and begin to rise, but from the other side of him, Lambient put a firm hand on his thigh and pushed him back into his chair.

"Do you now renew your vows to fulfill the laws of Azhwana and see justice done within the realm?" And a mumbling of "Aye, aye," went up from the various persons in the chairs. With this the crier saluted the prince, turned, and disappeared into the gallery.

Now a stiff sheet of thick parchment was brought to Tengo-maniah, who sat up and, attempting to sound royal, read, "You six are charged with unlawfully entering the sovereign realm of Azhwana in possession of military arms, with the mission of spy-ing out secrets within this land and with the intention of reporting them in Garlandium. How do you plead against these charges?"

Lambient rose slowly to his feet, walked calmly to the edge of the dais, and, placing his large thumbs in the loops of his pants like a lawyer, said loudly and cheerily, "Your highness, we plead guilty to all charges."

The uproar in the room was matched only by the cry of outrage that issued from Dashonae. All were on their feet shouting. Anna, however, could not stand. She had lost the feeling in her legs.

Chapter 34

Now the crier was back, banging his staff on the ground, but to little avail. The crowd shouted at them from the gallery. Dashonae attempted to throttle Lambient but was dragged kicking back to his chair and held there by two soldiers.

Anna sat in amazement, watching first Lambient, who stood there unmoved like a mountain with a little smirk on his face, and then Sazerac, who lay calmly on his cushion looking at Lambient with knowing eyes.

Ragundiae was the one who finally reasserted order. He stood and went to the center of the dais, raised his hands, and shouted above the din, "That is enough. Enough! Or I shall order the hall cleared." The noise subsided, and people returned to their seats. When a relative calm had been restored, the tara said to Lambient, "Am I to understand that you confess all these things that are said against you?"

"I do."

Dashonae cried out, "He does not speak for me. He lies. We are no spies! We are on a quest." But iron hands restrained him in his seat.

Ragundiae looked from Lambient to the knight and back. "You appear to have some disagreement within your own party as to the purpose of your journey."

"Not so, my lord tara." Lambient then turned to the room, and Anna got the impression that he was very familiar with presentations to hostile audiences. "I am quite sure the knight and I agree to the letter on the purpose of our adventure. The difference lies only in the sort of justice we each expect in this court." The crowd mumbled, the elders on the dais whispered to one another, and the prince looked as bored as the princess looked intrigued.

He continued with the air of an attorney who knows his case is already won. "The knight believes that the people of Azhwana desire the destruction of the southern lands, and as such he does not believe he can answer honestly the charges you raise. He dares not entrust himself fully into your hands. But I have no such doubts. I believe the people of Azhwana to be noble and just. I believe the two nations have for centuries thought each other the basest sort of savages, but from what I have seen of your city and your culture, I do not believe this to be so." The room was in his hands now, and Lambient knew it.

"I believe you fear Garlandium, not because you are cowards but because you have never seen that land with its gentle people, who fear you in mutual ignorance. I did not fear to tread upon Azhionian land because I have never felt you to be my enemy. I expected exactly the sort of misunderstanding that this tribunal represents, but I welcome it. I hold no secrets from this court but admit freely that I have been about exactly what you have accused me of."

There was a renewal of mumbling, but Ragundiae stamped his metal-shod boot upon the floor with a silencing effect equal to the crier's staff.

"What have you accused us of? Did we enter this land without consultation or permission? Yes, but ask yourself if it could have happened otherwise. Do we carry arms with us? Yes, but again ask yourself whether you would brave Kavue without such arms. This angry knight saved our company in the depths of Kavue by single-handedly destroying two skerzak." There were small outbursts of disbelief around the room, but Lambient drove on. "Did we come probing a great secret in Azhwana? Yes, Vizuritundu is surely one of the great legends here as well and an object worthy of questing.

And was it our intention to proclaim to the world the results of this journey? Yes, we have conquered Kavue, not for Garlandium's glory or Azhiona's conquest, but because it was a thing thought impossible. And from this feat the world shall know that man is greater than Kavue . . . all men, be they of Garlandium, Azhiona, Rokan, or Mulek. And yes, we are the first of many to come, not of soldiers, but of explorers and dreamers. I would die contentedly at the hands of this tribunal if but one Azhionian child were to gain sufficient courage from my efforts to repeat my journey in the opposite direction. I would welcome with my best wine any Azhionian explorer to knock upon my door and extend his hand in friendship." And with this he held out his hand to Ragundiae, who stood above him on the dais, wearing a shocked and displeased look.

The room was silent. Every eye was on the tara. Anna leaned forward in her seat, wondering if this would be the moment the Ever-War ended. But no sooner had she thought this, than it became clear that she had seen too many movies. The sound of soft clapping rang through the hall. Every eye turned to the little pedestal next to the prince. The salamander had risen on its haunches and was banging its little hands together with an amused and cynical look on his face.

"A very good speech," it said in a hissing voice that reeked of sarcasm. "Well rehearsed and finely given. In all my years of service to the konings of Azhwana, I have not heard it given better by any Garlandish politician. But I have heard it before."

And with that the spell was broken. Ragundiae returned to his chair, where he slumped and stared hard at Lambient. He, apparently, had *not* heard such a speech before and was chewing on it.

The salamander, however, was just warming up. "Elders of Ishtagung, you may desire to believe this utopian sentiment, but real intentions are revealed with ease. Bring forward the knight."

Dashonae was hoisted to his feet. "Knight, tell this assembly why *you* have come into this realm."

Dashonae threw back his shoulders. "I am on a quest to locate Vizuritundu."

"Why do you seek the lost well?"

"Because it is lost." This brought some tittering from the gallery.

Even the salamander smiled. "You are clever, Therran, but not entirely precise. How did it come to be lost?"

Dashonae's eyes narrowed. "I will not be mocked, salamander."

"A man is mocked only when he is afraid. What of the well?"

"I fear no one in this place."

"What of the well?" The salamander pushed him gently but firmly.

"You already know my answer."

"What of the well?" People began to whisper to each other.

"You will answer the question," said Ragundiae firmly.

Dashonae's patience was overtaxed, and he blurted, "Need I tell you of all creatures the cause of the dry death in my country? Is the cause of the whole bloody Ever-War unknown in the land of its birth? Has Azhiona so easily forgotten its sins?"

People rose in alarm, but this only goaded the knight to speak more loudly. "I seek that well by which Azhiona sought occasion against my country. It was your people who destroyed it in the beginning and brought the Ever-War down upon us all."

The room erupted again into shouts and cries of anger. His work done, the salamander settled back down onto its palette, buried its head under its tail, and seemed to go to sleep. Lambient gave Dashonae one disgusted look and marched back to his seat.

When order was restored, Ragundiae addressed the room. "I believe we have heard enough to ascertain the spirit of the knight and the scientist. And now, what of the canine?"

The dog rose, trotted in front of Lambient and sat down between his large feet. He barked three times. Though Anna did not understand him, when he turned and looked at Lambient with trusting eyes and made a final bark, a lump formed in her throat.

"Professor," said Ragundiae, equally touched, "you have a loyal friend there. So be it." And he turned to the elders. "Let the dog's fate stand with the professor's. And finally, what of the children?"

It was not exactly an invitation to speak, and so Eli and Anna sat, looking at one another, unsure what to do. It was Rose who saved the day. She had not followed much of what was taking place around her, but she knew that terrible things might happen next, and with all the yelling and shouting, she found this the perfect moment to have a meltdown. Her head fell into her hands, and she sobbed loudly, "I just want to go home!" It was probably the best thing that could have happened, for the whole room fell into a hush, and small expressions of pity were even heard from the balcony.

From her throne, Ahvorazhie saw an opportunity to needle Ragundiae. "I do not believe, tara, your honor is well served by making little girls cry. Perhaps we should have assumed that was her desire from the outset?"

Ragundiae spun around angrily to respond to the princess, but Tengomaniah said lazily, "I've heard enough. Tara, have the accused dismissed while we deliberate."

Consigned to the council chamber, Sazerac and the girls listened to Dashonae and Lambient argue about their respective handling of the tribunal.

"You just had to dredge up all that mythology," complained the professor, pacing back and forth, "right when I had them ready to let us go."

"Ha!" scoffed the knight. "They were no more ready to let us go than that stymphalia they're searching for. They've got a salamander, and those things can turn anything you say against you."

"Stymphalia?" Lambient's pacing came to an abrupt halt.

"Yes," said the knight casually, "that impundulu they're looking for. I've never seen one, but I'm guessing it's a stymphalia."

"What's a stim-fala?" asked Rose.

"It's one of the Avonian sylphs like Finch or the skerzak, but nastier. They're more inclined to forests or jungles and birthed by rainstorms amid great lightning and thunder. It has the form of a great bird with metal claws that are quite poisonous. Terrifying by all accounts I heard in Landembrost."

"That salamander was a longaevi too," muttered Eli. Anna knew she wasn't really aware of what she was saying. She was scared, and when scared, she babbled.

"Yes, one of the vulcani formed in fire by Lermerrus himself. Very cagy and wise, with little sense for humor. That one's clearly been in Azhiona's pocket for a long time."

"But it is far younger than the Old One at the Farwell foundry," said Lambient from the corner.

"Oh, by a millennia at least." The knight shook his head sadly. "If only Garlandium were able to solicit the Old One's cooperation on anything!"

"Yes, I would give a great sum to know how they negotiated that little thing's allegiance," said the professor, fiddling absently with his moustache.

"A millennia! How long do they live?" Genuine surprise roused Eli from her fear.

The knight was shocked "How long? Why, forever, unless they're killed. They're longaevi, I tell you—"long lived." The longaevi—whether sylph, gnome, undine, or vulcan—do not die."

"You mean that Finch won't ever . . ." Anna was incredulous.

"Not until someone wrings his little neck," said Lambient, "which I plan to do at the very next opportunity."

The door opened, and Ondertara Djerack beckoned them.

When they were back in the throne room and all were seated and silent, Ragundiae rose and addressed the hall.

"Let it be henceforth known in Garlandium that Azhwana is a just land and full of mercy. It is the decision of this council that each of the accused shall be taken at the value of their words. The professor and the dog, in view of their peaceful and universally beneficent intentions, shall be given safe passage to the coast. So too the children, who were doubtless brought either against their will or in ignorance of the consequences. The knight alone, having shown himself to be in all wise hostile to this realm and its people, shall die." Thunderous applause exploded from the balcony and the floor. Anna was horrified, Lambient was already on his feet shouting, Sazerac was barking wildly. Dashonae alone sat calmly in his chair, wearing a grim but satisfied look.

Chapter 35

"His execution shall take place at sundown." It had taken several minutes for the crowd to calm down and several more to restrain Lambient in his chair. The tara resumed his seat, and Tengomaniah waved to the crier, who stepped forward with his staff in hand to dismiss the tribunal.

"Wait," said Dashonae, calmly but loudly. The crier hesitated, looking toward the tara.

"The dead have no voice." Ragundiae waved the crier on.

"But surely," said the princess quietly from her chair, "this is not the usual circumstance. I for one should like to hear what bargains this southern knight would make in exchange for his life."

Her husband chuckled. "How truly perverse, my bride. You wish to further humble the knight? Very well, let him speak." He waved lazily in Dashonae's direction.

The knight stood and cleared his throat. "I offer no bargains. My life was forfeit when I agreed to this quest. I would merely make an observation on the nature of Azhionian justice."

Ragundiae's eyes flashed, but he said nothing.

"While it is true that I have no love for this land nor for its history of villainies against my people, I have heard of great warriors among the Azhionians. Your archers are feared in Landembrost, and Garlandian memory recounts great exploits among your mounted knights. So I had expected to meet my death, if Therra willed, in honorable combat against my enemy. But it appears that even the small good I have heard of this people was a lie, for not one of you will dare meet me in clean battle. I can only gather that honor is a word now unknown among the warriors of Azhiona."

The room remained silent, but Anna could see murder in the eye of every soldier. The knight turned with complete calm from speaking to the room and looked directly at princess Ahvorazhie, who sat wide-eyed upon her throne in all her beauty. "Princess, since Azhionian men appear to be cowards, perhaps your highness ought to look to the south for more suitable fathers for your children . . . assuming you have not already done so." And he winked at her.

Anna thought it was a foolish thing to say but realized a moment later that it had been a precisely calculated insult. Dashonae knew nothing about the princess, whether she was of upright or base character, but he understood the nature of a courtly insult and the corner into which it would paint every honorable soldier in the room. The effect was instantaneous. The room exploded. Every soldier, regardless of rank or stripe, leapt forward, volunteering to defend the princess's honor. Decrepit elders struggled to their feet, leaning on canes, declaring their intentions to duel "the young infidel." But Ragundiae outdid them all, for he leapt from the dais, sword drawn, and rushed upon the knight to redress the insult then and there.

A high, clear voice stayed his blade a mere foot from Dashonae's unflinching face. "Wait!"

Ahvorazhie was standing, her hand extended. Ragundiae's sword paused above the knight's head. "Do you not see his game? We have surely wronged this knight. We have denied him the right of monomachy. We have forced him to say these disreputable things. But if so many noble Azhwana would risk their life for the sake of *my* honor, then surely there is one who would meet his challenge for honor's sake alone."

Slowly the tara turned, his sword still held high. His met the princess's penetrating eye and knew what she intended.

"Your highness . . ." He lowered his sword slowly. "If it be your pleasure to risk the life of your servants for honor's sake against a defeated knight, then I would risk no life but my own. I shall meet the Garlandish knight in clean combat."

The princess sat back down on her throne and eyed the tara, one eyebrow raised. "I knew you would."

Chapter 36

Anna and her sisters sat in the top set of benches in the great civic arena, watching Dashonae down below swinging his sword through a series of graceful arcs, his eyes closed. The sky was clear and blue overhead. Merris was descending, and in an hour she would be below the rim of the arena behind them. An hour after that, Dashonae would fight for his life.

He was alone on the grassy field, having been granted the right to prepare himself. He desired solitude, so the girls did not disturb him. Having been freed, Lambient was elsewhere still trying, in his words, to "breathe a little sanity into this unenlightened folly."

Periodically Dashonae would lay his sword down and assume some complicated yoga-like position or perform some minor gymnastic feat. Anna still could not decide if he resembled more a Chinese warrior monk from the old movies or a medieval knight. The girls spoke little. They were free to go where they willed now, but they could not endure leaving.

It was all both magnificent and horrible. Anna could see the beauty and glory of Dashonae's knightly code, but she was equally repulsed by the ease with which people could be steered into mortal peril. Any possible future could be turned tragic at a moment's notice. Every lesson she had learned at school since kindergarten had been aimed at shunning violence:

"War solves nothing."

"The pen is mightier than the sword."

"Use your voice, not your fists."

And so on. But none of it seemed to fit here. These maxims simply did not work in this world. All Anna's youthful pacifism had no hook within this culture on which to hang. Were there times when fighting was necessary? Did she resist using her fists because she really believed fighting was wrong, or was she deep down just afraid? Was this what cowardice was all about? She felt arrogantly enlightened and barbarously out of touch at the same time.

As she sat dwelling on these things, tossing a small stone from hand to hand, a shadow fell over them all. She turned and felt her innards drop. The great tara, Ragundiae himself, was standing behind them with his hands on his hips, watching Dashonae.

"He is magnificent," he said in a low tone.

"Yes, I suppose so," said Eli. She looked at Anna and shrugged nervously.

"Is it true, what the professor said? Did he destroy two skerzak by himself?"

"Yes," said Anna. "I was there."

"One of them almost got Anna," began Rose excitedly, "but then he—" and she waved her arms as if holding a sword—"and its head flew right off."

The tara said nothing but continued watching the knight. Rose was never put off by anyone and never seemed to remember a slight or a wrong done to her longer than ten minutes. She treated everyone alike, friend and foe, and was candid and tactless with all of them. So Anna was hardly surprised when a moment later she added, "Mister, why doesn't the princess like you?"

Ragundiae looked down at her, and there was sadness in his dark eyes. "Small one, you are not old enough to understand such things." But she did not move or look away, unwilling to let go of the question once she had asked it. Eventually he sighed. "She hates me because I would not marry her."

"But she's already married," said Rose in confusion.

Ragundiae laughed. "No, small one, this was long ago. I was

offered her hand before my brother. But I refused because I would not have my honor given to me by marriage." He leaned on the railing with both arms. "Titles can be given by marriage, but not honor. I insisted on going forth and winning mine before accepting the proposal. I would be worthy of her in myself, not simply by the koning's decree. But he was angered and did not understand. He desired a quick and convenient marriage. So he gave her to my brother instead. She has never forgiven me for . . ." His voice wavered ever so slightly. "I believe she loved me."

"Gosh, that's terrible," said, Rose wide-eyed.

"Yes, but now she has moved me to destruction, so her vengeance will be complete." He sighed again.

"But you might still win," said Rose hopefully.

"Rose!" Eli was aghast. "That would mean Dashonae loses." Rose went pale as she realized what she had said. Anna rolled her eyes. Never was there a creature who lived more in the moment than Rose, and it apparently had never occurred to her to do anything other than wish good upon the person she was talking to—regardless of the consequences.

But Ragundiae just laughed. "I have done you a disservice, small one. I have made you care, and now you will mourn no matter the outcome. But this I shall do—I shall leave orders with my ondertara to escort you personally to the coast and see you safely embarked toward Landembrost." He turned to go.

"But what about the well?" said Eli. Anna credited her circumspection for not mentioning their real destination.

Ragundiae said gently, "Young lady, I do not know what the knight or the professor said to you to make you come on their mad quest, but Vizuritundu is a myth created by Garlandish kings so they may prosecute their wars against Azhwana. It does not exist. It cannot." And he left.

Rose pulled out her compass and tentatively held it up. The needles pointed stubbornly toward the mountain peaks looming in the west.

"Even if the well doesn't exist," said Eli thoughtfully, "we still have to go that way."

"Yeah, but with or without Dashonae." Anna chucked her stone at the green grass below them.

Chapter 37

As upset as he was, Lambient was in his glory. The sun was near setting, and the Azhwana had powered up huge spotlights that flooded the arena with bright white light. The inventor ran from fixture to fixture, asking anyone within earshot how such illumination was achieved and the source of its power. When he joined the girls in the stands, he was all abuzz about waterfalls and rotating wheels that created powerful currents that could be sent miles away.

"My word, I had no idea that such things were possible!" As he sat down, the wooden bench creaked under his weight. "Just wait until I tell the Lemerrian Academy about this." He was like a child at the circus seeing elephants for the first time.

The stands were awash with bright colors. A festive mood hung in the air. People were eating and singing. Every so often a large assembly of drums would break out into earth-pounding rhythm, and people would dance. Anna saw that many people had even brought their own drums and joined in. She had seen drum circles on the lawns at her father's university, but they were nothing compared to this. Vendors of food and drink wandered about the stands. And Anna had an amazing view of the whole thing because no Azhwana citizen would sit within ten feet of them. Seen from the field below, Lambient and the girls must have looked like a stationary eye in the middle of an undulating sea of rhythmic color.

For all the energy, Anna felt sick. This was not a Bulls or

Blackhawks game. In a few minutes, two men would try to kill each other with the approval of this crowd. Nothing in her life had prepared her for this. She looked at her sisters. Eli was pale and motionless. Rose bounced up and down, eating a pastry she had gotten somewhere. Anna shook her head. Rose was cheerful now, but when the first blows fell, she would probably cry and hide her face in Lambient's shirtsleeve. Even Sazerac was back in the guest house, refusing to participate in what he considered a repulsive human spectacle.

Suddenly from behind them great trumpets sounded. Anna followed everyone's gaze up to the skybox-like booth at the top of the stands and saw Tengomaniah with Ahvorazhie waving at the crowds. The people cheered and danced, and the drums pounded out a response to the trumpets. Then the prince spoke, his voice unusually audible, and Anna couldn't decide if it was being amplified artificially or if the stadium just had great acoustics.

"People of Ishtagung," he said loudly and confidently. "You have heard by now of our strange visitors from the south. They have been examined and found to be of no threat to our prosperous land. Yet one has ventured to impugn the honor of the princess Ahvorazhie." The crowd began to boo and hiss. "I, your onderkoning, have not sat idly by and allowed the infidel's insult to pass unanswered, but I have found for you a champion—the tara of the Ishtagung garrison, Tara Ragundiae!" And the crowd screamed and applauded and threw streamers. Anna saw Ragundiae appear at one end of the grassy pitch. He was bare-chested and wore long, tight, black knicker-like shorts with silver embroidery. He held a sword with a slightly curved tip in his hand and had a long knife strapped to his hip. He did not even acknowledge the crowd but marched resolutely to the center and saluted the prince and princess.

"The defamer of your court is a Garlandish knight, a follower of a false goddess, and a man committed to southern dominance. Sir Theodore au Dashonae!" As Tengomaniah said this, Anna saw

Dashonae enter the lists from the other end. He was also bare-chested and wore skin-tight knee-length pants and high leather boots. He carried his own sword and had a knife identical to Ragundiae's strapped to his side. When he approached the center, he too turned and saluted the princess. This stunned the crowd into a relative silence for a moment before they broke out in collective harassment.

"Each knight shall prove his honor on the body of his foe," the prince continued. The two men were squaring off now a dozen yards apart in the middle of the pitch. Anna watched two dozen soldiers, half with spears and half with bows, enter the lists and station themselves around the perimeter in groups of two—in each pair a bow and a spear. Whatever the rest of Tengomaniah's speech was, it was lost to Anna, for the entrance of the perimeter soldiers signaled something to the crowd, and their shouts redoubled. The spearman directly below the skybox, the same one from the tribunal, lifted his metal-butted spear and slammed it down on a plate of metal at his feet. The resounding clang filled the arena, and Ragundiae leapt toward Dashonae with a cry.

Dashonae was driven back several paces under Ragundiae's blows, but he remained untouched. Ragundiae was taller, thicker, and stronger, but Dashonae was more nimble and faster.

What followed over the next five minutes was something Anna would never forget. The two men leapt and spun like ballet dancers; they threw themselves at one another; swipes of the sword were dodged or answered with high spinning kicks. Dashonae was graceful and delicate and felled Ragundiae with a roundhouse to the chin, but was felled in his turn by a brutal blow to the chest from Ragundiae's iron fist when their swords were otherwise engaged.

The crowd roared as Dashonae's sword was wrenched from his hand when Ragundiae got him in an arm lock, and they roared again when he forced Ragundiae to release him by pulling his own knife against him. Dashonae now held two long knives; Ragundiae, his sword.

In the next engagement, blades whirled at such speed that Anna could not see who struck and who blocked. Suddenly the crowd let out a collective cry. Dashonae was down, his pant leg slowly turning crimson. Ragundiae had nicked him, but he had received blood for blood. A long streak of red appeared over the tara's right eye.

Dashonae hobbled upright and stood upon his good leg like a crane. Ragundiae repeatedly wiped at the blood that ran down his forehead and into his eyes. It was a terrible sight.

And as Anna had predicted, Rose was sobbing into Lambient's shirt, and Lambient appeared torn between watching the match and comforting the child who had attached herself to him. Eli sat pale and motionless.

Partially blinded by the flow of blood from his forehead, Ragundiae prepared to rush Dashonae. As he took the first step, however, a piercing shriek sounded from somewhere above Anna, and she had to cover her ears. It went through her like a knife and turned her fingers and toes to ice. The crowd screamed, but no longer at the match. People began running in every direction with their hands over their heads. The screech came again, and a black, bird-shaped shadow blocked one of the floodlights. A light post toppled and crashed into the bank of seats, leaving part of the arena in shadow. The thing shrieked again.

Lambient picked Rose up in his arms. "Come!" He began making his way down the bleachers toward the exit.

"Professor, professor!" cried Eli, stumbling behind him. "What's going on?"

The shadow swooped over their heads. The professor ducked. Behind them someone screamed. He turned with wild, fearful eyes upon her and said in a hoarse panic, "Stymphalia!"

Chapter 38

There was nowhere to run. The exits were glutted with people trying to get out. Anna and the rest stood exposed on the bleachers. All they could do was hunker down between the rows of benches and watch. The great menace swooped again, and Anna saw it in all its terrible form—black as midnight, its eyes bright like lightning. Thunder seemed to peal from its flapping wings, and its serrated beak clicked hungrily as it passed overhead. It was as big as a Cessna—more like a feathered dragon than a bird—and it was diving toward the center of the arena. Anna looked down and saw the archers shooting arrow after arrow at it, but they left no mark.

Ragundiae and Dashonae both turned to flee, but the bird was already on top of them. Dashonae made a fantastic leap to the side, but Ragundiae, too big for such a maneuver, dove for the ground, and one of the great metallic claws grabbed at his shoulder as he fell. It failed to clutch him, but the hinder talon raked a long furrow up his shoulder blade. The tara cried out in agony and collapsed on the grass.

The exits began to clear, and people were flowing out of the arena. Lambient hoisted the girls to their feet and began dragging them—not toward the exit, but toward the grassy field where Dashonae was rising and looking about.

"Where are we going?" cried Eli, looking toward the exit.

"To the only place we'll be safe," he said, and pointed at the knight, who was now leaning over the fallen tara. He looked up and met Lambient's gaze.

"Here! To him! To the tara!" Dashonae cried, pointing at the wounded Azhwana commander. He then bolted away toward the edge of the pitch as fast as his wounded leg would carry him.

"Where are we going?" cried Eli again as they left the relative protection of the stands for the openness of the field.

"Following orders!" Lambient grabbed her hand and dragged her forward onto the grassy field.

"But that's in the open," she cried, drawing back.

Lambient wheeled around and shouted at her. "I trust the knight. If you don't, then you are welcome to run the other way." And he let go and carried Rose to the fallen man. Anna pushed past her sister and made for the same place. Eli hesitated only a moment before following. The screech sounded again from the top of the arena and another spotlight crashed into the seats.

Anna, searching for Dashonae, was dumbfounded when she saw him. Only one pair of soldiers was still present at the far end of the arena. Dashonae ran straight for them. The archer was crouching on the ground in terror, letting arrows fly indiscriminately into the darkness. The spearman saw him coming and had wits enough to step up to the charging knight. Dashonae lifted his sword and swung it at the soldier's head. Anna gasped, but just before it connected, Dashonae rotated the blade so the flat came hard again the soldier's helmet. Anna heard the clang of metal all the way across the arena, and the soldier sank like a stone dropped into a pool. Without a moment's pause, the knight stooped, wrenched the bow out of the terrified archer's hand, along with its nocked arrow, and began to race back to the girls.

The black shadow of the stymphalia appeared again over the grass in a dive, bearing down on the girls. Anna saw the hideous red eyes flicker at her and felt that same swooning sensation she had felt in the desert when the skerzak was atop her. But this time it was cut short by Lambient, who, like the brave fool he was, picked up Ragundiae's fallen blade and positioned himself between the girls and the screeching shadow. He began yelling at the top of his lungs and waving the sword wildly.

The bird attempted to rake him as it passed, but Lambient swung the sword with all his might at the dark form. The blade made contact with the bird's claw, erupted in white light, and shattered like glass. The black shadow screeched away unhurt. Lambient lay on the ground examining his hands. Anna rushed to him; his hands were red and puffy with burns.

Ragundiae began to come around just as Dashonae reached them. The tara rolled over and began to sit up, but the knight tackled him, forcing him back onto his stomach, putting his knee in his back and wielding the arrow over his neck.

Ragundiae cried out in pain and anger. "Is this your sense of honor, Garlandian? Is this how you slay all your foes, wounded and in the back? You coward, you—"

"Shut up and lie still." Dashonae was remarkably calm, but Ragundiae fought to rise. "Lambient! Hold him."

Lambient stared at him horrified. "Dashonae, you cannot do this." His voice was rife with hurt and betrayal. Surely this was the greatest possible test of Lambient's trust in Dashonae.

"Hold him, or we all die!" the knight cried in the sort of voice that is difficult to disobey. The scientist responded and lay clumsily across the fallen man's legs and torso, grabbing one of his flailing arms. The black bird cried again, but the arena was empty now. There was no prey but the small knot of humanity in the middle. It bore down on them, its wings thundering.

Dashonae thrust the arrow into the gash in Ragundiae's shoulder—not far, only enough to cover the barb with blood. Then he rotated the arrowhead and pressed its other side into a different part of the wound. At each thrust Ragundiae screamed, more from rage than pain, but his cries were weaker than before. The knight paid no mind but leapt to his feet, setting the stained arrow to the string.

A few seconds later the bird reappeared in the remaining

floodlights, aiming right for Dashonae, its talons extended for the kill. The knight did not flinch or falter but calmly drew the string. A mere moment before the great claws would reach him, he loosed the arrow. It caught the stymphalia squarely in the breast and stuck soundly. The monster screamed, veered, crashed into the stands, demolishing several rows of seats and shaking the ground below them. Screeching in agony, it tried to rise. Anna could hear its metallic beak snapping. One wing beat up and down in the dusty haze of light and shadow. It gave one final, hideous croak—and then lay still. A profound quiet stole over the empty arena.

Dashonae turned to face a wide-eyed Lambient, still sprawled on the tara. Ragundiae was faintly moaning now, and the skin around his wound had taken on a blotchy gray appearance.

"Bring him," said the knight, "and hurry. He must not die."

Chapter 39

Back in the guest house, Dashonae prowled like a caged animal. No one dared speak to him. Rather than being praised for killing the stymphalia, they had all been rearrested as they came out of the arena. Two soldiers had borne the wounded tara away, and the rest had forced them back to the guest house. Dashonae had protested at first, then swore oaths, then cursed, saying that unless he spoke with the healers, Ragundiae would die. But to no avail. They were herded back to the house and shut up under double guard.

The night wore on. No one could sleep with the knight stomping about on his bandaged leg and occasionally yelling at the locked door.

At about midnight, they heard the bolt of the door being drawn. Two guards entered and stood on either side of the door, and Princess Ahvorazhie appeared in the framed light behind them.

The knight leapt forward but found himself facing the points of spears.

"The impundulu," she said impassively, "has plagued us since the later rains last fall when a great storm gave it birth. We have hunted it with every resource. We have lost a score of brave men to it. It has borne off children and plundered our herds. Now it is dead. How?"

The knight fell back onto the couch, his demeanor suddenly changed, and answered calmly, "Has your beloved tara joined it yet?"

The soldiers grunted, and the spears quivered with their anger.

"Do not tempt me, knight," said the princess with equal calm. "The tara still lives, but barely."

"Unless I talk to your healers, he'll be dead soon," said the knight. Anna was confused. The knight had been ranting for hours to be heard, and now he seemed to be trying to repel the one person who was taking an interest in him.

"So I am told." Her voice quivered a bit. "But what is that to you? Do you not desire the death of all my people?"

The knight shook his head. "No, I desire only justice. He was my opponent, and by rights, his life was mine if I was strong enough to take it from him. And he was strong. A great warrior. He does not deserve so senseless a death."

"And that is the question," she said. "Before I take any thoughts from you on his treatment, I wish to know how that which has been the bane of Balungorah for eight months has disappeared so quickly at your southern hands. A suspicious person might wonder if this had not been orchestrated toward some end."

Dashonae began to laugh. "Yes, princess, you've solved it at last. I planned the whole thing. The stymphalia was born and died at my command."

"I am not a suspicious person. Outside of the current situation, I would honor you for your bravery. But for now, I must simply know if I can trust you to save my . . . to save the tara. Now answer me, or I shall lose my patience, how did you kill the impundulu?"

The knight scrutinized her for a moment and then said simply, "Chemistry."

She seemed lost.

"Chemistry," he repeated. "The claws of the stymphalia are poisonous to men. But they are even more poisonous to the stymphalia. When the tara was scored by the bird, the bird's poison entered his system. By applying his tainted blood to the tip of the arrow, I did nothing but return to the bird its own gift. And since the stymphalia's feathers are so densely layered, the blow had to be delivered at close range." And he threw his hands apart in a sweeping gesture. "Poof! No more impundulu."

The princess stood thinking for a moment. "So the tara has been infected by the bird's poison?"

"Yes."

"And is there a cure?"

"Yes."

"Then tell me!" She stamped her foot impatiently.

Dashonae leaned back on the couch and spread his arms. "You free my friends, and then at the first opportunity cast them back into kennels like dogs. You first deny me honorable combat, then grudgingly grant it, then when I save your whole city, you lock me up like a criminal. Based on the way you treat those who help you, I'm not sure I can be of any further service and still protect the lives of my companions." He put his hands behind his head and shrugged helplessly.

"If the tara dies—"

"It will not be my fault."

The princess stood openmouthed. She shifted, she thought, she shifted again. "Very well, knight, you have my word. If you keep him from dying then I promise, you and your friends shall be released."

"And Vizuritundu?"

"Yes, yes. You have my word that you shall be permitted to continue your quest." She added as an afterthought, "I shall see to it that you are fitted with horses and provisions and letters of passage through the realm."

"Well, now," said the knight, rising, "that's more like it. The first thing we'll need is a dwarf."

Chapter 40

"If you continue to taunt me and waste time . . ." the princess began, incensed by the knight's apparent flippancy.

"Madam, do you want me to save him or not?"

"Yes, but . . ." And her eyes betrayed that her feelings for the tara were not dead.

"Then you will need to find me a dwarf, or perhaps a giant. A troll or goblin would work too, though they may prove even less cooperative."

"But why these creatures?"

"It would be obvious to anyone who understood the gods," said the knight calmly, but clearly intending an insult, "or the sciences." He looked sidelong at Lambient, who suddenly lit up.

"Of course!" The scientist jumped to his feet. "They are all of the Berduccan gnomi class of longaevi. It *is* simple chemistry." He clapped his hands at the apparent simplicity of the answer.

Anna was still lost.

"Exactly." Dashonae snapped his fingers. "You, princess, need an antidote to the poison of a sylph, a creature of the air born of the goddess Avonia. So the answer lies in its elemental opposite —the earth, which lies under Berducca's authority. You need an elemental creature born of earth to restore the balance in the tara's blood."

The princess hung her head in thought. "I wouldn't know where to find one—but I know who does." Her eyes narrowed in a calculating way that Anna did not much like. "Come with me!" she said suddenly, "all of you."

She turned to leave, but the guards hesitated. "Stand aside, fools, and bring them with me. Do you *want* the tara to die?" They jumped aside, and the whole troop of them followed the princess out of the guest house and on to the palace. She marched straight to the great doors of the throne room, laid her hands on the brass handles, and paused. Her head fell in concentration. She clenched her teeth, and her knuckles whitened. And when she finally threw the doors open, Anna was amazed to see an entirely different person step through them.

The bowstring tautness of her frame had dissolved into slinky and voluptuous curves. "Your most royal highness," she said to the lounging figure of Tengomaniah on his throne. "I have interviewed the knight as you suggested, and have some interesting news to report." She sauntered through the doors. Anna could almost see the smirk on her face as she spoke.

The onderkoning started. "Suggested? It was *your* idea to consult the southerners." He looked neither upset nor grieved, only suspicious. His eyes darted up and down the sensuous form of his wife, but she melted into the chair next to him and said in a voice that ought to have melted *him*, "It was for love of you that I made the suggestion. I care nothing for the life of the tara. But surely your highness realizes the troubles that might arise with the koning if he should die—considering the favor the tara still holds in his eyes."

Tengomaniah nodded absently and mumbled to himself, "Troubles, yes. Troublesome in life and even more so in death." Then he rallied himself. "Very well, Ahvorazhie, what have you learned."

"It seems that his case is terminal, and we are powerless to save him."

Lambient started forward, ready to contradict the princess, but before he could speak, Dashonae caught his arm and whispered,

"Quiet, Professor. Here is a master at work. Her tongue is far sharper than my sword. Let's see where this goes."

Tengomaniah was torn. Ragundiae's death would clearly not be mourned by his usurping brother, but it was equally clear that he did not relish telling the koning that Ragundiae was dead.

Ahvorazhie cut through the tension by increasing it. "I am sorry, my love, that you will be forced to explain to my father why his most trusted tara is dead from a simple scratch."

The prince squirmed. "Nothing can be done then?"

She smiled sweetly, turning to the guards. "You see the noble heart that exists in your onderkoning? How tenderly he desires to draw the tara's life back from the brink, even though his place would be more firmly assured by his death."

Lambient turned openmouthed to Dashonae, who only smiled in return. It was a preposterous assertion. So clearly were Tengomaniah's motivations self-centered that if Ahvorazhie did not seem so innocent and confident of her husband's nobility, the pretense would have been insulting. Every person in the room knew quite well that Tengomaniah was more concerned with his own reputation than his brother's life.

The prince writhed in discomfort. "Yes, well, uh . . . it is a terrible shame to lose . . . so, uh, valuable a soldier." Apparently deciding to embrace Ahvorazhie's offer to ennoble him, he brightened. "Yes, it is a shame that there is nothing to be done for my poor brother."

"Oh," said the princess, turning back to him with the innocence of child who has forgotten to deliver a message. "I didn't say *nothing* could be done, only that it is not in *our* power to heal him."

Tengomaniah's face fell. He seemed to Anna oblivious of the metaphorical ring in his nose by which Ahvorazhie was leading him.

"There is one possibility." She shook her head. "But it is absurd."

The trapped prince could not respond otherwise than he now

did. "Absurd or no, I must do all within my power to save the noble tara."

"I'm sure you will find it funny," she laughed, "but I will tell you what this knight claims."

When she had finished telling the prince Dashonae's description of the cause and cure for the tara's fever, concluding with a little titter about its silliness, Tengomaniah waved her silent. He was on the edge of his chair now, mumbling to himself. "No, no, it makes perfect sense." His head shot up. "Is this so, knight? Will a dwarf really be able to cure him?"

Dashonae nodded. The prince fell back into his chair, thinking hard. "How?"

The knight squared his shoulders and ignored the question. "We must go to the dwarf and return with the cure. The princess has given us her word, and I assume we have yours as well that if we cooperate, we will be free to continue our quest?"

The prince looked as though he'd just been slapped. He turned to his bride in astonished horror. But she just smiled sweetly and said through pouty lips, "Oh yes, I told them that your love for your brother was so deep and so noble that in exchange for his life, you would surely let them continue their pointless little journey into the mountains."

The prince rose to his feet angrily. "I will not! I *will* not! I will *not!*" He stamped his feet, and Anna thought he looked like Rose throwing a tantrum.

"Very well," said Ahvorazhie, rising to go. "You always do the right thing. I shall go and make the arrangements for the tara's internment. You will be commissioning a statue of him for the square, I assume?" She said it with such innocence, such ignorance of the slap that it was to the prince that Anna wanted to laugh. And Eli did gasp softly.

"Stop!" cried Tengomaniah, his voice rising slightly, his hand extended to her more in entreaty than command. He stood frozen like that for a full minute thinking, then he turned and looked at the travelers. "*They* may go. *He* must stay." He pointed at Dashonae. "He does not leave this place until I am assured of the tara's recovery."

Anna watched the princess and Dashonae exchange a look of understanding, and the knight stepped forward. "It is acceptable."

Lambient began to protest.

"No, Professor." Dashonae put out a soothing hand. "It is good this way. I can explain the cure to you, and I can wait here for your return. I trust the onderkoning's word." But the knowing look he cast was toward the princess.

"Well, I never," huffed Lambient.

"The real question," said Dashonae, turning again to the prince, "is where to find a dwarf. I do not assume they are more common here than in the south."

Tengomaniah had resumed his seat, wearing an odd, satisfied smirk. "You are correct, oh knight. But I, Tengomaniah, onderkoning of Balungorah province, know of a single dwarf by which I may save my brother's life." And he sat tall before his subjects, like a grand messiah come to offer them salvation. Anna was stunned that he could take any credit for what had just transpired, but she understood little of the pride that infects the adults of her race.

BOOK 5

Into the Dark Mountain

The madness of a dwarf alone
Is the epitome of gnome!
While he won't trick you in his home,
Beware the moment you are not.

Though he might seem quite insane
You must not doubt what's in his brain
For dwarves were here before men came
And remember secrets we've forgot.

FRANKO RAZHAMANÌAH,
"On the Madness of Dwarves"
in *Sweet Songs of the Longaevi.*

Chapter 41

The horses' hooves pounded over the trail. Anna held onto the broad back of the rider with all her strength. She had ridden a horse only once at a fair when she was little, and she didn't understand how anyone could enjoy it. She bounced and teetered so precariously that she almost wished she were being carried over a soldier's shoulder again. Anna was numb at both ends—her mind was a jostling vacuum, and her nether parts had lost feeling half an hour ago.

She felt sorry for Rose, who had never ridden anything except a bicycle. But perhaps Eli had it worst. She had been paired with Lambient, whose great size must have presented difficulties for her encircling arms. Still they rode on at a ridiculous speed. Nothing but the peaks of the Alappunda Mountains could be seen ahead as they rounded the bends of the steeply ascending trail, and what brief glances she dared take over the edge of the occasional precipices showed only forest spreading out below. Even the desert was just a periodic strip of nothingness in the remote distance between gaps in the forest as they ascended the foothills.

They had been released with the knowledge that if they didn't return with an antidote, Dashonae would be executed like a common criminal, and the same would happen if they delayed returning and the tara died. The knight had passively accepted the verdict, believing wholly in Lambient's resourcefulness and the princess' good word.

"She is both deceitful and utterly trustworthy in the same

breath," he had said to Lambient. The professor had wept in grief over their forced parting, but the knight was confident that they would eventually resume their quest together. Sazerac had agreed to stay behind with the knight to safeguard his welfare.

So before first light they had left Ishtagung with a contingent of six soldiers, riding full out and exchanging horses periodically at way stations. Late in the afternoon the trees began to thin, and the pale sky began to darken with evening. They entered a clearing that backed up against sheer rock cliffs. The horses were reigned in and stood stamping in place. Anna's rider, the broad-shouldered Azhwana lieutenant, Djerack, dismounted and gently lowered her to the ground. Anna looked around as Eli and Rose stumbled up to her, grimacing from the effects of the journey.

"Is that a dwarf house?" Rose pointed to the small, shanty-like structure backing directly up against the rock face with a door about four feet high. It could not have been a house; it was far too small even for a dwarf. It looked more like a breezeway between a garage and a house. This made sense to Anna, for in all the stories she had ever heard in her own world and now in this one, dwarves were creatures who lived underground. This small, ramshackle hutch had the look of a transition area from the open air to some deeper cave dwelling. No attempt at landscaping had been made. It was as though the inhabitant cared nothing for the world out-side his door, knowing only that a door was necessary.

"No, that is but the place of meeting," said Djerack, confirm-ing Anna's thought. "The dwarf lives deep within the mountain and only comes when he is summoned . . . and in the mood." He pointed at a bell that hung next to the door, and to a heavy chain that wound through a pulley and disappeared through a hole. Lambient hauled down on the chain with all his weight. He did so again . . . the chain squeaked, the pulley groaned . . . and from far below, a gong like a church bell sounded deep within the mountain.

"Have you ever seen the dwarf?" Rose asked the lieutenant.

He looked down at her with raised eyebrows. "No. No one has. He has not been seen for a generation."

"He could be dead," said Rose with wide eyes.

The lieutenant smiled. "I doubt it. Dwarves love the darkness. They would not emerge at all if they were not summoned."

"Why would he come at all?" asked Eli. "Do you really have the power to summon him? Does he really obey you?"

Now the lieutenant laughed aloud. "No, no. He is his own creature. But I was taught that dwarves, though they dislike all men, still speak of an ancient obligation to them. I do not understand it. That is for the deep thinkers. All I know is that if we beckon and he is willing, we shall meet. If not . . ."

"Ragundiae dies," said Anna soberly. "And Dashonae too."

"Yes," said Djerack with equal sobriety. "And it would be a double loss. The Garlandish knight is an honorable and worthy foe. I would regret having him dishonored by execution."

Lambient heaved the bell pull again. They waited in silence for several minutes.

The professor beat on the door and shouted. But only silence was returned.

The lieutenant spoke. "Learned one, he does not come. We shall set up camp and await him."

"But we need to speak with him now!" cried Lambient. "Can't you do something?"

"Yes, I can. I can wait," replied the lieutenant. And the other soldiers began to unpack the saddle bags.

"But . . . but . . . there must be something . . ." stammered the scientist.

"What would you have me do? Break down the door?"

"For starters," mumbled Lambient.

"And this would incline him to help you?"

The professor's shoulders fell. "Very well. But I shall continue to ring the bell every half hour, even through the night."

"As it suits you," said the soldier, turning to attend to his men's work. "But it will be dark soon, and we shall want fire." Then he added as an afterthought, "Do not be mistaken. No one is more desirous of saving the tara's life than I. He is deeply loved by his men, and by me most of all. We will not leave without his cure. But patience is often harder than steel."

The evening passed without movement or sound from the door, despite Lambient's arising every half hour to ring the bell. The only result was that no one slept well except Rose, who had once slept through a Midwestern tornado.

Chapter 42

The sun was up, but the little band still lay in relative darkness. The peaks of the mountains rose so high and close that it would be nearly noon before they would see Merris herself. A red-eyed Lambient was just ringing the bell for the thousandth time, it seemed. Dejected, he returned to the fire, which had been stoked to prepare breakfast.

He flopped down and cursed. "If we don't reach this dwarf soon . . ." and he shook his head. But as if he had issued a command by the waving of his shaggy whiskers, a rattle sounded at the little door.

Everyone leapt to their feet and rushed to the tiny building. A series of bolts and latches was being drawn. Anna, torn between her concern for Ragundiae and Dashonae and simple curiosity at meeting a real live dwarf, realized she was holding her breath and tried to breathe normally.

The door opened, and a tiny face appeared. Well, a nose actually—a long, thin, crooked nose. It was followed by a pair of black eyes, deep-set in a puffy face surrounded by so many bushels of black hair that it was hard to tell where the face ended and the body began.

"Dwarf!" began Lambient in a hurry. "We must speak with you—"

"He sees humans have not learned any manners since last he spoke to them," the dwarf grumbled. His accent was strange and broken, and Anna thought it sounded oddly like . . . French.

Lambient was stunned to silence. He gave the lieutenant a helpless look.

"Monsieur dwarf," said Djerack with a low bow. "The onderkoning of Balungorah humbly requests your assistance in addressing a matter of great urgency."

"Onderkoning, eh?" the dwarf sniffed. "Just an onderkoning. He remembers days when the koning of Azhwana himself would come and prostrate himself on this very ground simply because a pretty jewel was desired." He then fell silent and eyed them, grinning mirthlessly. Anna could see that Lambient wanted to punch him in the nose. But he looked again at the lieutenant, who nodded slightly, and slowly they both got to their knees and bowed low. The soldiers followed, then Anna and Eli. The oblivious Rose was last to fall.

The dwarf chuckled and threw the door open. He was a three-foot study in contradiction—dressed in filthy knickers and a soiled leather tunic but wearing gold rings with immense gems on his knobby fingers. Rubies dangled from his ears, which must have been huge because they were visible despite the masses of hair that seemed to cover every inch of his hide—even his forehead was hairy. He was thickly built and looked very strong even though he was no taller than Rose. He shoved his fingertips into his trousers and puffed out his chest. "How little it takes to be the tallest one at the party, eh? Very well, very well, rise, oh strangers. Be blessed of Berducca and make your request." His voice was thick with sarcasm, but it was still as promising a sign as they had yet seen. But no one rose. From his knees, Lambient told him of the stymphalia's attack and the tara's injury. The dwarf listened dispassionately to the story, chuckling only at the point where Dashonae's arrow felled the bird.

The professor finished by saying, "And so, noble dwarf, in order to effect the cure, we must ask you for a small but most precious gift—an ounce of blood and a drop of saliva."

The dwarf was already laughing. "Just that, eh? Only his life's blood, eh? Just a tiny gift, eh?" He laid his hand on the door, and began to push it closed. "There is no oblation," he whispered.

"Wait!" cried Djerack. "I come with gifts." The dwarf paused, and Lambient looked at him in surprise. But before he could ask the lieutenant what he meant, Djerack loosed a leather pouch from his belt and threw it on the ground before the dwarf. Out spilled a single diamond, but from the remaining bulges, Anna inferred that it had several companions. The dwarf sniffed with mild interest. The lieutenant raised his hand. Each of the other five soldiers added a similar bag from their own belts.

The dwarf waited, but when no more came, he sniggered, "That? That would not buy two hairs from his beard."

"It is our total savings!" cried Djerack in disbelief. "We have sold—"

"Just a minute." Lambient went to his horse and returned with two additional pouches, which he added to the stack. "Here are 160 Garlandian gold dynars, a half year's wages."

"Yes, he knows what the dynar is worth," snapped the dwarf. "Do you think he is so poor as to need such pretty pebbles?" He reached back into the darkness of the hovel and produced a bag, heavy enough to require both hands to lift it. He upended it. Rubies, diamonds, and amethysts tumbled out and piled themselves up on the threshold. "This is but one bag within his easy reach. Take these back to your onderkoning. They will mean more to him than to me." The door creaked again.

"Wait!" cried Djerack with renewed urgency. Slowly he unfastened his belt knife and laid it on the ground. Anna could not see much of it in its sheath. But it was an odd weapon—not very like a knife at all. More like a long, lead-colored stake slightly curved at the tip. It lacked both cross-guard and quillon, and the hilt seemed too short while the pommel looked too large. It was not a pretty weapon but did look very old. "It has been in my family for generations," said the lieutenant.

The dwarf was already waving his hands dismissively without

even looking at the blade. "Pah! What use is a knife to him? The work of human hacks. No man-blade would endure a single blow from his hammer."

Lambient's patience was spent. "Then what do you want, dwarf? What can we offer to gain your help?"

The dwarf smiled a cruel smile. "Now you have reached the point of true negotiation. He shall consider your question. Await his return." And the door began to close again. Just before it shut, the dwarf's nose poked through the crack again. "And leave this pile of goodies for him to consider." And the door snapped shut.

"Why that dirty little—"

But Djerack laid his hand on the professor's arm. "Guard your words, learned one. He can still hear us."

They returned to the fire to wait. An hour passed, then two. Lambient paced, grumbled, and periodically uttered vivid imprecations against the dwarf. The frequency with which the various gods appeared in his oaths caused Anna to wonder if the scientist had found religion after all.

Rose was watching Djerack intently as he sat at the smoldering fire with his eyes closed as if in meditation or prayer. Realizing she was about to ask him a question, Anna started to tell her not to disturb him. She wasn't fast enough.

"How do you know so much about dwarves?"

The lieutenant's eyes popped open. "Longaevi courtesy and ritual are learned in school when we are very young. Every Azhwana child of your age knows that dwarves must be placated before they will lift so much as a finger to even the most urgent need."

Eli said, "But I didn't think there were many dwarves left."

"That is true," said the soldier.

"Then why do they still teach that stuff? I mean, isn't it just a waste of time?"

The lieutenant was silent for a moment. "Courtesies and rites should not be lost simply because one generation does not happen to find them useful. That would leave the future empty of many deep and noble things. And who knows when they may be needed again." And to make his point, he gestured at the closed door. "Are they not still taught in your land?"

"Um . . . no," said Eli, truthfully enough.

He shook his head. "We believe that one day the longaevi will prosper again. Garlandium will be greatly disadvantaged in that day."

They sat in silence. Suddenly Rose said, "It's like Naggie." Eli and Anna looked at her in surprise, but she said no more.

Still, it set Anna to thinking. Yes, it was a little like Miss Heavernaggie. She kept an old-fashioned foreign house; she served tea at four o'clock every day; she was absorbed with keeping up the appearance of a whole way of life that just did not exist in the world any more. But it suddenly did not seem quite so ridiculous to Anna. Well, yes, it was still ridiculous, but it also made sense in a way it hadn't before. It was unsettling to think that all those manners and traditions, so out of place in modern America, might still have some mysterious value and be worth preserving.

She was not permitted to think about it anymore, however, for at that moment the little door rattled, and they assembled before it once again on their knees.

"It is a tedious world," began the dwarf in a shabby attempt at melancholy. "In his 2,416 years of life, he has seen all this world has to offer. He is convinced that nothing new exists under Merris's light, and he is indescribably bored. He would give even an ounce of his blood and a drop of his saliva if someone could simply show him something he has not seen before. For such a gift, you could even keep your worthless bobbles." And he grinned, gesturing at the pile of gold and gems at his feet.

Anna could almost feel the current generated by the shock within Lambient and the soldiers. They were struck dumb before the dwarf for a full minute.

"That's it?" said Lambient. "That's all we have to do—show you something . . . new?" But even as he said it, he cast his eyes about the empty glade, and his tone changed. "But . . . but, where are we to find something in this gods-forsaken place that you've never seen before?"

The dwarf sighed again with exaggerated ennui. "Ah, monsieur, that is the difficulty of old age. When one has lived as long as he has, one despairs of ever seeing anything new."

Anna too was shocked. With the gravity of the situation, she could not believe the dwarf considered his boredom as lamentable as Ragundiae and Dashonae's death. But she was also at an utter loss as to what to do about it.

She heard Eli inhale and mutter to herself, "That's it. I can't take it anymore." And she stood up and stepped forward. No one stopped her. They were all too taken aback by her sudden assertiveness. The dwarf too stood on his stoop, eyeing her with a mixture of wonder and suspicion.

"Do I understand you, dwarf," she said in clear defiant tone, "that if we show you something you've never seen before, you'll give Dr. Lambient what he needs to save Ragundiae?"

The dwarf drew back apprehensively. He clearly did not like this new and aggressive opponent. He preferred the kind who groveled.

"Yes . . ."

"Very well," she said in a withering voice. "Rose, come here. We have some business with the nice dwarf."

Rose looked to Anna. Anna grabbed her hand and led her to the front of the group. Anna thought she knew where Eli was going with this, and it was crazy dangerous. But she didn't have an alternative.

"Inside," commanded Eli.

The shock on the dwarf's face was absolute, bordering on terror.

"Miss Eli," began Lambient with concern.

"No, Doctor. I know how to meet the dwarf's demand, but you have to trust me."

The professor stepped aside.

It was so out of character for Eli, so unexpected, that everyone complied. She took Rose's hand and pushed past the dwarf into his shanty. The dwarf stood stock-still, like a sign nailed to his own door. Anna followed more out of instinct than anything. Then they were inside, and the dwarf stammered to the men outside, "He'll, uh . . . be back in a moment."

And the door creaked closed behind them.

Chapter 43

The tiny room was dry but filthy, like the opening to a mine shaft. Burlap bags were piled against the wall amid broken digging tools. A single, dingy lantern swung from the ceiling, casting a grayish yellow light that was absorbed by the close air before hitting any of the walls.

The dwarf turned to them and wrung his hands fretfully. Eli did not give him time to think. "Take us to a place where we can sit and talk." While Anna felt apprehensive about going anywhere with the dwarf, she was already feeling cramped from standing shoulder to shoulder in the tiny space.

The dwarf, so absolutely out of his element, obediently pushed past them and opened another door built directly into the rock face. As he passed he shrugged his shoulder in a way that suggested they should follow. They did and found themselves in a low tunnel. Rose and the dwarf could walk upright, but the other two had to stoop to keep from cracking their heads on the stone ceiling. The tunnel sloped downhill abruptly and steeply.

A strange light beckoned from the far end of the tunnel. It looked only a few yards away, but they actually walked for several minutes before they reached it. And then the three girls gasped. This was not the low and dark mine shaft they'd thought they were entering. Instead, there was a surprising amount of light and room. The ceiling shot away from them to a vast and invisible height. Lights of various shades of white, amber, and bright blue shone from what looked like large jewels set in the walls. Great stone pillars stretching up into the gloom gave the impression of a great hall. They could not see the far end, for it disappeared into a murky darkness. The sense of dry, decrepit grandeur increased when Anna looked down and saw a floor of polished marble tiles, each several feet square.

"Moria!" Eli whispered. Anna rolled her eyes, but it did look like something straight out of Middle Earth. Some of the gemstones in the wall were dark, like burned out bulbs. Off to her left she saw a seven-foot spike of collapsed column, pointing upward like a finger with shattered fragments scattered all around it. Thin dust covered the whole floor except for a small, scuffled path that went straight forward into the depths, beyond the reach of the lights—apparently the only part of the floor the dwarf used.

But the dwarf did not follow this track. He veered to the right, leaving a new patch of dusty foot prints. He made for another door and disappeared through it. The girls followed him into a small gathering room. Wooden chairs lay piled about before a great black stone hearth. A rug covered the floor, shabby, thin, and dust-covered. A painting hung precariously above the mantle, but it was so faded that Anna could make out few details—a winged creature and what looked like tongues of fire surrounding it.

The dwarf plopped himself down in the only upright chair and stared at Eli with a malicious look that dared her to continue pushing him now that he was on home turf. Eli rose to the challenge by saying nothing. She simply righted a chair and gestured for Rose to sit. Then she did the same for herself, and Anna followed suit.

"What is your name?" she asked.

The dwarf smiled mirthlessly, showing small pointed teeth. "He is called Girondin-jacobous-mochecouteau."

Anna shook her head numbly. She was not even sure she'd heard all the syllables, which again had a garbled French sound to them. Eli plowed on, not even asking him to repeat it.

"And what is this place?"

"This?" he waved his hand carelessly about the room. "This is nothing. It was once something, but no more. They are gone. Only he is left." And for a fleeting moment something like wistfulness crossed his hairy face.

"And you are lonely?" Eli's voice had become oddly sympathetic.

He eyed her suspiciously. "It does not matter. What is, is. He remains. They are gone."

"Where did they go?"

The dwarf shrugged. "Time is long. It changes even the earth. Mountains rise. Mountains fall. All things change." Anna could see they were not going to get anything useful from the dwarf this way. Eli realized it also and changed tactics.

"So you want to see something new?"

The dwarf said nothing.

"I can show you something very old. So old it would be new even to you."

Still the dwarf said nothing, but again showed his humorless smile.

"Rose, give me the compass." Rose produced it. Eli held it out with one hand for the dwarf to see. "I'll bet you've never seen this."

The dwarf leaned forward with little interest. But after a hard look at the small orb in her hand, he jumped up and grabbed at it. Eli was ready and yanked it back out of reach. Her other hand came up, holding her belt knife. Anna hadn't even seen her draw it, but the tip of it rested on the dwarf's leather shirt.

"Where did you get it?" he snarled.

"So you do know what it is. I thought you might," said Eli, maintaining the knife's pressure against the jerkin. "But first things first. Have you actually *seen* it before?"

The dwarf paused, licked his lips, then sat down reluctantly. "He must look at it again . . . to be sure."

"No, perhaps later. You've seen enough to answer the question."

The dwarf squirmed and seemed to Anna to be holding his breath. But after a minute of writhing indecisively on his chair, he deflated. "No, he has not."

"Then you will give Dr. Lambient what he needs?"

The dwarf hesitated.

Eli pressed, "If I cannot trust you to keep your word, then we have no further business here." And she began to put the compass into her pocket.

"A promise!" cried the dwarf. "He made a promise! Yes, yes, he will help the big rude man. He always keeps a promise."

"Very well," said Eli, producing the compass again. "You may look at it, but you may not touch it."

"No, no!" said the dwarf, raising his head. "He must touch it, hold it. He must know if it is—"

"Very well," said Eli, smiling. "But that will require a new promise."

The dwarf stopped fidgeting and looked at Eli with a mixture of dislike and grudging respect. Anna too was experiencing an unexpected regard for how well her sister was handling this. She was not used to the feeling and was not sure she liked it.

"What do you want of him?" the dwarf asked, now trying hard to look accommodating.

"What do you know of Vizuritundu?"

The dwarf was nonplussed. "That? Just an old ruin. He has not been up that way for a century. Dull, most dull. Let him show you something interesting instead."

Now it was Eli's turn to be amazed. "You know where it is?"

"Yes, yes, a day's journey at most." He waved his hand dismissively. "But further down he can show you whole veins of jewels and reefs of diamonds. Where the gold bleeds from the walls like—"

"You will show us how to find it," Eli interrupted.

The dwarf went silent and looked at the ceiling as if trying to remember. "This is all you want from him? To find the old well? For this you will give him the relic?"

"No," said Eli. "We can't give it to you. We need it. But if you will promise to show us the way to the well, you may examine it.

But you must promise to give it back to us immediately when we ask for it."

The dwarf thought in silence for a whole minute, then a wicked grin broke across his face. "He promises. He promises on the horns of Berducca herself that he will give back the relic and show you the way to the ruin."

Anna did not trust the dwarf any further than she could toss him, and started to say so.

But Eli waved her silent. "Very well. Now we must go out and leave with Dr. Lambient. But we will return soon for your assistance, and at that time you may see the—"

But the dwarf had leapt to his feet. "No! You must not leave. He must examine the relic."

"But we will return," said Eli, trying to maintain her hold on the situation.

The dwarf began looking around the room frantically as if hoping for aid from unseen comrades. "No, no!" he moaned repeatedly. Then the answer apparently materialized for him. "The rude man can go with his blood token, but you must stay. The relic must not go away from him."

"Absolutely not!" said Anna, deciding this had gone too far. Eli was losing the position of power.

"No promise!" He waggled a finger. "No promise if the relic leaves. He will not help you find the well."

Eli looked helplessly to Anna. Anna wanted to shout something snide at her, but she could only get out a choked, "But we *can't* stay. It isn't . . . safe."

The dwarf must have known what she feared and made a concession, but pleadingly with his hands together in almost a prayer, "He promises again. You will not be harmed in his house or his halls. You may stay here. You will be safe here. And he will tell you things—things about the relic. He promises to show you the way to the well—a short way. He promises. He promises on the horns of Berducca." He began nodding violently, looking from one to the other as if to persuade them by the sheer force of his bobbing head.

Eli sighed and looked at Anna.

"Don't even say it," said Anna in disbelief.

"What choice do we have?" said Eli.

"He did promise," said Rose.

"So did Gollum," said Anna hotly. "Next he'll be calling it 'his precious.'"

"Yes, yes," said the dwarf, trying to help his case, "it is precious, very precious."

"Be quiet," said Eli in frustration. "Look, we can either wander around the mountains forever looking for the well, or we can take a risk and—"

"We're not looking for the well!" cried Anna. "They are. We're trying to get home! They're two different things."

Eli went ashen, and Anna knew the blow had gone home. Leave it to Eli, for all her smarts, to forget the basic point of the journey. Eli lowered her head in thought for a moment, then she turned to the kneeling dwarf. "You've promised to give it back when we ask for it?"

"Oh yes, yes," said the dwarf, giving what he thought to be a reassuring smile.

"Then look at this and tell me—" and before Anna could stop her, Eli had thrust out her hand to the dwarf, who in turn had snatched the compass—"and tell me, if you can, how close the arrows are pointing to the location of the well."

Anna gritted her teeth as the dwarf greedily turned the orb over in his hands.

"Hard to be sure," he said after a moment, "but very close. Within the passage, perhaps. Very close, he is sure of that."

"Very good," said Eli, holding out her hand. The dwarf hesitated. "You may examine it again after the doctor has what he needs. But this is the first test of your trustworthiness." Anna could see Eli was scared and trying not to show it. But the dwarf dutifully put the compass back into her hand, and tried to smile again.

"We must see the rude man now," he said cheerfully, "so you can know that he keeps his promises. Always does. Then you eat, and he will tell you things." And he began nodding again.

Anna was beaten. Whatever was going to happen was going to happen. Eli had committed them. As Anna trudged out of the room after the others, she thought, *How could someone be so brilliant and so stupid at the same time?*

Chapter 44

Lambient waved nervously to them as he rode out of the clearing, the small vial of dark blood and saliva stowed safely in his saddlebag. He was clearly conflicted, wanting to hasten back to Ishtagung and yet unwilling to leave his three charges behind. He had not been easily persuaded to accept the arrangement, which would require at least a day to make the trip back to Ishtagung, arrange for Dashonae's release if possible, and beat a path back to the girls so they could all go with the dwarf. Even when Djerack had confirmed the general reliability of the dwarf's promise, he had held out for other options. This only further incensed the dwarf, and finally even Lambient realized that his continued protestations were only making the inevitable parting harder.

While the dwarf did technically complete his part of the agreement, it was clearly against his will. He called down great maledictions from Berducca upon "the rude man" when Lambient made the incision in his ruddy arm to collect the blood, and he spat with all his might into the little bottle afterward.

Now the three girls stood on the threshold of the little causeway between the light and the dark. They held their hands over their eyes in the face of the late afternoon sun and waved goodbye to the doctor. Rose was sniffing back tears, and Eli's jaw was clenched resolutely shut. Anna could hear the dwarf within still cursing about the "mortal wound in his extremities," and she dreaded the return to that desiccated underworld.

But return they did, and when they entered the great hall

once again, the voice of the cursing dwarf sounded far away. He had apparently followed his little dusted path back into the dark depths of the hall.

"Come on," said Eli firmly. "They'll be back for us as soon as they can." And grabbing Rose's hand, she began to walk forward. As it turned out, the hall was not actually dark. Wherever they went there was dim light around them from crystals set in pillars or in the floor, but everywhere else the hall seemed to swallow up the light like an inky liquid. So after about fifty yards, Anna turned around and saw that the entrance through which they had come was lost from sight. A shiver rippled down her back. The desert had been friendly compared to this cold tomb.

Suddenly Eli and Rose jumped back. A small figure holding a beat-up lantern had suddenly emerged from behind a pillar. It was the dwarf.

"He thinks you are hungry at this time," he said in a voice straining to sound pleasant. And without waiting for an answer, he turned and began to walk away.

"So what do we do?" whispered Anna.

"Follow him—what else?" said Eli.

"Okay, you're the boss," shrugged Anna. "But remember the way back, or we won't be able to meet Lambient." Eli had taken them underground, and Anna did not want any of the blame for it splattering on her shoes. So she continued to shuffle along behind them.

The great hall eventually came to an abrupt end at a large, gaping archway. Beyond it lay pitch blackness, without even the faint comfort of the gem lights. The three girls balked at the mouth of it, but the dwarf continued without hesitation. Eli and Anna realized that if they intended to follow, they would have to stay close to him. His dirty little lantern was their only source of light. So they plunged headlong into perfect darkness.

The yellow light bobbed along before them in the passage. They could tell it was a passage from the sound of their footfalls, but it was a very big one. Anna could see neither walls nor ceiling in the light of the lantern. The ground was paved with smooth, brick-like stone, giving the impression of an underground road, but the brick had fallen into disrepair. This made for treacherous going, and more than once the girls stumbled. Once Anna thought the lantern had gone out, and her heart jumped sideways in her chest. But the dwarf was only rounding a corner, and a few hurried steps brought the light back into view.

They walked this way in silence for ten minutes . . . or twenty . . . or perhaps more, how could one tell? Then the light halted before a door, intricately carved with images so foreign to Anna that afterward she never could remember any of them.

"He decided long ago that he should have the best room in the kingdom," the dwarf said, lifting the latch and pushing with a grunt. It must have been a heavy door, for it swung slowly back on its hinges. Anna waited for the bang of the door against the wall, but it made only the softest thud. The dwarf took a little candle off a nearby table and lit it from the lantern. Then he thrust the lit candle into a small metal box that hung on the wall. Instantly a flame leapt from the box and began to race diagonally up the wall in a little track like a lit fuse—or fire racing along a thin trail of gasoline, thought Anna. (She had tried that experiment a couple times in the driveway of their Chicago house until Dad caught her and chewed her ear off.) The flame reached the corner of the room, turned, and sped back toward the middle, then out over their heads on a suspended track to the center and burst out in a dozen directions until it touched off two dozen candles in a chandelier. The room erupted in candlelight.

Squinting and shading their eyes in the sudden brightness, the girls found themselves in a large suite. Like the meeting room, it looked old, dry, dusty, and unused. But it had once been as comfortable as a Victorian sitting room, to which it bore a resemblance. Several high-backed chairs and a sofa surrounded a low table. Bookshelves lined the rock walls, along with spaces for paintings, though neither books nor paintings were there now. Threadbare carpet covered the floor, and the ceiling reflected the light as if covered in tin or copper plating. The back wall featured three doors—or rather, two, for the door of one doorway was missing. Any hominess the room may have offered was further undone by a large, roughly hewn hole in one wall. Stones and chips of rock lay all about it, as though the workmen had tired halfway through cleaning up the rubble and let it lie.

The dwarf motioned for them to sit and went through this hole, mumbling something about having made a shortcut to the kitchens. The girls sat stiffly on the couch and looked at each other. No one said anything.

He returned in a bit carrying a large silver tray somewhat bigger than himself. It contained a pot of lukewarm, weak tea (thanks to Mrs. Heavernaggie's diligence, Anna could now appreciate how insipid the tea really was) and bowls containing all sorts of earthy foods—foods Anna associated with being underground: raw mushrooms, cold boiled potatoes, and a thin stew of parsnips, turnips, and carrots. Also a plate of salted fish. Everything was way too salty, but Anna realized that salt was probably the only seasoning the dwarf had access to.

"Fish?" said Eli. "Where do you get fish?"

"There is a lake far below," said the dwarf, popping a mushroom into his mouth. "He catches them there, and sometimes eels."

Rose shivered and would not touch the fish. But Anna was hungry enough to eat nearly anything that did not still crawl or swim. And in fact it was not bad except for the mushy texture and heavy salt. Unexpectedly, pity arose in Anna's heart for the wretched dwarf, living all alone in a once-populous place—for all she knew, the last of his kind. Whittling away ageless hours here in the dark. It would make her a bit batty too, she thought.

"Do you ever go outside?" she asked before she thought.

"Eh?" he said, pulling a fishbone out of his mouth and picking his teeth with it. "Outside? Yes, sometimes at night, when he gets a taste for meat or treats. He hunts for things or finds berries."

They finished eating in silence. The dwarf finished everything on the tray and even cleaned up the untouched fish on Rose's plate. He then belched loudly, sat back on his chair with his hands resting on his paunch, and eyed Eli.

"Well," said Eli awkwardly, "thank you for dinner. It was very nice." While this was not exactly true, it probably had been as good a meal as the dwarf had to offer. Anna cringed to think of the sorts of creepy-crawly foods that he *might* have served them.

"You don't know what it is, do you?" said the dwarf. They all knew what he was referring to.

"We know some things," said Eli. "We know how to read the arrows."

"You stumbled into this world, didn't you?" The dwarf yawned. "Didn't know what you were doing, did you? Never thought of the consequences, did you?"

"I don't know what you mean," said Eli.

Anna was not surprised that the dwarf knew of their other-worldly origins. If he knew what the compass was, he probably knew a good deal about the kind of person who would possess it. "No, we didn't know about this world before we found it. But we are trying to use the compass to get home again, so anything you know that would help us—"

The dwarf cackled. "They do not even know the story they have entered! I often wonder why men were brought into the world to begin with. They have no memory, no sense of perspective. They do not see the pages being turned right before their eyes. Do you know how many ages have passed since the Great Heavenly Procession?"

"No," said Eli flatly.

The dwarf laughed again. "Do you know the prophecies that are written on the walls of the temple in the holy hill? Or of the coming war?"

Eli looked at Anna for help.

"Look," said Anna, sitting forward. "We don't care about any of the religions in your world or any of the wars. We just want to get home."

But the dwarf leapt up and ran around his chair, waving his hands with excitement. "They don't even know! They don't even know!" he sang in a horrid, croaking voice.

"Now, that's enough," said Anna firmly. "I'm tired of listening to your craziness—no, I'm just plain tired. So get on with it already." And she realized in that moment just how tired she actually was.

The dwarf sat back down on his chair and said curtly, "He must examine it first."

Anna sighed and made a gesture of helplessness to her sister. "Back to you."

Eli produced the compass and held it out to the dwarf. He didn't snatch it this time but took it calmly in his hands and rolled it around. He smelled it, knocked on it with his fist, shook it, licked it ("Ew, gross," said Rose), and did a host of other odd and seemingly useless things with it. His finale was to place it on the floor and stand on it, balancing on one foot.

Anna was growing impatient again and cleared her throat loudly. He looked up at her and sniggered. "Since you want none of his craziness, he'll not tell you the best things. Only the dull things."

Eli was about to protest, but at that moment the dwarf handed the compass back to her. This act of voluntary surrender so surprised her that she forgot what she was going to say.

The dwarf sat back in his chair. "It was made by his oldest ancestors in the days before men came into the world. During the dark time of Hamayune. It is the shemaroon-demageen. It was made in order to draw forth men into the world. It created a bridge between the worlds so that men could come, so that they could do battle with Hamayune and restore the world to order—their order." His final words contained more than a touch of spite.

Anna knew nothing about the story the dwarf was telling, but she had understood something. "So this thing actually creates the window that we came through? But we were told—"

"Foolish children of men do not listen! The relic creates the bridge, not the chasm it crosses. There are chasms between the worlds. They open, they close. But only with the shemaroon-demageen can one pass over safely."

"So it is true that without the shemer . . . uh, the compass," stammered Eli, "we can't get back?"

The dwarf nodded.

"What would happen if we tried?" asked Anna.

"What always happens to those who cross chasms without bridges." The dwarf grinned as if he had made a joke.

"What are these markings on it?" asked Eli.

"They are of two different kinds from two different worlds."

"How do you mean?"

"The bronze band was made of ore mined in this very mountain, and it bears the marks of Merris, her mate, and her children."

"Let me see it," said Anna with sudden interest. Eli hesitated. "Oh good grief. I promise to give it back when you ask for it," she said in imitation of the dwarf. Eli grimaced and handed it to her, but the dwarf found Anna's retort very funny and clapped his hands.

Anna examined it closely in the candlelight. None of the bronze band's symbols meant anything to her except the goblet-shaped one that was also etched on her amulet—Therra's symbol. She counted the symbols—seven total. The bright steel band had eight, and those looked suddenly familiar. One was a little crescent like a moon; another looked like the symbol for male—a circle with a diagonal arrow projecting from it; and there was one that looked like the symbol for female too.

She handed it back to Eli, who had begun to fidget with impatience. Rose yawned and looked bored. "What's the other band?" Anna asked the dwarf.

"That is a strange metal from the other world, the world of men. It does not tarnish or rust. It is not a natural ore, but is man-ufactured in a way even the dwarves do not understand. Its marks reflect the emissaries of that world," said the dwarf.

This did not clarify things for Anna at all.

"Emissaries?" Eli peered at the band with squinty eyes. Then she got excited. "Do you mean like gods?"

"Only men believe in gods," said the dwarf. "They are emissar-ies, nothing more. But, yes, in the words of men—the gods of that world."

Anna was about to remind Eli that their world had no gods when Eli burst out, "Yes, of course! This one is Mars, and here's Venus and Jupiter. And that's the moon."

"But the moon's not a god." Rose was apparently still listening.

"And if the moon is on there, then it's a planet short," said Anna, who felt Eli warming up for another demonstration of knowledge.

"But not in the ancient times he's talking about," Eli went on breathlessly. "For centuries they didn't know about Neptune, Ura-nus, and Pluto. And they grouped the sun and the moon with the planets for astrological reasons. So the planets were Mercury, Venus, Earth, Mars, Saturn, and Jupiter, which makes eight. The ancient gods."

"Yes," said the dwarf, "because the shemaroon-demageen pos-sessed the metals of both worlds, it belonged to both worlds and could cross over the chasm safely. And by it men first came into the world."

But Eli's face had fallen. "Wait a minute. That can't be. If you need this thing to travel from world to world, how did both metals get to this world in the first place?"

"Someone brought it," said Rose.

But Anna saw that Eli was right. It was the same chicken-and-egg problem Whinsom and Cholerish had described. How did one get to the other world to get the material that allowed you to travel to that world?

"Where did the dwarves get the metal from our world to use in making this?" asked Anna.

The dwarf was unruffled. "It was given us."

There was a moment of dumbfounded silence before Anna burst out with, "But that's crazy. It's the same problem. Who *could* give you the metal?"

The dwarf seemed to be enjoying himself now. "One who does not need the shemaroon-demageen to travel between the worlds."

Anna sat there open mouthed. But Eli was thinking hard. "Do . . . do you mean . . . Thes?"

The dwarf leapt to his feet and ran around the chair with his hands on his ears crying, "The name, the name! Do not speak the name! The Maker! The Holy! Do not say it before him. He cannot stand to hear it! It is not permitted."

"Whoa! Whoa!" shouted Anna. "Okay! Okay! Don't go all Voldemort on us! We won't say it again." And she looked at Eli. "Geez, who knew?"

"But is that who you mean?" she asked again.

The dwarf leaned against the arm of his chair, panting, and nodded his head. But he was so unnerved by Eli's use of the name that he refused to answer any more questions. He held his hand to his chest and complained of pains and said he had to sleep now.

"First we sleep, then the well," he panted, and turned to go through the doorway with no door, which apparently led to his sleeping quarters.

"But where are we to sleep?" said Anna.

The dwarf turned around, his hand on his heaving chest, and pointed at the other doors. As he went into his room, he pulled a little cord on the wall. The chandelier shook slightly and all the candles went out, leaving lit only a single, melting stump of a candle on the table.

The three girls looked at each other across the little flame. There could only be a few minutes left before it burned out, and no other candles were to be found. Carefully, Anna gathered up the candle and slowly walked to the first door. Inside they found a small guest room furnished with an old dusty bed—very wide but short like a toddler bed, as if several dwarves were intended to sleep together in it. Eli closed the door behind them. It just would not do to leave that door open all night with who-knows-what-all crawling around in that underground world. Anna put the nub of the candle down on the bed stand, and they all lay down on the squeaky bed. The flame sputtered, and they all turned to stare at it.

Lost inside a mountain with a crazed dwarf, and the only source of light dimming, dimming, gone. Utter black, utter silence. The weight of a million tons of earth and rock to muffle their cries and bury their bodies. It all settled slowly upon their minds. No one would ever find them. If they ever got out of here, thought Anna, she would always look back on this as the most terrible moment of her life.

She lay awake on the bed. But was she awake? How could she tell? Were her eyes open or closed? She didn't know. How long had she been that way? Was there anything beyond this blackness?

Oppressive doubt descended on her mind. It was as though the darkness were a living thing seeping into her mind and clogging it up. She was having trouble remembering things . . . things like the color red or the meaning of *up*. She couldn't remember her name or what she looked like. Her mind was growing slowly blank in the inky blackness. Something cried out in her that it would be like this from now on—forever.

Despair was overtaking her when she felt warmth. For a moment she could not identify the source or even, as strange as it sounds, what part of her felt it. She had no body left with which to feel. This warmth was reaching her mind by some direct route. But she concentrated, imagined her body—her neck, her round shoulder, a length of arm, elbow, hand, fingers. That was it—her hand. She felt warmth in her hand. It was Eli. She had put her hand into Anna's. There followed what seemed a deafening explosion in

Anna's mind—but it was only Eli whispering softly, "It's okay, we'll get through this."

Anna's mind reclaimed its perspective. Her hands could feel. Her ears could hear. The sky was up, the earth was down, water was wet. She squeezed her sister's hand and reached out to find Rose's. And so they slept, hand in hand, in the tomb-like darkness.

Chapter 45

A loud pounding awoke them. Anna's eyes opened—or at least she thought they were open. They were still in utter blackness. Rose stirred. Eli yelled, "Yes, what it is it?"

The door of the room opened, and oh! Glorious candlelight shone into the room. Anna's eyes were moist; it was the most beautiful thing she had ever seen. But the wonder of the moment was dampened a bit when a gravelly voice started to speak.

"He wakes you now. It is time to go to the well." It was the dwarf.

On the table in the main room sat several small lanterns, skins of water, lengths of candles, and some dry biscuits. He gave them each a small bag, like a purse, and instructed them to take provisions for themselves and a lantern apiece.

"So we're not going back out to wait for the others?" asked Rose, looking plaintively from one sister to the other. Deep down, Anna was glad Rose had asked. She had thought it last night as they climbed into bed, but then things went . . . well, the way they did, and she had more pressing things to occupy her mind. But now that the question had been asked, she realized how desperately she wanted to be out of the dark mountain—to see the sun and feel the breeze on her face.

But the dwarf stamped his foot. "No, we go now, or we do not go."

"But you promised to—" began Eli.

"He promised to show you the way to the well. He did not

promise to wait for the rude man to return. He will keep his promise whether you come or not." So they had to follow or be left behind.

"We'll just have to hope they can find us somehow," said Eli in a choked voice as she picked up her pack. Without another word, they trooped out the door into the hall, or rather, the road. For that was more and more what it looked like to Anna now that she could see by her own lantern.

"Is it far away?" asked Rose, the only one who might have found the weight of her bag troublesome.

"We will walk all day," said the dwarf. "Then we must emerge and walk a bit more. Then we shall camp. Then you will be close."

"Do you mean," said Anna, a lump rising in her throat, "that we have to walk all day in the caves?"

"Of course," said the dwarf indignantly, as though he had never considered that there might be an alternative to underground travel.

Anna could never have recounted all that they saw in those caves during that long underground march. They passed through great halls similar to the one they had first entered by, and down passages with hundreds of doors lined up one next to another like motel rooms. They descended long, winding staircases and walked next to a great, black lake in a cavernous hollow in the mountain (not the same lake from which he fished, said the dwarf, but much like it). And for a long while they walked through what was clearly an abandoned mine. Ancient pickaxes with wooden handles dried and hardened to the consistency of iron lay strewn amid carts filled with dirty, rough gems and hunks of gold the size of the girls' fists. Evidence sufficient to persuade the most skeptical archeologist that a mighty culture had once flourished beneath these hills.

Only one incident disturbed their travels—and it *was* disturbing. They were ascending a passage intersected by many other large passages on either side. They were natural caves created by flows of water or lava, not carved by dwarves.

Rose, who was walking immediately behind the dwarf, slipped and fell. "Ow!" she cried—then, "Ew!" She leapt to her feet and began brushing off her pants.

Anna shined her lantern where Rose had slipped. What initially looked like a stream of water turned out to be more like a trail of slime. It crossed their path and disappeared down passages to the right and left. Anna called to the dwarf, who tended not to slow his pace for anything.

He turned and yelled back, "We must continue if we are to emerge today."

"But we found something . . . odd," was all Anna could say.

The dwarf returned, bent to examine the slimy trail, and shrugged. "It is only the lou carcolh." And he walked away.

"The what?" said Eli after him.

He called over his shoulder, "The lou carcolh, the great mollusk. But the trail is many hours old so he is probably not near."

"Would it be bad if he were?" asked Anna.

The dwarf paused. "He would swallow you whole and consider it a treat."

Rose made a small gurgling sound.

"But you never said there would be—" began Eli.

"You wanted him to take you to Vizuritundu. He does so. He was never asked how dangerous the journey would be. But do not fret. The great mollusk does not attack. He is not smart or brave. He only sends out the tentacles from his mouth to catch what prey he can. If you see them, run. You may get away."

"May?" said Anna.

The dwarf shrugged and continued his march.

They stopped to rest only twice. Anna had no way of knowing how long they had been marching, but Rose was losing strength and starting to straggle behind. Anna grabbed her hand. "Come on. Not long now." She had no way of knowing this, but it was the first thing that came to mind to say. As it turned out, she was very nearly right.

They had been going uphill steadily for some time, and now Anna saw far ahead a small patch of light, like candlelight, but it didn't flicker. As they drew closer, she realized it was daylight.

They emerged from the side of the mountain and stood blinking in the late afternoon sun. Merris was full in their face, and they welcomed her warmth and light—feasting on it like hungry men at a banquet. As their eyes grew accustomed to the brightness, they also saw that they were high in the mountains. The whole plain of Azhwana was spread out before them to the horizon. They could not see the desert.

The dwarf paused only long enough for them to get their bearings again and then began to descend by a small stone staircase, which led to level ground below. Upon reaching the clearing at the foot of the stairs, Anna realized they were not so high as she had thought. They were not even above the tree line. Looking up, she saw that thousands of feet of mountain still towered above them.

The dwarf stowed his lantern in his bag and started off through the forest. The sisters were tired by now, and the path was once again ascending. Anna's feet hurt, and so did her back, and she was thirsty, and . . . oh, she just didn't want to think about how much farther they had to go.

The sun was near the horizon, and the sky was changing from blue to gold to red, when the group came to a clearing. Less than an hour had passed since they had emerged from the caverns. Anna saw that the mountain split in two before them, and between the two peaks lay a slender passage, like the crack in a sidewalk from an ant's point of view.

The dwarf threw his bag on the ground. The others did the same. Then he walked toward this fissure. Exchanging looks, the girls followed him. Though long, the passage was just a few feet wide. No vegetation grew in it, so it was not hard going.

The path emptied into a clearing—a rock-strewn hollow in the mountains about the size of their old backyard in Chicago. In its center, a hole in the ground a few feet wide opened like a chimney in the mountain. And straight out of it—the oddest, unlikeliest thing to see in such a forsaken place—ascended a long metal pole, like a fireman's pole.

The dwarf walked to the edge of the hole and pointed down into it.

"That's the well?" said Eli, sounding disappointed, and not without cause. Anna too was struggling with the idea that they had come all this way to find something that looked like a manhole in the street.

"No, not the well, but the way to it," the dwarf said matter-of-factly. The girls approached and looked down. The shaft descended into darkness. The pole showed no signs of visible support but seemed to hover in the middle of the opening.

"We have to go down that . . . into there?" asked Eli.

"Yes," said the dwarf, "and when you reach the bottom, if it has a bottom, the passage will take you to the well."

"What do you mean, 'if'?" said Anna.

"He means it has been many years since he has been here," said the dwarf. "He does not know if the pole is sound all the way down or if the land has changed."

"But you'll go first, right?" asked Eli, her voice rising slightly. "You'll see if it is safe, right?"

Anna knew the answer before the dwarf spoke.

"He promised to show you the way to the well. That is the way. He goes no further. But you need not do it tonight. Return with him to the clearing and set camp. He shall go home in the morning, and you . . . may do as you wish." Turning, he disappeared back through the narrow fissure.

The girls stood looking down into the blackness for a few minutes.

"Ain't this just ditty!" said Anna, glaring at Eli, and then stomped after the dwarf. Rose followed.

Back by their packs, Anna threw herself down to sulk, fighting back hot, angry tears. A few minutes later Eli trudged by with her hands in her pockets and collapsed onto a stump, looking miserable.

The dwarf had a fire blazing in no time. Unfortunately, Rose decided to help by throwing a large, wet pine branch on the fire! Smoke and steam choked them all for several minutes and billowed high into the sky before the dwarf managed to pull it off. Even after, it continued to smolder and smoke.

During the afternoon's march, the dwarf had shot a wild goose with his bow, so dinner was unexpectedly delicious. Even Rose, who had complained loudly at having to watch the dead fowl bounce along on the dwarf's back, ate her weight's worth.

The sun was now below the tree line, and the evening's deep shadow made the fire seem brighter. The dwarf, after picking most of the bones clean, lay down on the ground and in two minutes was snoring. The girls were left to stare at one another and decide their course of action.

"What do we do?" said Eli. She sat with her hands crossed between her spread legs, looking regretful and apprehensive.

"Won't we wait for the others?" said Rose.

"No good," said Anna. "They don't know where we are. And even Sazerac couldn't track us, 'cause we left no scent. We were underground most of the way."

"I guess we have to go on or go back," said Eli without looking up.

Anna felt hot annoyance bubble up. "It's a little late to talk about going back! As I remember, that suggestion was made this morning, before following this dwarf up into the boonies. How are we supposed to go back now, even if we want to? We have no idea where 'back' is."

Anna realized she was itching to have it out with her sister and waited for her to respond. But Eli did not flare up. She just dragged her toe around in the dirt and whispered, "I know." This so surprised Anna that the edge of her anger was blunted.

"I just didn't see any other way to save Dashonae, and then one thing led to another, and . . . well . . ."

Compassion welled up in Anna. She remembered Eli's hopeful words to her in the midst of her own dark crisis the night before. Reaching out, Anna embraced her sister. Eli began to cry on her shoulder. Rose's arms reached around them both, and the three of them sat that way as the fire burned down and night fell around them.

Chapter 46

Anna awoke with the horrible feeling that something was wrong. It was just a feeling, but it was very strong. She was lying on the ground, facing the fire. She opened one eye slightly. The fire was nearly out, but a slightly waning Lemerrus was bright overhead, so the clearing was bathed in the amber moonlight of that world. Anna saw the figure of the dwarf squatting by the fire. He was mumbling to himself. Without moving, she strained to hear what he was saying.

"Kept his promise, he did. He showed the way to the well, he did. And no harm came to them in his home or halls. Safey waifs they were. But now they're outside." He seemed to be rambling, but the longer she listened the more frightened she became. "Now the shemaroon-demageen can be his. It is his by rights. What do they know of it, of the prophecies, of the war to come? Mushrooms—they're just mushrooms, tiny and ripe for picking. Snick, snick goes the blade, off at the neck, all done, no mess to clean. He's back to home, safe and sound. Home to dwarfish halls it comes. Sleepy deep they do. Now's the time."

To Anna's horror the dwarf rose and drew his belt knife—a long, thin blade curved slightly like a butcher's knife. He took a step toward the sleeping Eli. Anna's mind raced. Could she get her belt knife out in time to do any good? What if she yelled and woke the others up? Then it would be three on one? But she remembered what Dashonae had said about the unnatural strength of the longaevi. He was surely stronger than any of them and probably all of them together.

All this raced through her mind in a moment, as such things do in a crisis. She decided that leaping up and yelling would be the best hope and was about to do it when the whole scene became confused.

A shadow descended upon the dwarf. It looked like something falling out of the sky. Whatever it was, it knocked the dwarf to the ground. The knife went skittering across the rocks. Anna jumped to her feet and yelled. The other two sat up, bleary-eyed, but very quickly Eli was on her feet too. A jumble of small arms and legs had developed before them. The dwarf was wrestling with something they could not make out and cursing all the while. Suddenly the thing broke away and zoomed into the air.

"Come back here, you coward," cried the dwarf at the heavens. "You fight like a man!" He then looked down, scanning for his knife. But his challenge was answered as the thing fell upon him again.

Rose said it first, in a voice completely devoid of surprise, as if she had expected him. "It's Finch." The fairy was a third the size of the dwarf, but the fight was evenly matched, for the fairy was quicker and could fly. But if the dwarf got a hand on him, he could break Finch. They battled as mortal enemies, without rules. The fairy pulled the dwarf's beard and scratched at his eyes; the dwarf tried to rip the fairy's wings off. The movement was so furious that the girls could do nothing but watch.

The end came in an unexpectedly dramatic way. At a moment when the fairy's wings and arms were both free, he bolted behind the dwarf, grabbed him by the back of the jerkin, and attempted to take off. Realizing what the fairy was doing, the dwarf fought desperately to free himself. But he was so stocky he could not reach the fairy's hands, and Finch managed to stay behind him no matter how he swung or turned.

Despite his strength, Finch struggled to get the dwarf off the ground; it was as if some strong force bound him to the earth. But finally, with a mighty lunge, the fairy succeeded. The dwarf's feet came off the ground with a jerk, as if being pulled out of the mud. His jerkin tore at the seams as if under incredible strain, but it held. The dwarf began screaming as if in agony—crying, begging, pleading to be released. By inches the fairy dragged him upward, his wings beating wildly. So pitiable were the dwarf's cries that Anna almost forgot that five minutes earlier he had wanted to kill them all in their sleep.

The dwarf thrashed in the fairy's grasp, throwing himself around, trying to break free. He was only about eight feet off the ground, but Finch seemed unable to gain any more height. He was even starting to lose altitude. But the dwarf's cries were weakening. His writhing grew less vigorous—until finally, the dwarf grew still. His thrashing became a twitching and then ceased altogether.

The fairy was coming down now whether he wanted to or not, drained from holding the dwarf aloft. He hovered a foot above the ground for another minute and then dropped the dwarf to the earth like a sack and collapsed himself beside him.

Girondin-jacobous-mochecouteau was dead.

And Finch nearly was as well. He lay facedown, panting. His wings drooped as though drenched with water. He tried to rise once and collapsed.

Anna ran to him, followed closely by her sisters. "Finch! Finch! Are you okay?"

The fairy raised his head and smiled. "I will be, but I'm swearing off dwarves. That one sort of upset my stomach."

Rose giggled. "You were wonderful, Finch. I knew you would come."

Anna and Eli stared at Rose, bewildered. She just stared back. "What?"

"How did you know he would come?" asked Eli.

"Figured he'd see the smoke."

"Smoke?"

"From the fire. I threw the wet branch on the fire so it would make smoke."

Rose was so matter-of-fact that Anna actually believed her.

"But what made you think to—" Eli began.

"Well—" Rose helped Finch sit up and gave him a drink from her canteen—"I figured the professor would send him out looking for us, and I knew he had to find us before the dwarf got us."

"So you heard him too," said Anna, but Rose looked at her blankly. "You know, just before Finch attacked him? He was talking to himself about killing us. Right then."

Rose's hands went to her mouth in surprise. "He was going to do it right then? Oh, Finch, how wonderful of you! You were just in time."

The fairy shrugged, but Anna wasn't satisfied. "I don't get it. You didn't hear him planning it? Then how did you know he'd try to kill us?"

Now Rose looked at her sisters with her "duh" face. "Come on—what did you think he was going to do? You saw how bad he wanted the compass. He said he wouldn't hurt us while we were in his house, so I figured that once we got out . . ." She nodded knowingly.

"So you threw the branch on the fire, hoping Finch would find us, because you knew the dwarf was going to kill us?" Eli spoke the words back to her slowly, struggling to believe they were all true.

Rose responded with her "duh" face again.

Anna and Eli were speechless. They looked at each other. They looked at Rose. It was incredible. Absurd. Rose just wasn't that . . . and yet, there was Finch and the dead dwarf.

Anna felt dizzy and sat down. It was too much. Only Rose could have found it in her heart to put any faith in the fairy after their past experiences with him. And if she hadn't . . . Anna shuddered.

The fairy was breathing more easily now. "She's right on all fours. Sir Teddy found the loophole in the dwarf's promise as soon as Lambient told him. Sent me out directly, told me to scan the mountain and return with your location soon as I found it. Said they'd set out at full speed as soon as they slipped out of the noose."

"So he made it back in time?" said Eli, hope-filled again.

"Well, the terrible tara was still alive when I left, and I found the Doc and Sir Teddy already on the road when I flew back to give them your location. So I guess it went well. They should be here by sunrise if they ride all night."

"But how *did* you find us?" asked Anna, to which Rose harrumphed.

"Your li'l sissy's smoke did the tricky." He rose and tested his wings. He fluttered up and hovered like a hummingbird. "You got any eats?"

"There may be some goose left," said Eli, but the fairy was horrified at the idea of eating something that flew. So Rose offered him some of the hard biscuits they had brought. He grudgingly accepted the "dwarfy food" and said he would take care of the "unsightlies," by which he meant the dwarf's body. This amazed Anna, for Finch now flew the body away with no more effort than picking up a doll. What's more, he did it with one hand; the other one was busy stuffing biscuit into his mouth.

He returned a few minutes later, empty handed, and asked for a drink of water. Then he alighted by the fire, which Eli had stoked up. Finch said it would be morning in a few hours, but no one felt like sleeping.

"Finch . . ." Now that the danger had passed, Anna was thinking things through again. "How did the dwarf actually die? It looked like he just . . ." She realized she had no a word to describe it.

"Like he drowned in mid air," Rose whispered, with a sort of muted terror. She was not a good swimmer and had an active imagination on the subject of drowning.

"True 'nough, missy. I broke his ——." He used a word Anna didn't catch.

"Broke his what?"

He repeated the word. "You know—what Lambient calls his *vinculum*, his link with Berducca. The dwarves belong to the deep earth—born of rock, soil, and clay. They can't leave it. They are linked through her to it. For him, being lifted up into the air was the same as being held underwater." He shivered. "Not by me, of course. By a merman."

This suggested other questions, but Anna didn't get to ask them. Eli had assumed her "I've figured it all out" demeanor. "Of course," she said. "It makes sense. Dwarves have one environment in which they survive—the ground, just like a mermaid in the water. If you took a mermaid out of water, she'd die."

"Not exactly, but if you put a fairy *into* the stuff, he would . . ." said Finch, snapping his fingers.

But Eli was just warming up. "Every one of the longaevi have their environment. Dwarves have the land, mermaids the water, fairies . . ." She hesitated.

"The sky," finished Rose, and the fairy nodded.

Eli paused. "But that salamander back in the city wasn't in fire when we saw him, and you're sitting perfectly happy here on the ground, so—"

But the fairy waved her off. "No, no, the surface of Errus, the world, is common to all. It is the common element, the center. Even the merfolk can endure on the earth, though they are not well-suited to it. The skin of Errus is the meeting place of the longaevi. The dwarf's habitat is not the surface of Errus, but *under* it."

"But why was he so heavy?" asked Rose.

"He would have found me equally heavy if he had tried to pull me down into one of his nasty holes. We're all bound to our element with strong bonds—strong vincula, as the men say. He did not expect me to attempt to draw him up into my element. I only won because of surprise and fright." He heaved a great sigh, and Rose patted him affectionately on the back. The fairy was too tired to talk any more and announced that he was going to sleep.

Perhaps all the longaevi had the power to go to sleep at will, for not a full minute later he was snoring softly.

Rose lay down next to him and gazed at her sisters, smiled, and closed her eyes as well.

"She probably saved our lives, you know," said Eli quietly.

"And we'll never live it down," said Anna.

Chapter 47

Anna awoke in a coughing fit, opened her eyes, and shut them immediately. They burned and watered from smoke. She leapt up and tried to figure out what was going on. When she could finally see again, she found Finch piling wet leaves onto a blazing fire. The smoke had all of them coughing and seeking clear, breathable air.

"Finch!" she hacked. "What are you doing?"

"Gotta help Sir Teddy find his ladies!" he cried with delight, and then zipped off into the sky.

The girls consumed the last of their biscuits, and before they had finished, they heard shouts and the thudding of hooves. Two horses broke through the trees. They bore the knight and a very red-faced Lambient. Sazerac accompanied him in a carrier strapped to the horse behind the professor. He looked a little like a child riding behind its parent on a bicycle, complete with tongue hanging out. They pulled up short when they saw the girls.

"Ladies!" cried Lambient, bounding down from the horse and crossing the final yards at a trot. His big arms managed to embrace all three in one sweep, and they were crushed and mangled with affection. Then he held them all out at arm's length and waggled a finger at them. "After all we've been through—tsk, tsk! You've been keeping secrets from me."

Anna didn't know what he was talking about. Neither did Eli, or else she was faking it really well. Once again it was Rose who surprised them. "Was it Finch or Sazerac who told you?"

"Both." The professor feigned a hurt expression. "And to think that all this time we've actually been about different journeys. And yet here we all stand—me on the verge of a scientific extravaganza and you on the verge of a window between the worlds."

Now Anna understood. She had forgotten about discussing all this in front of the dog in the SkyCricket and a little later being forced to tell Finch. It seemed like a hundred years ago, even though it had only been a few days.

"Enough sandbagging," he cried. "Let me see the little wonder." With no hesitation Rose produced the compass and held it out to him.

"Sorry, Doctor," said Eli. "Whinsom thought we shouldn't tell you about it. Said you might try to crack it open or something."

"That old fussbudget." Lambient shook his head and then smiled. "He was probably right, you know."

Sazerac, freed from his carrier by Dashonae, bounded up, barking, and nearly flattened Rose and her sisters, each in turn. Anna still couldn't understand what he was saying in his barking voice, but she didn't have to understand canineish to know he was happy to see them.

"Naughty dog," cried Rose as she nuzzled his neck. "Telling secrets on us." And Anna was in for a third shock when Rose responded to the next series of barks with, "Oh, a likely story. I don't believe it." This appeared to be the day for underestimating her younger sister.

It was wonderful to have the whole company reunited again. After Dashonae had thanked the horses and released them to go home, he produced food from his saddle pack—cured jerky, dried fruit, dark bread with butter, and a skin of cool fruit juice. Then they sat around the fire and rehearsed all their adventures together. The dusty heat of the desert, the crash of the SkyCricket, and even the struggles of Ishtagung, now that they were in the past, were daring exploits to be relished by friends who had shared them. They toasted each other's health as Merris's light pierced the crevice between the mountains, chasing shadows and framing a glorious entrance before them. They fell silent in the bright warmth. Anna looked around the circle and wondered at the mystery that perfect strangers, enduring even stranger adventures, should be made such fast friends. She met Eli's eyes. They were misty, and though Eli nodded and smiled, she said nothing— allowing, for the first time, the silence to speak for her. And Anna loved her for it.

Eventually each wanted to know what had happened to the other during their separation. The girls went first, explaining all about their night in the dark, their day's journey underground, and the vast, empty dwarfish kingdom. Rose gave a glowing rendition of the battle between Finch and the dwarf, for which the fairy sat perfectly still and listened with glowing eyes, as if it were the first time he had heard it. Then everyone drank the fairy's health, and Finch turned so red that he looked like a salamander.

Lambient told about his reckless ride back to Ishtagung with Djerack and the soldiers, and of arriving just as they were binding Dashonae's hands to take him to the executioner.

"But Finch told us that Ragundiae lived," said Anna.

"Oh, he did," said Dashonae. "But no one believed he would, especially Tengomaniah. Apparently he allowed Lambient to go on his errand only for show. He never thought for a minute that he would succeed in getting anything useful out of the dwarf. He figured Ragundiae would die, and he could execute the 'Garlandish dog' and be all the tighter with the koning for having done so."

Dashonae then knelt before Eli and took her hand. "Young lady, I must thank you. You risked much, and for that, I have my life." And he kissed her hand.

Eli turned the color of raspberries. She tried to speak, but nothing came out. Anna realized that she didn't mind Eli getting such credit. She had resented Eli taking the risk, so it seemed only right to let her have the kudos for how it turned out.

Lambient, however, had grown serious. "But still there was a debate as to whether we should be allowed to leave."

"Why? Didn't Ragundiae recover?" said Anna.

"Yes," said Dashonae, his face falling a bit, "but there were complications. By the time we administered the cure, the poison had worked its way down his left arm to such a degree that it began to . . . well, die anyway."

"Just his arm?" Rose was horrified.

"Yes. They had to amputate his left arm at the shoulder, which means he could no longer be a tara."

"How terrible!" cried Rose.

"Truly. But it has worked one favor for him," said Dashonae with a wry smile. "Since no one could bear to have the credit for the slaying of the stymphalia go to a Garlandian, and since no one else was there to see what actually happened, the story has been revised so that Ragundiae was the one who ultimately brought the bird down, receiving his injury while saving the city. It was the only credible story they could manufacture. So Tengomaniah was forced by the koning to make him an elder in Balungorah province—the youngest one in living memory."

"But the koning wasn't there, was he?" said Eli, "I thought he was—"

"No, no, of course not." Lambient waved his hands. "But they have a way of making words travel all the way to Arzhembala in a moment." He grew excited, and Anna could tell that a long story was about to be born. "They have this remarkable machine that can send little beeps along a wire all the way to Arzhembala. I don't know what they call it, but the one who operates it is called the umemelugha—it means something like 'quick mouth' or 'speedy lips' or something like that. Anyway, it—"

But Anna interrupted. "What about the princess?"

"She's still married to Tengomaniah," said Dashonae, "but he's in rough shape. He thought he had ensured his position, but now his brother has outflanked him."

"You're actually the one who did the outflanking for him," said Lambient, grinning.

Dashonae thought for a moment and then one corner of his mouth turned up in an ironic smile. "Yes, it's strange. I would have killed him in combat without a second thought, but I'm actually pleased for him. He was a worthy opponent."

They continued for some time, swapping stories and laughing a great deal. Sazerac even told a joke, which everyone found funny except Anna and Eli, who exchanged mystified looks.

But eventually Lambient tossed the compass to Rose. "I understand, young lady, that you are the one who discovered this treasure. So it seems only right that you be the one to lead us to the next stage of this adventure." Rose pocketed the compass, stood, curtsied, and walked into the mountain crevice.

The six of them stood around the hole looking down into blackness. Finch would not go near it, and Anna now understood why. To go down it, to traverse down under the earth like a Berduccan gnome, would mean his death. He sat on a ledge and occasionally shouted down rude remarks, comparing them to groundhogs, moles, and other burrowing creatures.

Rose's place at the head of the procession turned out to be purely ceremonial. Standing at the edge of the pit, her knees shook, and she teared up at the idea of being the first to go down. Dashonae stepped up chivalrously, but placing one hand on the pole, he found that it wobbled and shook and gave every sign of snapping under his weight. This excluded Lambient as well. And Sazerac would have to go down on someone's shoulders, if he went down at all. Anna knew before anyone else that she would have to do it. She looked and saw that Eli already looked pale and woozy. She didn't like heights, and this was as likely to end in her falling as anything else. She had used up her allotment of courage on the dwarf affair and was back to her old, apprehensive self.

"Oh, all right, I'll do it!" Anna snapped. Lambient and Dashonae looked at her with surprise. "Well, I'm the only one who can," she said miserably.

Eli caught her eye and mouthed a silent "Thank you."

"Okay, so where's the rope?"

The two men's faces fell in unison. And she knew without their saying—they had none.

Lambient pawed the ground with his toe shamefacedly. "We, uh, left in such a hurry, that we didn't think of bringing any."

"Ditty!" Anna threw her hands up. She stared another minute at the hole with its metal pole sticking up like the finger of a sun dial. It had to be done, and she knew she'd have to act before she lost her nerve. So she bit her lip and jumped, grabbing the pole with both hands and wrapping her legs around it. It wobbled under her weight, but stayed straight.

"Now don't just slide down," warned Dashonae. "Go as slowly as you can. You don't know what's down there. And keep shouting up what you see."

" 'kay," said Anna in a choked voice. She gripped the pole tightly and held herself still for a moment, looking down into the blackness below her. Then she took a deep breath and began her descent. Slowly, hand over hand, with her legs squeezing the pole tightly to keep from sliding, she left the world of light and air—again.

The hole wasn't wide—just wide enough that she couldn't reach the sides with an arm or a leg. The pole was all she had. She continued her controlled descent, losing all sense of how far she had gone or how long her hands had been grasping, sliding, releasing, grasping, sliding, releasing. But they were starting to cramp. The circle of light above her grew gradually dimmer and dimmer until it was just a small halo of light somewhere above. The darkness became oppressive.

Perhaps it does goes on forever, she thought. She knew this was unlikely, but then other alternatives began to present themselves. *Perhaps it comes down into water*. This, the more likely end, brought real panic.

Then she froze. Both hands seized the pole as tightly as they could. The pole had ended—not in water or on ground or on anything else. It simply ended in midair. She had felt it disappear first around her foot, and then her knee slid off. Another few inches and she would have been hanging only by her weary hands. The pole wasn't connected to anything! It just hung in midair in the center of the shaft as if by magnets. Had she been less frightened, she would have found it a miraculous thing, but she couldn't even think about that now. She pulled upward with all her might and got both legs wrapped around the pole again, but the effort made her real plight all the more clear.

No climbing up that again, she thought. *And I can't go down either.*

But that wasn't really true. She could let go, but there was no way to know how far off the bottom was or if it was solid, liquid, or steaming gas. It was a horrible minute. Her hands were screaming now, and she knew that circumstance had conquered choice. In a moment she *would* fall. It was now only a matter of doing it smartly.

She screamed her situation back to the others, not knowing if they could hear her.

She thought, *If I fall for more than a couple of seconds, it won't matter after that. I'll land . . . messy. But if it is a short fall, I have to be ready.* She vaguely remembered a story of someone who had broken an ankle falling only a few inches because he had thought it was farther. So she visualized that she was only jumping off a kitchen chair, intending to hit the ground immediately.

From nowhere, the image of an old Cuban fisherman pulling on a fishing line for all he was worth blew into her mind. All he had to do was hang on; all she had to do was let go. The irony would have struck her as funny if she had been able to think about it. "Come on, old man," she grunted, steeling herself.

She told her hands to let go. They hesitated, then obeyed. There was no point in closing her eyes. She was blind in the dark anyway.

Chapter 48

She was standing. She was standing on her feet. Her legs weren't broken. She was alive. Relief poured through Anna and out her tingling fingers. She looked up at the tiny dot of light above her. She reached up and felt the bottom of the pole just above her head. The jump had only been about five feet.

"I'm okay! Come on down!" she shouted to the others, her voice made ghostly as it echoed up the shaft. She listened and heard a shouted reply, but she couldn't understand what was said.

She felt the end of the pole again. It really was suspended in midair. She had not encountered any supports on the way down, and here was the bottom. But she did not take time to think about it. She fumbled in her pack for the lantern, feeling all around the base to see if any of the fuel had leaked. Then she fumbled again to find and turn the flint on it.

Twist . . . a single spark but no flame.

Twist again . . . and this time the spark caught the wick, and a tiny flame bloomed in the darkness.

For a moment Anna was as blind as if the sun itself had come out suddenly on a cloudy day. She held up the lantern and looked around her. It was very like the bottom of a well—solid rock all around. No, not so. A tunnel led away in one direction. She knew she would have to venture some way into it, if only to make room for the others to come down.

So she took a few steps into the passage and shone her lantern around. It was a long tunnel, straight as an arrow, intersected by many other passages, and it went slightly uphill. The main tunnel looked carved, but the first side passage Anna came to appeared more like a natural tunnel, smoothly worn on the bottom as if by water. She went to the next, and the next, and these too had the same natural look. Then she came to a very large passage—and stopped.

A trail of viscous slime crossed the main passage. It suggested something horribly familiar. What had the dwarf called it? She couldn't remember the proper name, but "giant mollusk" doesn't easily escape one's imagination.

Anna's heart stopped. Something was moving in the passage to her right. She turned slowly and held the lantern out into the passage. At first she thought it was only an earthworm that crept into the circle of light, then two, then five. But they were not worms, and as they slithered along the floor, they grew thicker. She backed away toward the pole. They seemed to move randomly, searching without direction or guidance, until one of them happened across the place where Anna had been standing. Then it began to quiver. The others immediately joined it, as if sniffing at her footprint. Then . . . oh, horror! They all turned and began to move quickly toward her. Panicked, she backed way. More of the tentacles appeared. Anna saw movement above her. They were on the ceiling too now, all tracking her.

She ran back to the pole and began screaming with all her might. But she could no longer see the circle of light above her. Before she had time to wonder why or to listen for a reply, the first tentacle reached her ankle. She jumped, but it sprang to life and wrapped around her foot. Several more wound around her arms and waist. They threw her to the floor and began dragging her backward. Anna clung to the lantern and tried to scream, but all that came out was a hoarse "Help me!" Behind her she could hear something—a slurping, inhaling, suctioning. She struggled with all her might, but it was no use.

Then came the most beautiful sound she had ever heard—a

bark, an angry bark. A mass of fur and teeth rushed in next to her and began biting and tearing at the tentacles. A horrible screeching resonated deep in the caves behind her. Then—a flash of metal, and her right arm was free. Dashonae's calm voice rang out. "Don't worry, little lady, it's a coward. It'll give up in a minute."

Another slash of the blade. Her legs were free. The screeching continued—and the next moment, all the tentacles let go and slithered back into darkness. Anna lay breathless on the floor of the cave.

The knight helped her back to her feet. Sazerac licked her hand reassuringly.

"Was . . . was that . . . ?" was all she could get out.

"The lou carcolh? Yes, it was." He grabbed the lantern out of her hand and held it up to the mouth of the passage. "One of the less palatable Berduccan gnomi. But it won't be back this way. At least, not before it grows a few new tentacles." He shone the lantern around, but there was no sign of the searching tentacles.

Sazerac barked and trotted back toward the pole. Dashonae followed. Anna came last, wobbly and weak. Her recovery wasn't complete until she stood again at the foot of the pole and looked up. She would have burst out laughing if the knight hadn't waved her silent with a finger over his mouth.

By Dashonae's upheld lantern she could see Lambient's immense lower half dangling from the pole with one of her sisters clutching each thick arm. He began bellowing at the top of his lungs, "So what happens now? Dashonae, don't leave me like this! What do I do from here?"

Dashonae smiled mischievously at Anna. He reached up, grabbed the professor's ankle, and gave a gentle tug. The huge man let out a high-pitched scream and attempted to scramble up the pole again, but the weight of the girls proved too much. His hands slipped, and he fell with a hard *wump* onto his backside, the girls tumbling onto the ground next to him.

When they finally compared stories, it turned out that the rest of the group, not understanding Anna's first yell, felt concerned for her safety. So Dashonae attempted the pole with Sazerac on his shoulders. Anna's subsequent view up the pole had been blocked by the knight, who, hearing her scream, slid down the rest of the way at full speed and nearly broke his leg upon landing. Now one of his ankles was badly turned. He insisted it was nothing but winced with every step.

Lambient, retrieving a bandage from his pack, soon had the knight's ankle tightly bound. Then he examined the pole, fascinated. "Must be held in place by some sort of natural magnetic polarization."

"Or perhaps . . . faith," offered Dashonae.

"Yes, that's it, faith. That answers everything," the professor replied with friendly sarcasm. Dashonae only smiled.

"Let's have a look at the compass, Rose," said the knight. They examined it by the light of all the lanterns. Both arrows pointed firmly at the main passage, and one was slightly elevated, as they would have expected. They all embraced again, for they were now sure this was the last leg of both quests. So in a close line, with Dashonae at the front and Sazerac sniffing along in the rear, they ascended the main passage.

After about fifteen minutes of carefully picking their way forward, Dashonae called back that he could see natural light ahead of them. Five minutes more and they stood in the archway of a great cavern. It was easily as big as one of the dwarf halls, but it had not been carved; it was natural. Damp stalactites and stalagmites grew toward one another and in many places kissed in graceful hourglass columns, in their way as beautiful as anything the dwarves had made. Morning sunlight poured in from fissures in the vaulted granite roof, filling the whole hall with a dusty twilight.

The vastness and lonely silence of the cavern were working a strange enchantment on them. No one felt like talking. They were on the verge of a great, even holy, event before which words would have seemed an intrusion.

The cavern's central feature was a hill, broad and imposing. Silently, they began their ascent. Nearing its crest, they glimpsed a second, smaller hill set atop the one they were climbing. At least, a hill is what it seemed at first—but like none they'd ever seen, strangely white and glowing in the mottled sunlight. What on earth could it be?

The answer —far beyond anything even Dashonae could have imagined—awaited them at the summit. There, fully revealed, it stopped them in their tracks, staring in open-mouthed astonishment.

Lambient whistled softly. Dashonae drew his sword.

Before them rose a tall, circular pyramid constructed of massive, concentric stone disks, each a foot deep. Surrounding the pyramid like ancient stone sentinels were the remnants of numerous pillars, connected here and there by archways, like the gates to a Roman plaza. In millennia past, these had once formed a complete and imposing structure, but now that structure lay in ruins. Stumps of columns and broken arch stones lay strewn about the hilltop.

Surely this was Vizuritundu.

It had to be.

No trident stood upright in its center, but a neon sign could not have made it any clearer.

Yet for all the wonder of that sight, the groups' attention was focused on an even greater marvel. For the well and its shattered superstructure were not the only things occupying the cave.

What they had taken for a smaller hill earlier was actually a tremendous skull—that of a great lizard. Its long, jutting open jaws seemed to bite the very top of the well, and the rest of the skeleton, a hundred feet long if it was an inch, stretched down the far side of the hill. Its spine arched upward like a skeleton in a museum or like the Gateway Arch in St. Louis.

But there was more. On either side of the back lay a pair of gigantic, sweeping bones, like great wings—bat wings with a span that rivaled the creature's length. Some of the bones in the left wing were partially encased by a large stalagmite. The skeleton must have been lying there for centuries.

Dashonae finally whispered the word Anna had been thinking —"Dragon."

Lambient stared at him. "But that's impossible. Dragons are pure fiction."

"Even now you doubt, Doctor? Even here, with the evidence you so desire within your reach? A 'fictional' dragon impaled upon a 'fictional' well? Let mythology and science meet in friendship for once, and believe."

Dashonae approached the well of Vizuritundu, stopped a few feet from its base, and knelt. Laying his sword down upon the ledge of the first stone ring, he bowed his head in devotion.

Anna felt compelled to join him—she could not say why. She came to the knight's side and knelt. She did not pray; that wasn't her way. But she knew she was meeting something bigger than herself, something worthy of respect and even reverence.

She felt her sisters' hands on her shoulders. Sazerac came and stood next to her, and she laid her hand on his back. Dashonae took her other hand. Whether Lambient had joined them as well or still stood afar off like the skeptic he claimed to be, it did not matter. Here was the well. Come what may after this, Anna had seen a myth become a reality.

And anyone who has ever experienced such a thing knows they will never be the same again.

Chapter 49

How long they remained on their knees before the well, Anna never knew. But after a time, reverence turned into curiosity. They began to examine the well—a task for which Lambient was more than ready. He circled the tower of stone, hmmm-ing to himself like a doctor doing an exam.

The well was curiously carved with every sort of image and rune in languages none of them recognized. Around the top surface of each great ring of the pyramid, completely encircling it, ran a trough, doubtless meant to hold water. A lip allowed water to pour down to the next ring below once the trough was full. Presumably, the water would bubble up at the very top, fill the uppermost trough, and then proceed, ring by ring, toward the bottom. From there it flowed into a small aqueduct that projected from the side and ended in a carved fish's head about a foot wide. It was a miniature of the amplabium in Halighyll. Pouring out of the fish's mouth, the water would flow down the hill into the unknown depths of the mountain.

"Oh, look!" said Rose, pointing to the massive skeleton. The bones of its right foreclaw were neatly splayed out on the ground—but where was the left foreclaw? At first glance, it appeared to be missing. It was there, though; it was just badly stunted. The limb was short and stumpy, like that of a tyrannosaur.

"It must have been a defect," said Lambient "How interesting."

"The poor thing," said Rose with sympathy.

"I wouldn't pity it too much," said Dashonae. "Even with one shriveled limb, that beast was probably a terror."

"So you think it was . . . um . . ." Eli searched for a word. "Mean?"

Lambient laughed. "Missy, I doubt it was someone's pet."

But Anna was only half listening. She was staring at the top of the well and feeling the same beckoning that had overcome her in the desert. She wanted to climb to the top. She *had* to.

Lambient thought this a very sensible next step, and they began the ascent. It was tricky, for the great lizard's jaws surrounded the final eight rings at an unnatural angle—like a dog gnawing on a bone, Anna thought. The great twelve-foot-long mouth, with its row after row of teeth, had been unnaturally wrenched to one side, and its upper part was level with the top of the well. This ultimately worked to their advantage: once they reached a place where they could access the jaw and confirm it was stable, they were able to use it as a stepladder.

More hazardous were the creature's upper teeth, which covered much of the top of the well and hung out into space beyond it. A single fang protruded downward from one side of the jaw, as if precariously balanced on the very top of the well. The opposite fang was missing, and the result looked strange indeed.

"Another defect?" mused Dashonae.

"Perhaps," replied the scientist, "or maybe dragons just lose teeth periodically, like other, uh, reptiles."

They reached the summit at last, hunched somewhat inside the dragon's mouth. But Dashonae, who should have been in his glory, instead gave a cry of dismay and covered his face.

The well was more like a fountain—just a two-inch hole in the center of the topmost circle. Clearly water once bubbled out of it. But it had been blocked. The single fang of the dragon was jammed so deeply and tightly into the opening that it had effectively sealed off the flow. Time had further married tooth and rock. By no means could the two be separated without destroying the wellhead.

"What in the world could have happened here?" said Lambient.

"Don't you see?" said Dashonae in a choked voice. "By whatever death this creature died, it has sealed the well. And that means . . ." He shook his head and could not continue.

"What? What? Speak, man!" cried Lambient.

"Azhiona did not stop up the well, as we have been taught. They could not have done this. They did not start the Ever-War. Which means . . ." He groaned. "We did."

Lambient was aghast. "All these centuries? All that horror? But who could have known?"

The knight gave a dismayed laugh. "No one. It could not have been foreseen or guessed by either side."

"The dwarf knew," said Rose quietly, but no one was listening to her.

The men dismounted from the well, sat upon the stone floor, and wept over the centuries of sorrow and waste that had consumed both lands. Sazerac joined them, baying like a wolf, and his howls echoed eerily in the desolation of the cavern.

The girls, still atop the well, looked at one another helplessly.

Anna's gaze wandered over the circular surface of the well. Around its edge was a series of markings . . . seven of them, arranged in clock-like succession . . . so familiar . . .

Anna drew her breath sharply and pointed. The symbols were identical to the ones on the bronze band of Rose's compass. They were the symbols of the emissaries. Rose produced her compass. They were all there. Merris, Vercandrus, and their five children.

But one was different. Six were simply etched into the rock, but for the one nearest Anna, a shallow geometrical hole had been carved out.

Eli looked at her with a stricken face. It was Therra's sign. The small goblet rune was etched into the bottom of the divot, and the shape of the divot was unmistakable. Anna's hand went to her breast. The amulet! How little she had thought about it in the last few days. But there was no question about it. The indentation in the well's top surface matched perfectly the shape and size of her amulet.

Yet they could not have been made together. The amulet was metal; the well was stone. Yet the shapes were the same. One had been made before the other, and the other made to fit it. But which was which?

It did not seem to matter, for in that moment she felt the amulet grow heavy, as it had in the desert. She struggled to get the chain over her head. The amulet fell with a thud that seemed to shake the whole structure. The girls looked at it, and it was clear they were all pondering the same question. The men and the dog continued to wail at the foot of the column.

Rose broke the silence. "Curious George."

"What?" said Anna.

"Curious George. He's always curious what will happen if he does something."

"And he always gets in trouble for it," hissed Eli.

But Anna was looking at the amulet. She picked it up; it had become light again. She fiddled with Whinsom's harness, trying to undo it, and with unnatural ease, the amulet slipped out of its bonds and fell into her hand. It seemed to tremble in her palm as though happy to be freed.

Anna knew what she had to do. "And he always makes it right in the end," she said softly.

She looked at her sisters. Rose nodded immediately. Eli looked apprehensive, but after a moment, she bit her lip and nodded also.

Anna's hand hovered over the indentation momentarily—and suddenly the amulet went heavy again and was ripped from her fingers. It fell evenly and easily into the cavity, united at long last with its mate.

The tower that was Therra's Well began to tremble as if under some terrific force. Sazerac ceased to bay, and the two men below looked up with terrified faces.

"What in the . . . ?" began Lambient. But the whole room heaved sideways and nearly threw the girls from the top of the well. They watched as the throbbing earth upset the delicate balance that held the massive skeleton together. As if in slow motion, it crumbled before their eyes into a desiccated ruin. Clouds of dust billowed like smoke. Massive vertebrae tumbled and rolled to every corner of the cave like colossal dice. Only the skull remained affixed at the top of the well. But even there, things were changing.

The amulet began to tremble in its new home. Suddenly it popped out of its place as if spring-loaded. Anna caught it as it leapt. It was wet in her hand. She looked down. The rock orifice in which it had lain had filled with water. As with the sand hole she had dug in the desert early in their adventure, the water bubbled up and filled the indentation. And now it was gushing. It filled the trough at the edge and began pouring down into the level below, filling it with unnatural swiftness.

Lambient and Dashonae were scrambling back up the side of the well. Their eyes went wide as they saw the water.

Dashonae's face clouded over. "What have you done?" he demanded darkly.

"We just . . . we just . . ." began Anna, taken off guard by the knight's response. Surely he of all people would be excited about this turn of events.

Eli jumped in. "But this is a good thing! The amplabium will—"

"Did you not think of the consequences?" he cried in despair. "Did you learn nothing of the stories we told you of the Ever-War? Do you not remember that the Flow irrigated such a wide track of Kavue that it allowed armies to travel between Azhiona and Garlandium? Do you not know that if this well reestablishes the Flow, open war will again be possible between our people?"

Anna felt as if she had been slapped. None of this had entered her mind.

"But you said that the Ever-War was all based on a lie," said Eli. "And you have proof now. You can stop the war with the truth."

But even as Eli spoke, Anna knew what a terrible thing they had done. If she had learned one thing from her adventures, it was that truth was often insufficient to avert catastrophe.

Chapter 50

The water had filled all the levels of the well and was flowing copiously, disappearing to unseen places. The volume pouring from the fish's mouth was inexplicably far greater than what was bubbling out of the top of the well. It was more like a small brook. Lambient and Dashonae stood soberly with their arms crossed, listening as the girls explained how the well had been restored. When they had finished, Lambient turned to Dashonae.

"You are right about what could now happen, but what they did has the ring of fate to it."

"It's not like you to speak so," said the knight through tight lips.

"Not fate as you're thinking, but fate in the sense that the ladies did as was intended. Obviously that cavity in the well was made for just such a circumstance, and the amulet was designed to be so used. If I found a nail partially driven and possessed a hammer uniquely made for that kind of nail, would you blame me for driving it in?"

Dashonae looked at him, thinking deeply. "But this is so much more than a nail."

"It is the same! Ancient things are at work here, plans laid long before the first blows of the Ever-War fell. I do not understand them, but they are facts. There is no possibility that the well and the amulet match by chance. Where there is a plan, there is a planner. Where there is a design, there is a designer. The ladies were rash, yes, but in the end, these two artifacts were meant to come together."

"Meant by whom?" said the knight.

"I do not know, but now that the well has been reopened, I doubt we shall need to wait long to find out."

"But wait," Eli said. "Whoever made the well or the amulet wouldn't still be around, would they?"

Dashonae said only, "You've met the dwarf. Do you think he is the oldest creature in this world?"

Eli opened her mouth to respond, then shut it again.

Anna surveyed the pile of bones. "What about the dragon?"

"That is at least as big a mystery." Lambient fiddled with the corner of his moustache. "The position of that brute is unlikely to be a result of chance. I am at a loss. I must make haste back to the science institute in Garlandvale and consult other experts—perhaps those of the Lemerrian school."

"Why Lemerrian?" said Dashonae.

"I do not know what elemental aspect would govern a dragon, but I am guessing it would be Lemerrus—that is, fire. It is, after all, like a great salamander."

"But they fly too," said Eli, pointing at the wings.

"So it could be Avonian as well," said Dashonae, "and it is also clearly underground, so Berducca cannot be excluded either."

Lambient sighed. "There is a lifetime of work in this discovery." But he trembled with excitement as well.

"Hey, come here!" Rose's voice sounded from a distance. No one had noticed that she had slipped away. They all turned and scanned the cave, and saw her at last down the far side of the hill amid the piles of collapsed bones. "I think I found it!" She held up the compass and pointed at the other end of the cavern.

They all climbed down the pyramid and joined her at the foot of the hill. Rose stood with her index finger pointing at the wall of the cave. There, hovering in space, a few feet in front of the rock wall, was the window, illuminated by a shaft of light from a fissure in the roof.

They all gathered before it. Unlike the girls' first look through

—into the forest glades of Garlandium—this window looked simply dark, like looking into a hole . . . at night . . . with their eyes closed. In fact, so cave-like was it that they would never have recognized it was the window if not for the change at its edges, where the rock walls showed through hazily.

Anna was disappointed, and it was clear the others were too. Dashonae said, "So that is your world?"

His voice full of concern, Lambient said, "That doesn't look very inviting."

Reasonable Eli answered. "Well, when we first came through to your world, we were in a cellar on our side, and there wasn't much light there. So maybe we're just going back to where we came in."

"Assuming it's even still our century," said Anna wryly.

Sazerac, however, was not content and began to bark. Anna's jaw fell open. She understood him! She couldn't explain how or why, except that it involved not translation but a certain kind of listening. They had been through a lot together, and she was deeply bonded to Sazerac. Now, as he spoke this final time, Anna was simply in a frame of mind that allowed her to perceive his intention. She knew intuitively that from here on she would be able to understand all dogs in that world. Would it be so back in North Carolina?

Sazerac had asked how they knew this door led back to *their* world.

Elated at her new ability, Anna was about to answer him when Eli burst her bubble by saying, "I hadn't thought of that." Anna was not the only one who had come to understand canineish!

Sazerac's observation prompted a rather heated metaphysical discussion between Lambient and Dashonae. Lambient believed the risk was significant, while the knight insisted that Therra would not abandon the girls even at the threshold of the world. In the end, Eli silenced their concerns by asking what options the girls had. None, of course, except to brave the window and see what would happen. The adventure of this appealed to Dashonae, and the necessity of it made sense to the professor.

Anna, however, wasn't at all comfortable with it. She was worn out on adventures, and the idea of dropping into yet another unknown world wasn't so much frightening as it was plain exhausting. But she covered her apprehension by voicing her own concern for Sazerac and the two men. "How are you going to get out of here?"

Lambient dismissed the problem with a wave of his hand. "Oh, we'll send Finch for rope. He'll have no trouble hauling us up out of the hole."

Eli said, "Doctor, what are the chances that the window would end up in the same cave as the well? I mean, it seems incredible that we should just happen to be heading to the same place."

Dashonae opened his mouth, but Lambient cut him off. "Don't you dare say 'Therra!' There has got to be an explanation." And he stood there in thought for a minute. Then he yelled at Dashonae again, who had begun tapping his foot loudly on the stone. Eventually Lambient threw up his hands and said, "There must be some unique physical property of the well that is conducive to the window's appearance here."

Now it was Dashonae's turn. "'Unique physical property,' eh? That answers everything." They both burst into laughter and clapped each other on the back.

But the laughter passed almost immediately into sober silence. The friends all stood looking at one another.

This was it.

Anna felt a lump in her throat. After looking forward to going home for so many days, it seemed to have snuck up on them in the end. Their departure now seemed abrupt, leaving much unfinished. Rose already had a tear on her cheek, and Eli's brows were knit in a frown.

Lambient saw what was coming and tried to stop it. "Now, now, none of that. We made this whole journey for this moment. It was bound to come." But he had to stop because his voice cracked. Sazerac whined, and Rose immediately knelt and hugged him. Eli and Anna followed. Then Rose and Eli both embraced Lambient and then Dashonae.

Anna teetered with indecision, feeling for the first time in her life that she would not mind hugging someone unrelated to her on a non-holiday but fearful of the feeling. The decision was made for her as Dashonae stepped forward, embraced her, and kissed her on the forehead.

"Go with Therra, child, for she has blessed you," he whispered.

Lambient followed, nearly hugging the stuffing out her. His face was wet with tears when they separated.

"Thank Finch again for us," said Eli.

Dashonae nodded.

"Will we see you again?" asked Rose.

Lambient sniffed. "You still have that compass, don't you?"

Rose smiled and held it up.

"Then anything is possible," he said.

The time had come. The three girls held hands and, looking over their shoulders at the two men and the dog, stepped into the darkness of the window.

Of Things Lost and Things Found

When writing history, one must always keep an eye upon the larger story behind the one in the foreground. I have been forced to read many tediously myopic poems on Vizuritundu that were missing this vital element: a sense of wonder! Imagine the utter surprise of finding that the mystery of Therra's Well, just when nearly solved, was actually giving birth to even greater mysteries. Mysteries that seemed to yank loose the very pins upon which the world itself hung. These mysteries would take over twenty years to become manifest, and the price of that clarity would be more horrific than anyone could have imagined. Any 'Lost Well Ballad' (even one by the 'greatest living poet') that does not trade on that central emotional fact is not only unworthy, it is false.

> DR. SONJI RAZHAMANÌAH, *An Attempted History of the Halighyllian Prophecies and Their Fulfillment*, Vol 7: *Prolegomena to the Second Theso-Hamayunean War*, 4r.

Rose sneezed. They were not hurt, but they were not entirely unhurt either. They were lying in a jumbled pile of arms and legs in the dark. Apparently the window had not come out on the level with the world, but rather a step or two off the ground. They had stepped through onto thin air and fallen together onto a pile of rubble. They were well bruised but, thankfully, nothing worse. Wherever they were, it was dark, dirty, and musty, and it had the faint smell of rotting fruit. No light of any kind penetrated the darkness.

"Crud," said Anna, "I wish we'd brought the lanterns with us."

She felt Rose squirming next to her. Then came the sound of a turning flint, and light filled the place. She saw Rose smiling sheepishly and holding up her lantern. "I put it in my pack when we got to the well, and I forgot about it." Anna was surprised that it still worked. Their tumble had shattered the lantern's glass and bent its wires, and a wet spot on its bottom indicated its fuel was leaking. Remembering vividly the fleeting candle in the dwarf's bedroom, they scrambled down from the pile, which consisted of broken concrete blocks and wood timbers.

Anna took the lantern from her sister and began to look around. At first she thought their worst fears had come to pass. The room had that indefinable feel of a place where no one has been for years. It seemed indeed that a long time had passed since their departure.

Further inspection revealed they clearly were not in the same cellar where their adventure had started. This place was similar, but the shape was all wrong. There were shelves, but they were empty, rotted, and many had toppled over. There had even been a sort of cave-in at one corner, where damp earth had poured through a section of rotted boards. It took them quite a while to pick safely over the masses of timbers, crates, and other wreckage. It was all reassuringly familiar junk, and it meant almost certainly that they were back in their own world.

Eli picked up a stray board from a shattered packing crate. She scrutinized it in the partial light, then suddenly she went rigid.

"What is it?" asked Anna.

"I know where we are," she said in a frightened voice and held up the board to the light. Green stencil letters read, "ordeaux." Supply the missing *B*, and it was a reference to a region of France known for red wine. "I'll bet we're in the south cellar."

"But it's locked." As she said it, Anna realized the difficulty this raised. Easily in, but not so easily out.

"What will happen when we're found down here?" squeaked Eli.

Anna thought that, given the things they had been through in the past week, little could happen that would bother her much.

Rose called from ahead. They found her standing at the foot of a short cement staircase consisting of only a couple of steps. A vertical strip of light stood at the top of the stairs. And at a strange angle, horizontal to the stairs, was a set of metal doors.

"This can't be the south cellar," said Anna. "The staircase isn't long enough, and this is a double door."

Eli had put her eye to the crack. "No, this is a different door. I'm looking into the garden. This must be an outside storm door—like a tornado shelter."

All three girls recognized immediately how fortunate this was. If they could get out here, they might not get caught by Miss Heavernaggie. But when they stood on the bottom step with necks craned to one side, pushing up on the doors, they found them locked from the outside.

Rose chose this moment to make the horrible observation that they still didn't know how long they'd been gone. Any search for them might have been abandoned long ago. And anyway, there was no reason for anyone to ever think of looking for them in a locked cellar. This put them all in a panic, and abandoning caution, they began to bang and pound on the door, calling for help.

Almost immediately there was a commotion at the door. After a series of grating clicks, the doors flew open, and they found themselves looking into the bewildered face of Mr. Putterly.

"Crivvens!" he cried in the tongue of his Scottish ancestry. "Where have you been? Miss Heavernaggie's beside herself with—" He broke off, smothered in a triple embrace.

Rose rubbed her dirty face on his overalls. "Oh good, I was hoping you'd still be alive."

The fuddled gardener could only stammer, "Oh, uh, yes, thank you, to be sure." He peeled Rose off his hip and stared at her grimy face and matted hair. "What in the name of tarnation are you doing in there in the first place? Just look at the state of your clothes, child!" Not only were their clothes dusty and dirty from the cellar, but they had been branded with the blemishes of deserts, jungles, mountains, and slimy underworld mollusks. "Just what's Miss Heavernaggie to say to Master Hoover when he gets home?" He shook his head grimly.

"He's not home?" said Eli, glancing sidelong at Anna.

"What? No, he's off to his meetin's this very afternoon, he is," said Mr. Putterly. "Be back on Sunday. You know this for sure. You sent him off yourselves, you must've."

"So it's still Friday?" asked Eli.

"To be sure, it is." He looked at her with new concern. "And when you three didn't show for tea, I must tell you that the house was in such a state as I've seldom seen it!"

The girls stood in dumbfounded silence for a minute.

Then Eli asked, "What time is it?"

He fumbled about, produced a pocket watch, tried to read it, then paused to pull out a small pair of reading glasses. Anna nearly grabbed the watch out his hand in her impatience.

"Well, um, let's see . . . it's, uh . . ." He finally fitted the spectacles to his face. "It's, uh . . . about 5:30."

Eli turned to her sisters. "We've only been gone a few hours."

"But how . . ." began Anna, and then saw Mr. Putterly staring queerly at them. She shut her mouth and nudged Rose to do the same. The girls all looked at the old gardener and smiled sweetly.

"Well now," he melted, taking off his sun hat and scratching his weathered scalp. "You're in trouble enough as it is. No use addin' to your grief. But when she sees you in this state . . ." He shook his head. "Oh, well, come on. Let's see as we can get you to your rooms on the sly." They followed him around to the front door.

"But Mr. Putterly," said Eli, "won't Miss Heavernaggie be—"

He silenced her with a wave and gestured for them to stay put. He then mounted the steps and made a show of *not* wiping his muddy boots on the rug. He turned, winked, and stepped into the house. A moment later they heard a stomping sound, as if someone was grinding as much mud into the carpet as it could hold. And sure enough, he had not been in the house twenty seconds before Miss Heavernaggie's shrill voice shattered the silence. "Mr. Putterly! Come down those stairs this instant. Have I not told you a dozen times *not* to use the front door? Look at the dirt on the rug. Do you think I have so much time—"

"Sorry, ma'am," said the gardener, feigning contrition, "but I thought you'd want to see right away the blight on the squash. Got some new insect or other that's making things iffy for that welcome-home dinner the cook's got planned for Master Hoover."

"And a fine dinner it will be if his children have the decency to show up," she said.

"Can't know nothin' about that, ma'am, but if you'll just step out this way."

Anna froze. Why was he leading her out the front door? She would surely see them if they came this way.

But the housekeeper shrieked again. "Did I not just say—out the back with you, Mr. Putterly, this instant. Honestly, I never . . ." A door swung shut and the voices retreated, with Mr. Putterly offering a second round of apologies. The girls snuck into the house and up the stairs, noting that the gardener seemed to have stomped so much dirt into the carpet that their own grimy footprints would go unnoticed. They bathed, put on fresh clothes, and were sitting primly at the table at 7:00.

Miss Heavernaggie wandered into the dining room wringing her hands—and stopped abruptly upon seeing them. Her hands went to the hips and her face rearranged itself into an iron-clad grimace. "Well now, young ladies—and I use the word with great latitude—may I ask where you have been for the past six hours?"

Anna glanced at Rose. They had worked all this out in their room earlier, but she wondered if her little sister was going to crack. But Rose's face remained sweet and unreadable as Eli told the story of going wandering in the woods and getting lost—a regular Hansel and Gretel. How they were so hungry and had tried so hard to get back in time for tea and were so sorry for missing it.

When she was done, Miss Heavernaggie stared at her for a moment, turned up her nose, and sniffed. "If you do not wish to tell me what you were doing, that is your right, but do not insult me with nonsense. Make no mistake, your father shall receive a full report." And she stormed out of the room in a most dignified huff.

They had decided not to tell anyone about their adventure. It was just too strange and incredible. It was no good showing anyone the compass as proof. The two arrows swung around lazily with every shake. Anna had taken her amulet and carefully rejoined it to its chain, to which it meekly submitted without even a twitch. And both treasures were hidden away in their rooms.

When their father returned Sunday afternoon, he was regaled by Miss Heavernaggie with tales of their woeful conduct. He was very disapproving in her presence, but when she left the room, he seemed to forget all about it—much to Anna's relief.

Over tea, he recounted rather dull stories from the conference. His own paper had been warmly received, as always. But when Anna and Eli rose to go, Rose remained seated and asked, "Daddy, what did the lady say?"

"The who?"

"The lady you said you'd talk to about my compass."

Anna's heart fell. So after all that had happened, here was Rose picking right up where they had left off. She seemed determined to confess the chaos in the gallery.

But Teddy banged his head in remembrance. "Oh, yes, I almost forgot. Yes, I met her and asked if there was anything more to the Stemmathus legend. Turns out his original name wasn't even Stemmathus. That was a name his followers gave him. You'll remember, many had followed him all the way across Europe to Jerusalem and then back across Africa to the edge of the Atlantic.

He had hundreds of followers who all thought him a new messiah leading them to heaven. So they began calling him Stemmathus.

The girls looked at him blankly. He often forgot that other people did not know half the things he took for granted.

"Well, you see, they thought of him as a great leader, or even a king. So they named him Stemmathus, which in Greek means something like 'wreath,' 'crown,' or maybe 'garland.' And so they followed him right out to sea and probably . . . what's wrong?"

The girl's faces had all gone white.

"Garland?" said Eli in amazement. "His name means 'garland'? As in Garlandium?"

They looked at each other with open mouths.

Teddy seemed miffed at the interruption. "What? No, just garland, like you put on your head. Guys, don't take this stuff seriously. It's a legend. No one really believes he led all those people out to sea to die. There's no point in worrying yourselves over it. It's not real. It's just a myth."

Rose recovered first. "Some myths *are* real." She said it so innocently that contradicting her would have been just plain mean. "And I'm not worried about Mr. Garland, Daddy. I think his compass led him to heaven just fine." She smiled sweetly and left the room.

Eli, looking hard at the floor, remained an awkward moment longer, shrugged, and then followed her.

"I wouldn't worry about her, Dad. You know what Rose is like," said Anna. And she did her best to smile as sweetly as her little sister and ran after her.

About the Author

Gordon Greenhill completed a degree in theatre and communication in his youth, then went on to earn a Ph.D. in moldy old dead European men. After fifteen years teaching at university, he became a professional audiobook narrator and discovered he liked writing fiction more than lecturing on theology. Most importantly, he's a husband and father of four amazing kids, who like his reading of Harry Potter better than Jim Dale's . . . but they may be prejudiced.

www.gordongreenhill.com
www.relicsoferrus.com